THE MAGE'S DAUGHTER

THE STONE MAGE SERIES, BOOK 1

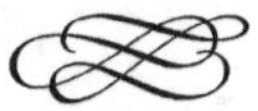

AMELIA G. SIDES

RIVER ROCKS PUBLISHING

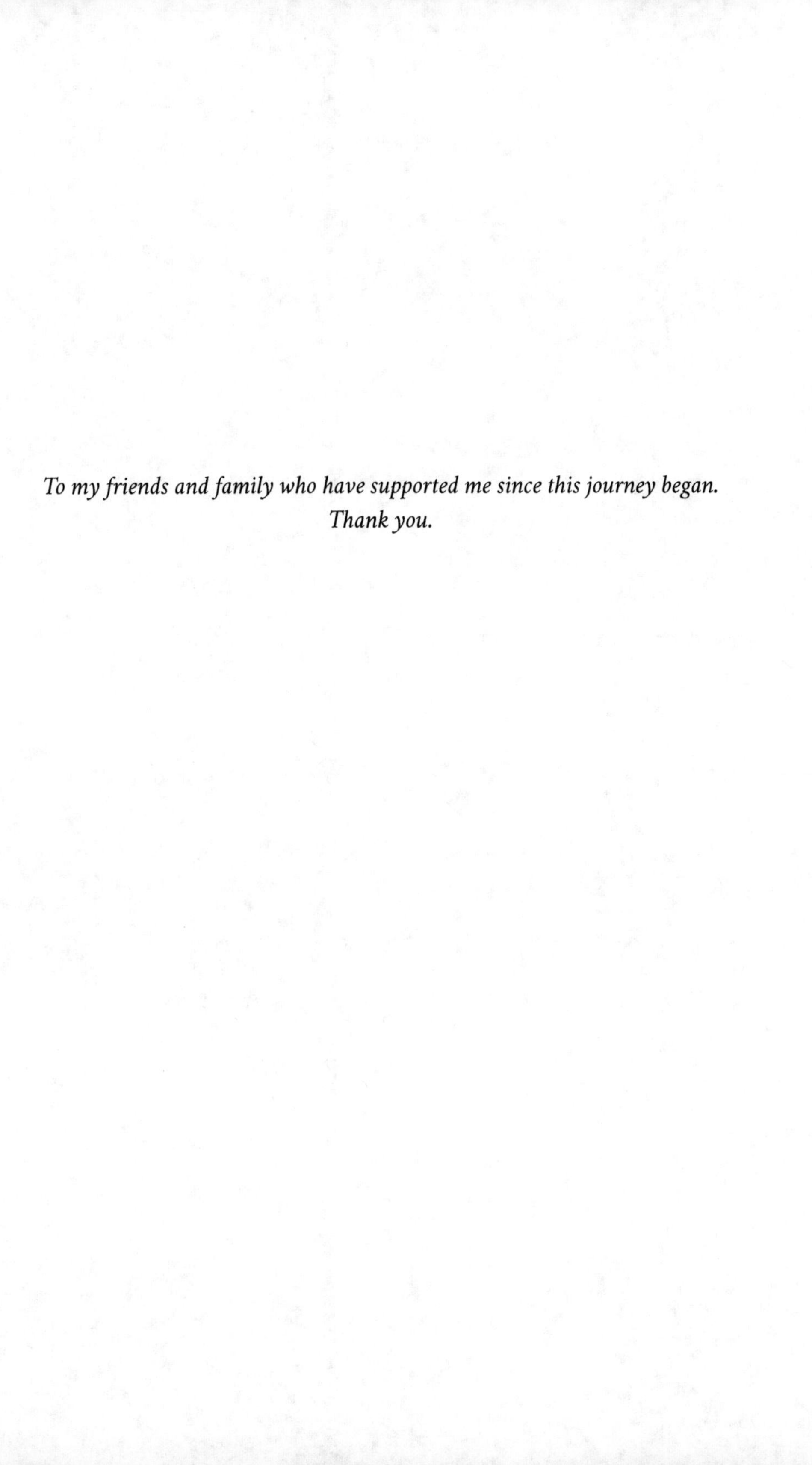

CHAPTER 1

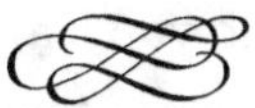

*B*eryl eyed the decaying wards on the town wall with pity; they barely had any glow at all, flickering in the corner of her vision. They would fail if the town was attacked before they were repaired. Refugees from nearby towns wandered the small town square, eyes dull with exhaustion and despair. Northern bandits and raiders had been attacking all season, pillaging what they could while the mountain passes were open. The army had patrols on the border, and the nearby towns, but the attacks continued.

"Six hundred," Jared snapped, glaring at the man before him.

"Four hundred is the most that we can pay." The Mayor replied, fidgeting with his chain of office.

"It's six or I leave your town as is. The most you would get for four is the stables warded."

"We would not be hiring a hedge mage if we had that much gold!" he sputtered.

"Then send a message to the Wizard's Council and see if they will cut you a deal. I doubt it." Jared sneered.

Beryl listened with half an ear as she wandered away from the pair. She could at least shore up some wards while she waited. Asking six hundred for warding a place this small was ridiculous. At the most she would have charged four, but a mage from the royal council would have charged eight. The Monarchy was stingy with their magical resources, claiming to save the magic for important problems like droughts and wars.

"Every drop of her sweat has a price! Every gram of energy spent warding your precious village is magic that can't be used on the next."

"Half the towns around here have been attacked. Our wards are not what they used to be. Would you leave us defenseless?"

"If you won't pay, then the next town will. Maybe they will take your sorry selves in when the raiders take your gold and your city."

The low wall circling the town was barely five feet high. A determined child could scramble over the rough stones in moments. The town had counted on the wards to keep the town safe, blocking out arrows or magical attacks aimed at the town.

Beryl doubted the wards could do much more than stop a handful of arrows without failing right now. She pressed a few small runes in where she could discretely. It would not do much, but it might keep the wards stable for a while longer.

* * *

"Five fifty," The mayor snapped, gesturing for a bystander to go collect the gold. He held out his hand and sagged once Jared gave it a perfunctory shake.

"Girl, get to work! The wall, inn, and stables are to be warded."

"Yes, Uncle Jared," she said with a frown, walking back and handing over her cloak at the man's impatient gestures. Gods, she hated it when he called her "girl."

"Thank you for your work, Mage." The mayor said, offering her his hand.

"Beryl Marcian," she said, fighting to keep the bitterness out of her voice.

The man would forget her name as soon as she walked away. It was her curse, something so small and simple that no one spared it a moment's notice. She glanced at the other townsfolk watching from their doorways and porches. Those around they would remember them, called by name when someone needed them. They would not be known as "Girl" and "Woman" for the rest of their days. The best she could hope for was that they called her "Mage." That, at least, she had earned.

Beryl pulled a coil of copper wire from her pack and got started. It took hours to carve and spell the runes needed to power the warding on the wall. Each carved rune was filled with copper and spelled to collect ambient magic. The more people that lived in the town, the more magic the wards would collect and the stronger they would become. It might take a few years, but the wards would strengthen.

She finished warding the wall and inn as the day darkened into night. The mist slowly turned to steady rain as she worked, drumming against the stable's roof in a steady thrum. A series of pattering clicks sounded as something struck the roof. She spun with a gasp as something buzzed past her shoulder, leaving a line of pain behind, thunking into the wall next to her. She fell back unbalanced as the next arrows slapped into the wet ground around her.

Beryl stood frozen, the sound of pounding feet and thudding doors ringing out around her as the villagers locked themselves in their homes or raced for weapons. Raiders charged silently out of the mist as arrows slashed down into the town. A scream rang out, snapping her out of her daze.

Lurching, she threw herself toward the nearest section of wall at a scrambling run. Striking the rough stone, she barely felt the pain of her scrapped palms as she poured magic into the old wall while shaping new runes and directing them to link to the old and new wards. She lost herself to the spell and runes as the fight raged around her.

She struggled to concentrate. Then, the wall glowed steady silver as she fed power into the wards. Silver fire lit the night as the runes connected to each other, bridging the openings in the wall and locking out the next wave of raiders, they threw those that tried to force their way through back with burns. Beryl sagged for a moment, catching her breath while looking at the chaos unfolding around her.

The runic shield stopped the incoming arrows but did little to help those fighting within the town. Townsmen fought against swords and crossbows with little more than axes and farming implements. The raiders left them dead and bleeding in their wake.

The clash of weapons, shouts of anger, and screams of pain bled into each other as she panted. She could not stay here. Snatching up handfuls of loose stones, she filled her pockets as she ran to the side of a house.

Pressing her back into the wet wood, she darted a quick glance around the corner. Chaos filled the streets of the small town. Several roofs smoldered, adding dark choking smoke to the falling rain.

She pressed a turning spell against her chest and whispered a prayer to Ruth that it would work. She had created the spell to turn unwanted attention away while she was traveling. Too many times she'd been cornered by either her drunken Uncle or a tavern patron looking for someone to hurt. The spell made people ignore her as long as she wasn't drawing attention to herself. She shivered as a fighter stalked past her hiding place, eyes passing over her.

Clutching a stone, she pressed a sleep spell into the rock, fighting to ignore how her vision blurred for a moment. She had already used too much magic warding the town. She would have to be careful; if she pushed herself too far, she could collapse mid spell. In the past, she had infused the spell into other objects for knocking out a drunk and violent Jared. Hopefully it would work the same tonight.

A raider lunged out of the gloom, slashing at a retreating towns-man. Shouts of pain and rage echoed in the dark along with the taunts of both the attackers and defenders. She shivered at the rictus of hate masking both men's faces.

"Don't run from your death, little boy! Fight me like a man!"

The first stone skimmed just above the man's shoulder, missing him and clattering to a stop against a house's porch. The raider turned to track the noise and the next stone slapped into his back with a slight thud. The spell flared for a moment as she activated it; he crumpled to the dirt, asleep.

Someone shouted over the roar of the fight. "Push them to the square!"

She wiped rain out of her eyes and tried not to shiver. Beryl was covered in mud and soaked to the skin. She pulled out another stone and tried to pick a target through the downpour. Blinking raindrops away, she sent her next target into the mud before she crept to a new vantage point.

Beryl darted from building to building, fighting to control how her hands shook. She wasn't trained in weapons or fighting. All she had were a handful of stones against men who were killing everyone around them. It was madness. Fighter after fighter collapsed into unconsciousness, helped along the way by her magic-infused stones.

Fighting to keep calm, she crept along the edge of a house toward the next knot of fighters. A whimpering cry drew her gaze to a slight form seated on the edge of the fight. A toddler sat bawling in the dust mere feet from where the men fought. Beryl started trying to clear a path to the boy but as quick as she took down one raider, another stepped up to take his place.

The child screamed as a fighter stumbled over him. She watched as the man turned and kicked the small body away. She was up and running, drawing at her magic before the blow landed. Her magic filled her body like bottled lightning, pulsing and clawing at her control. She pulled at the magic stored in her mage belt, recklessly draining the gemstones. Her vision narrowed until all she saw was the boy.

She needed it to stop. Everything needed to stop. Throwing herself through the fight, she pushed the fighters out of her way without a thought, slamming her body into them. The sword was just being raised to kill the small boy when she slid through the mud to snatch him up, sparks of magic crackling between her fingers.

"Make it stop!" she screamed, pushing the magic outward as she poured everything into the command. The magic exploded outward, slamming through the town like a shock wave. The town fell silent around her as the raider dropped his sword. Every fighter dropped into the mud, limp in sleep. Beryl hugged the boy to her and crawled to a safe corner of a nearby house before the magical depletion caught up with her, pulling her under.

* * *

"Up, get packed!" Jared snapped, shoving her out of the warm bed where someone had placed her.

"Yes, sir." She gasped, gripping her head as she fought her way out of the tangled blankets.

"Hurry and get breakfast. We leave as soon as the sun is up."

"Yes, sir." Beryl said, staggering to her feet, her head pounded as nausea clawed at her throat.

She was exhausted, magically depleted, and bruised from the battle. It would be an endless day if Jared was leaving at first light. Beryl thought he would take advantage of the grateful townsfolk while he could, but he seemed determined to be on his way, hangover or not. She wondered what he had stolen this time as she gathered up her wet, muddy clothes from the previous night.

She forced herself to eat the porridge they gave her for breakfast. Then, Jared rushed them out the door, snatching her wrist and gripping it hard enough to bruise as he rushed her out of the Inn. She trudged through the sucking mud after him, rubbing her wrist. Jared stomped away at full stride, each step spraying the surrounding air with gouts of mud and water.

One villager stepped forward stopped her for a moment, handing her a wrapped bundle, "Just a few things to make your journey easier, child," she said, her voice pitched low so not to carry to Beryl's snarling relative. She smiled her thanks and slid the bundle into a small bag. With a slight wave, she headed after her Uncle.

Once she caught up she asked, "Where are we headed next?"

"Breyton," Jared muttered, digging out a tin of ground betnut and filling his lower lip with the red narcotic powder. "They have a good crowd at the gaming tables in the Inn."

He shot a thin stream of red tinted spittle to one side, rubbing at the blackened gums he sported with a dirty finger, the mark of a betnut user. Beryl fought to keep her disgust from her face. It was a nasty habit. She shuddered as she avoided his spittle.

She didn't bother responding, moving to place her bedroll farther away. It was always the same. They traveled from town to town, Jared fleecing those he could at the gaming tables or negotiating for her to ward the town or people's homes. She was so tired of it.

She thought about her small horde of coin and supplies with a sigh. It was enough to get her to the coast, but she would need more for passage. She had her magic and not much else to pay her way; it would have to be enough.

"Just a little more, a few more months," she whispered under her breath. She rubbed one gem on her Father's belt, trying to ignore how many times she'd made that same promise to herself.

They reached Breyton two days later, just as the last bit of light slipped from the sky. Jared went straight to the inn, but Beryl dawdled outside. Jared would go straight to the bar to drink before gambling for the rest of the night. The wave of laughter and music that came from the open door was enough to keep her outside. The inn was packed with people, and she wanted some time to relax without having to ward a corner of the bar from intruders.

The tiny village sat at a crossroads. Glancing around, she turned down a side road. She walked along until she came to a small clearing with a pile of boulders. Climbing up, she fished out the small bundle the villager had given her. She might as well see they had given her.

Inside she found a pair of brown leather gloves that were a size too big. She set them in her pack and pulled out a wrapped packaged of honey bars, a slab of berries and nuts held together with honey. Happily, she broke off a piece and took a bite, letting the hard mass of honey and berries melt as she sucked on the treat.

Next, there was a small bag of herbal leaves that could be seeped to make tea, a small pot of healing balm, three candles, and a black pouch which was bound and sealed with wax. She tucked everything away but the pouch, feeling the rough leather and rolling the contents between her fingers as she crunched through another bite of berries and nuts.

Breaking the seal, she almost dropped the three stones that rolled into her hand, smooth spheres of onyx, jade, and moonstone. Each was about the size of a walnut. Where in the world had such a tiny village gotten them? They were stones without flaw, waiting for magic to be poured into them—blank wells waiting to be filled.

She hopped down after replacing everything in the bundle except for a last chunk of nut bar. Clearing a spot of ground near the boulders, Beryl wrote a quick circle of runes and prepared to call in the pack where she kept her handful of treasures and supplies she didn't want Jared finding. The actual bolt hole where she stored her pack was in a well warded cliff face near her old childhood home, originally a hideaway in the event of an attack by raiders on the village. It was well hidden and unused now that she was the only family left who knew of the location. After a few weeks of Jared's 'tender care,' she'd crafted the two-way sending spell to protect her things.

Writing the last rune, she paused. Her father had often spoken of magic having ways to correct wrongs. She had stopped believing in that soon after the news arrived. Tears built in her eyes as she remembered the day. She had been staying with a neighbor while her parents traveled. It had been their first big trip since the accident, but the creditors would wait no longer. Her father was sent off on a commission, and her mother went with him as a minor holiday; neither reached their destination.

Attacked by robbers, they were killed on the road. Her father was struck by an arrow before he could cast a ward; her mother died of her injuries soon after. The attackers were caught trying to sell the mage belt her father had always worn.

Dashing the tears from her eyes before they could fall, she finished the circle and sent her pack back to its hiding place. After scuffing the marks away, she headed back into town, fingers lingering on the gem studded chain belt she wore. She needed to make sure Jared had gotten her a room. In the last town she had to sleep in the Inn's stable, and she was still tired from the fight and warding two days ago.

. . .

BERYL SPENT the next two days doing what she could to avoid her Uncle. He was in a foul mood, and he dragged her from the room that first morning by her hair, tossing her clothes out after her. The small wards she cast around her bed had failed in the night. She was just too fatigued to try casting something stronger.

She spent her time wandering the town, trading small wards and charms for supplies they would need once Jared left the village. Her nights were spent in their room at the Inn or in a small, warded corner of the barroom. She waited through the hours, counting her savings, trying to decide if it was enough to run with. If she could get far enough away, eventually Jared would have to give up on her, and she would be free to do what she wished.

They had been at the Inn for two days when the visions caught up with her. She was walking across the main floor, heading toward the stair to the Inn's rooms when pain stole away her sight. She crumpled as the Inn faded from her sight and was replaced with a battlefield.

Her eyes were drawn to a bloody and sweat stained soldier as he fought his way toward a fallen comrade. Her head pounded a marching beat as she staggered her way to his side. She watched, unable to speak or touch the soldier as he tried to help his friend.

"Captain," the fallen man gasped, as he coughed and choked on the blood filling his lungs, his grey uniform stained black.

The man pulled the soldier over his shoulder and started fighting his way back to the camp they marched from hours before. The surrounding landscape was blurred, Beryl's only focus was the man and his burden. She followed as they wended their slow way through the fighting, watching as he fought through the debris and picked his way around the bodies.

A trumpet sounded in the distance and most of the fighters disengaged, pulling back to their own lines. Nearly every man was injured; they were all exhausted. Beryl watched in silence as the Captain staggered to the medical tents with his lifeless cargo.

CHAPTER 2

*C*harles Marshal, a Captain in Arden's Army and a member of the King's Guard, strode into Breyton's Inn fighting against a sigh. Thankfully, this trip was nearly over. He adjusted the red cuffs that proclaimed his rank and made his way to the bar.

Every garrison was running increased patrols hoping to limit Northern Raiders in the area. The fact was that many of the raiders were simply the farmers and ex-soldiers whose homes and crops had been razed in the pervious years. It impossible to track the accurate reports of raids from the near constant reports of attack or theft by those displaced.

"Can I help you, Soldier?" the bartender called out, gesturing to Charles to take a seat at the bar.

"It's Captain, Captain Marshal. I'm looking for the Innkeeper?"

"That would be me as well. Are you looking for a room, Captain, or an enjoyable meal?"

"I was told you had a mage staying here. I was hoping to talk with them."

A drunk at the end of the bar laughed, "That waste? What would you be wanting her for? Not even a proper mage, is she? She has fits, collapsing and bleeding all over the place." Draining the last of his ale, he slapped the mug down in front of the innkeeper. "Another."

With a sigh, the innkeeper refilled the mug and gave it to him. Gesturing the soldier to the far end of the bar, he drew up two mugs of cider. "I didn't know she was in any trouble," he mumbled, handing one mug to the soldier and taking a drink of his own. The soldier assured him she was not. "The King has declared that all mages must go to the capital to be registered. I have to give her a copy of the declaration and make sure she is headed that way as soon as possible."

The innkeeper finished his cider and began methodically washing the mug, "Well, you won't be telling her much of anything today," He said with a huff. "The drunk and the Mage walked in three days ago. He has been drinking and gaming his money away." The bartender continued with disgust, "The girl is a mage. She warded several homes here, wouldn't even take a coin for it. She only comes to the inn to sleep, walks the town the rest of the day." Topping off the soldier's cider, he eyed the drunk.

"Yesterday she came in and collapsed halfway across the floor, had some kind of fit, limbs trembling and jerking. We got her into bed and called the healer, but she's yet to wake up. Her room is at the top of the stairs," he said, gesturing to the landing behind them, "She is a pleasant girl, stuck with an ungrateful relative." He reached out to stop the Captain before he could move away, he entreated, "Is there anything you can do?"

"I have to report to the King at the end of this trip. If she makes it to the capital, I can make sure they know of her problems. The King does not enjoy seeing his subjects in such situations. He may help. If not, there are others who will."

After brushing off the Innkeepers thanks, he headed up the stairs to see the mage who inspired such concern. He doubted the King would have bothered with a normal civilian's home life, but Mages were all but considered property of the Crown. She would become a ward of the Crown or one of the nobles if she needed a new home away from her current guardian.

He found an older woman sitting next to the bed as he entered the room. The mage herself lay on her back with covers drawn up to her chin. A bloody bandage was wrapped around her head, the reason she hadn't awakened yet.

The woman leaped up, "Thank Ruth, are you here for the mage?"

Nodding distractedly, he surveyed the rest of the room. A pile of baggage sat in one corner. Lining the window sill were straight stacks of what looked like river stones, worn smooth by the current. The local healer stood next to the bed wringing her hands. "I've done what I can. She needs a true healer to see to the head wound. I'm just a midwife; I know nothing about fits like she had."

Turning back to eye the girl he interrupted, "Can she be moved? I can take her to the next town; they have a temple to Ruth there and healers."

"Yes, I'll start getting her ready now." She said, nearly crying in relief. Charles nodded and went to speak with the innkeeper; half an hour later they were on the road to the next town with a Healer's Temple with the mage cradled in a mass of blankets inside a borrowed cart. He'd left her uncle there insensible from drink and a well placed left hook. The bar owner could point him to the healers hall once he recovered his wits and manners.

* * *

"WILL SHE BE ABLE TO TRAVEL?" Charles asked, watching as the healer tended to the mage's head wound.

"The wound is superficial, just a slight cut and bruising. She's unconscious from magical exhaustion. She should wake up in the morning once her core recharges itself. The healing will help with that, but she will be tired for several more days."

"But she is all right to travel?" He pressed the healer, needing to know what orders to give his men.

"Yes." The healer said, sounding annoyed at the interruptions.

"Good," he said, sighing. The last thing he needed was to report to the crown was a potential mage damaged by her guardian and left to die in some backwater town thanks to the general incompetence of her guardian.

"Captain, if you are going to loom over my patient you can assist me," the healer snapped in exasperation, gesturing him forward.

"What do you need me to do?" he asked. He'd helped with battlefield injuries, but mages and magic was beyond his depth.

"Help me get her undressed so I can see if there are other injuries."

The healer directed him to prop the limp young woman up as she was unclothed and examined. Both drew a breath at the scars visible in the lamplight. The twined scars that ran up her arms resembled branched lightning forking across her back and chest. Charles laid her back down at the healer's gesture and tilted her head away from the light, exposing bruises along her neck and collarbone.

"Could she have done this in the fall?" he asked already knowing the answer in his gut.

"No, I've seen too many bruises like that from fights in the local inn, and here," she said, pointing to the girl's arm, "Someone grabbed her wrist hard enough to bruise."

"I will need to send word of this to my superiors. Can I count on you for a statement on this?" Charles asked, ignoring the glare his question earned.

"As a daughter of Ruth I cannot do anything less." She snapped, "The elders at the temple also need to be informed, however first, let's make sure this child is healthy."

Stepping back to allow the healer space to work, he surveyed the girl he had found. Her long brown hair was pulled back in a fraying braid with golden highlights left by the sun. She was thin to the point of looking starved, yet muscles showed their lean lines along her arms and flanks. She had pale skin with a light tan where she'd been exposed to the sun and weather.

He wondered how old she was. A faint tracery of old scars ran along her collarbones and shoulders, marking her back, chest, arms, and hands. He forced himself to list her injuries dispassionately. She had two cracked ribs, and a sprained shoulder according to the healer's quick assessment, a hand shaped bruise along one shoulder and finger shaped bruises along her throat. A black ring of bruises wrapped around one wrist.

A golden glow outlined the healer's hands as she dealt with the broken or fractured bones, the light throwing the mage's face into stark relief. Charles added another year on to his estimate. Even in rest there was a tension to the girl's features, a look that said she had seen too much, too soon. He had seen the same look on soldiers fresh out of battle and had worn the mask himself. He wondered if her eyes would show her wounds.

It was late when he rode back to the inn to deal with

The mage and her guardian had had little baggage, far too little for even a traveling peasant, much less a mage. He'd surveyed the pitiful pile with a sigh, he'd have to deal with the Uncle soon enough. Then, he turned to his next problem—the stones she'd stacked around the room.

"Can you tell me what the stacks of stones are? Are they important?" Charles asked, watching as the innkeeper laughed and scratched his head.

"We caught her building those all over town. When we asked about it she said they were for protection. We left her to it, figured it couldn't hurt." Charles nodded, picking up a stone and rolling it in his palm. Mages were known to work with different materials; the smooth river stones might just be what she used. He'd packed them up along with the rest of the belongings and hoped for the best.

It was a two-week trip back to Cardu, the capital. At every village he would inquire about local mages and deliver the proclamation to any mages nearby. None traveled with the soldiers, preferring to make their own way on their own time.

His supervisors might flay him for taking the girl away from her guardian. They had borrowed the innkeeper's horse and cart to carry the girl, but it was heading back with one of his soldiers now. He hoped that he wasn't making his life and job harder by keeping the girl with the troops.

The mage had been unconscious since they had arrived the day before, but the healer claimed she would wake up the next morning and be able to ride, if exhausted from the healing. Having brought her this far, she may as well accompany them the rest of the way to Cardu. It would not do for a young woman to travel without an escort, even if she was a mage.

Charles couldn't return her to the inn and her "Uncle," he thought with a snort, turning to take one last walk through the camped soldiers. The next morning, however, an empty bed in the healer's hall greeted him. A quick search found the girl kneeling on a clear patch of ground, a stone's throw away from the temple, drawing runes into the soil.

"Mage," he said, clearing his throat.

The girl glanced up at him. "Soldier," she replied in the same crisp tone he had used. Turning back to her circle of runes, she placed a stone into the center of the ring.

Taken aback, he opened his mouth to scold her before forcing out a breath and striving to be courteous. "May I ask what you are doing?" he asked, settling into a crouch near her.

"You may." She glanced at him after a moment, taking in his relaxed posture and huffed. "I am retrieving my things." she said, placing her hands atop two of the runes, her voice sounding tired.

"We retrieved your things from your relative…" he trailed off as the circle of runes glowed. With a flash of light, a pack appeared in the middle of the runes. Picking up the pack, she stood, scuffing out the runes. She placed the stone back into her pocket. He forced himself to stand his ground, swallowing as he tried to stop his legs from trembling under him; he wasn't used to such casual displays of magic. Arden hoarded its mages, and it was rare to see them cast at all.

"The healer said that you helped me. Thank you," she said, her eyes to the ground as she adjusted her pack.

"It is my duty, Mistress Mage, as it is my duty to deliver this proclamation to you." Taking out a scroll, he opened his mouth to read, only to be interrupted.

"Your pardon. May I?" She asked. Her grey eyes watched him intensely. Flustered, he handed the scroll to her murmuring, "Of course."

Reading through the proclamation, she saw it was a summons to Cardu, the capital city of Arden. Frowning, she perused the document. Jared would not be happy about this, but she could not ignore a royal summons. She would just have to deal with Jared when it happened.

"All mages are to report to the Capital to renew their vows and be tested," she read aloud before glancing up at the soldier. "It doesn't say that we must travel under guard." She looked at the other soldiers readying their mounts in the temple's courtyard.

"I could not in good conscience leave one of the land's Mages in danger. Now that you are well you may travel as you please," Charles said stiffly. Mages were often considered a law unto themselves; even if she was still a minor, there was little he could do to stop the young woman from traveling alone if she demanded it.

Beryl smiled and held up her hand, shaking her head. "I was asking if I may ride with you to the city? You helped me in a time of need, the least I can do is help your troops as I can along the way," she said. She extended the scroll back to him, "If you ride that way."

Taking back the scroll he relaxed a bit and smiled, "We are working our way back to the Capital. I would not turn down the services of a mage for the journey. I am Captain Charles Marshal. May I ask the name of the mage we will travel with? I'm afraid none of the staff at the inn could recall it."

"No, they wouldn't have," she said with a thin smile. "My name is Beryl Marcian. It is a pleasure to meet you, Captain."

"Charles, please."

"Charles, then. While your men are getting ready, I'll see about getting a horse and contacting my guardian," she said with a frown, turning to look at the village.

"Your guardian has already been informed that you are with me, and that we are planning to escort you to the capital," he said.

Turning back, she looked at him in surprise, "Really? That must have been an interesting conversation. He agreed to this?" she asked, her voice rich with disbelief.

"It was a royal summons. There was no genuine way that he could say no, since a group of the King's soldiers were escorting you, not that he didn't try." The mage hummed in response. "You can ask for a horse at the Inn in town. I'm sure they have a few to sell, or I can see about getting one from the messenger service if you need."

"I think I can find one on my own. Thank you for the advice," she said with a slight grin. She turned and started walking toward one of the side roads that circled the outskirts of the town.

* * *

WITH A SLIGHT SHAKE of her head, she headed down the road into town. It was beyond her to understand how soldiers worked. The man looked stunned that she would travel with his troops and had been waiting for her to fight him on the issue. All she had ever wanted was to get away from Jared and get some training in magic. This might be her chance to change her luck, Ruth willing.

Even if she left the soldiers, she wouldn't have many options. She could evade them easily, but she would be branded as a rogue mage. Nowhere would be safe if that happened.

For now she would have to travel with the Captain and be registered at the capital. Once she was tested and released, she could decide if she was striking out on her own or staying in the capital. Maybe she could stay and study or at least find a small shop to work in until Jared caught up with her. She doubted he would take her being snatched away by the King's soldiers kindly once he sobered up.

In her pack she had a small horde of coins and gems that could work as payment for a horse, but it would put her back if she had to leave the capital. Walking up to a fence on the edge of town, she traced a small rune of calling onto the top rail, releasing her question in a burst of spent magic. A moment later a small sparrow flitted to alight on the rune. She thanked the bird for answering and murmured that she was looking for someone with horses.

Cocking its head, it gave a peep before it flew down a few lengths of fence, landing and looking back at Beryl. Thanking the bird again, Beryl followed it to a side road and along that to a middle-sized farm that looked in good repair. She set a crust of bread on the ground for the bird and went to the farmhouse door. An older woman answered and Beryl straightened, hoping the woman would not see her injuries.

"Hello Ma'am. I'm sorry to bother you, but I'm trying to find a horse for sale. Do you know of anyone in town looking to sell?"

"What would a young woman your age be doing looking for a horse?"

"I'm a mage, Ma'am." She said, gesturing to her gem studded belt. "I have been asked to return to the capital and need a horse to do so. I can pay a fair price." Beryl insisted, wincing at how much of her funds this would cost. The woman eyed her for a moment before gesturing for her to follow.

"I have a horse for sale. My husband, Ruth bless him, passed away a few months ago, and the farm will soon be sold."

"I am sorry to hear that, Ma'am."

"Call me Ester, dear."

"My name is Beryl. It's a pleasure to meet you, Ester."

"You as well, dear. I am sorry for sounding skeptical, but you look like a runaway, child."

"I had a bit of an accident," Beryl said with a blush, wishing she could heal the bruises away herself.

"Life is full of accidents, child. Here he is," she said, stopping at a small field behind the house. "Expecting a used up plow horse, I see." The old woman laughed at the look of shock on Beryl's face, "My man used to be a royal messenger before he retired to farm his father's land. He always had an eye for splendid horses." Reaching out, she rubbed the nose of a sturdy white and brown gelding. Built for endurance and not speed, he looked like he could go for days with his heavily muscled hind end and chest.

"This here is Flox; he is a mountain breed cross. He'll truck through heavy mud and rain like no other." As they talked about the horse, they walked the length of the pasture. Flox followed for a few strides before stopping and snatching at the sparse grass of the field.

"Now, I have tack in the barn, let me show you."

"Ma'am, I'm not sure I can afford such a horse. He's too fine."

"Nonsense, my son will come in a few weeks to help me pack up and sell the farm. I would rather Flox go to someone who will care for him than to be sold to strangers at an auction," she said with finality. "Come, let's sort out which tack will work for you."

Shaking her head, the mage followed behind the old woman, who was telling of the various deeds her late husband had accomplished in the King's service. This thing often happened when you used magic to ask a question. The answer may not be what you thought you needed, but later was indispensable; you had to go as the Gods willed sometimes.

Soon she was on her way, her purse lighter but saddlebags bulging with things the old woman insisted she needed, from a currycomb, brush, and hoof pick, to grain for the horse and a packet of food for the rider. Along with the tack, light rope and stakes to picket the horse were included. The saddle "came with" a bedroll, and basic camping gear filled one saddlebag. There was even a small tin of fishing gear and a few jars of healing herbs and balms for the horse if he got injured.

Provisioned, Beryl headed out to meet the soldiers she would travel with for the next week. The horse was fresh and ready to be moving, striding out at a swinging, brisk walk. The soldiers were waiting when she arrived, and the Captain ordered them to mount up with a grin.

"Only a mage," he said with a laugh, taking in the sturdy looking mount. "Come, let's get the beast settled in the line."

They traveled at a trot, alternating with a brief period of walking to rest the horses, and reached the next town just after midday. Beryl dismounted, loosening the girth and walking her horse to cool the animal before he could have some water. Once he was cool enough, she let him drink and graze on a lead line to one side.

Charles came up and offered her a mug of broth with a slab of toasted bread and cheese balanced on top. He watched her stake the horse so he could graze in peace while she ate. They sat next to each other in silence for a long while, both content to enjoy the simple meal.

"There are no mages here so we will move out after everyone eats. It's a day and a half ride to the next town. Would you be willing to ward the camps at night?" he asked, watching as she chewed with obvious pleasure a mouthful of bread and cheese dipped in broth.

Swallowing, she nodded, "Of course. I can ward the camps, keep the fires contained and burning all night, and assist if we encounter raiders."

He gestured away the last part, "The soldiers are here to do that, don't you worry. But I never turn away a hand in a fight."

CHAPTER 3

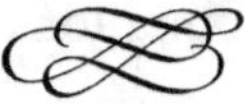

*C*harles watched the young mage riding ahead of him. She was not like any girl he'd ever encountered. After a night of watching the bruised and broken child healing, he was not prepared for this awakened mage. The scar-covered girl held a fire and spirit that could rival all the girls he knew. The girl, no young woman, stood tall and confident, speaking with assurance and poise; this was not a beaten youngster who would cower before him.

With a frown, he edged her mental age closer to his. His superiors may flay him when he got back; he'd expected to return with an abused child who was being used for her gift. Instead, he had a confident mage who, while still used and abused, seemed more mature than the other adults around her.

The question of her age bothered him. Why had she put up with this "Uncle Jared" if she was old enough to have married? Fifteen-year-old girls were often married, and a powerful mage would have been welcomed in almost any family, as it would increase the chance for magical children. Compared to the demure girls and women he was used to, this girl was a mystery.

His own sister had babbled nonstop of babies and marriage as long as he could remember, yet this girl seemed to have actively avoided it.

Some mages dedicated their lives to Ruth and would forgo marriage and their family names for the rest of their lives. He could not name one girl, who if asked, would not jump into a marriage. He didn't know of any that lived alone, much less dressed and worked as this mage did. It simply wasn't the way things were done.

The key thing that stopped his tongue from calling her a spirited child and dismissing her presence were her eyes. Those grey green orbs stared out of a face too young for them. Those eyes belonged in the face of a battle hardened warrior or an ancient scholar, not on the face of a girl less than twenty summers.

Once they had been on the road for a few days, the soldiers were much more relaxed around the woman. Charles pulled a small bag from his saddlebags and handed it to Beryl. "In all the commotion of finding a healer, I forgot about this."

With a hum she opened it, breaking into a quick laugh at the contents—the stones she had placed on her window sill at the inn to form part of a protective ward sat nestled in the bag's bottom. "This is the last thing I expected you to find. They have a forgetting spell laced into them."

Charles sputtered, "But the midwife and innkeeper knew about them!"

"They saw me building them, so I explained. A few days after I left they would have had no memory of the stones. After that, anyone that saw them who was not a mage would simply ignore them." Turning one over in her palm she asked, "Do you have any mages in your family?"

"In a soldier's family? No, no magic at all." He said looking shocked.

She shook her head with a smile, "I would not say that too firmly. My father was the son of a fisherman. No one had ever had magic in my family until him, but my cousins and uncles have a knowing about how the sea will run that day and many of the women are midwives and small healers who helped with the day-to-day illnesses of the village." Turning back to face the road she smiled, "Not all magic has to be large and showy."

He laughed, making her glance back at him. "Most magic I've seen is showy, all lights and smoke, loud bangs and lots of hand waving." She laughed. For such a serious girl, she had a beautiful glow about her when she laughed.

"Some people enjoy the spectacle, they expect a show. My father always said casting a good spell was show enough. He thought it sloppy to waste so much energy on theatrics. A man plowing a field can see how much he has completed without lights and smoke to announce it. So can a mage," she said with a wry grin.

"Your father was a wise man," he murmured with a smile.

"Yes, though many looked down on him because of his ancestry and contempt for most of the common trappings of magic." She said with a snort, "Most of the gestures are wasted; you don't need the priceless gems and golden instruments and bowls or robes that most affluent mages use."

That night Charles dropped to a seat next to the woman. She'd claimed a prime spot next to the fire after warding the camp for the night. She had spent much of the last day talking to several members of the squad as they traveled. None of his men were openly against magic users that he could tell, and so far they all seemed at ease with the young woman.

"My men are saying we're traveling with a cursed mage. No one seems to be able to remember your name, Mistress Mage. Not even me."

"Maybe I am cursed," she said with a bitter smile, "Cursed with an unremarkable name, forgettable."

"I doubt that. Somehow I think you are all too memorable." They sat in silence for a moment while she shredded a piece of grass. "And your scars?" he asked. "Those are not the marks of a gentle life. Even in all the battles I have seen, I've never seen scars like that."

"Few people would," she said, crumbling the dry stalk between her fingers until nothing remained. "They attacked me when I was little. A rogue mage stole me away and tried to cast a spell on me. The spell failed, and the mage left me for dead."

"Yet you survived."

"Yes," she agreed, her voice soft. "I was found and healed, but the healing reacted with a spell meant to prevent me from speaking of the attack. It strengthened it and twisted it until no one remembers me or the spell."

"But you are speaking of it."

"And in the morning you will not remember," she said with a bitter laugh, tears pooling in her eyes. "The healing twisted the spell, and now no one remembers my name, no matter how many times I tell them."

"Surely it isn't that bad. We could call you whatever you wanted."

"No," she said with a sigh, shaking her head, "any name I claim as my own is forgotten. When I die no one who ever knew me will know who I was. They will think I was just some random person they knew."

"I don't believe that. Tell me your name again," he insisted, watching her with eyes reflecting the light from the fire.

"Why? You know you will not remember it."

"Maybe I will. Tell me, and we will see in the morning. I will spend my night reciting your name to seal it within me," he said with a grin, teeth flashing in the dark.

"That's nonsense."

"Perhaps. Tell me anyway."

"Beryl. My name is Beryl." She said it like she was reminding herself as well.

"Beryl, a lovely stone and a lovely name. Thank you for telling me, Beryl."

"You are a fool, Charles," she said with a slight laugh.

"Perhaps, but only fools can move a woman from tears to laughter. Ask me in the morning, Beryl, and we will see," he said with a grin, his teeth flashing in the firelight. "Goodnight, Beryl."

"Goodnight, Charles," she whispered, watching as the man moved to his bedroll next to the other soldiers.

In the morning Beryl ate a small bowl of porridge with the other soldiers while she waited for the captain to finish his morning rounds and gather his own bowl.

"Good morning, Charles." she whispered, eyeing the sleep mussed man.

"Morning, Miss Mage. Did you have a good night?"

"It was fine," she mumbled, turning away to get her horse ready for the day's journey.

She had been foolish to hope that the spell could be broken so easily. She had lived with this curse since she was five years old, and in the last ten years no one had broken it. Not even her father, whom everyone had said was a powerful mage. Why would one soldier's reassurances matter?

The mage sat wearily in the saddle as their horses plodded along. Watching the Captain's back, she pondered the man. He was young to be a captain, looking to be in his late twenties or early thirties; however he was good with his men and had their respect. He had taken the risk of taking her away from her guardian and letting her travel with his soldiers before he knew how she was injured or even how she would react to waking up surrounded by soldiers.

She kept trying to dismiss his kindness as a soldier doing his duty. However, if that was the case, he could have left her with the healer and continued on his journey. Instead, he had stayed and helped with the healing, waiting for her to wake up so he could explain what had happened. He had stayed to give her the proclamation, but he could just as have left it with the healers and continued his journey. He was a conundrum, and she was not sure she wanted to solve it.

* * *

THEY WERE STILL a week from Cardu when the mage reined her horse to a stop and turned like she would say something to the soldier next to her. She slid boneless from the saddle between one breath and the next. Charles muttered thanks to several Gods as her horse stood without shying, giving the nearest soldier time to untangle her foot from the stirrup. Two men pulled her to a patch of the grass beside the road as she started twitching and jerking.

Once she had stopped shaking, Charles snapped a gurn from the medicine kit. The branches of a gurn plant released a foul-smelling stimulant; cut into small lengths and sealed with wax, were carried them in most healers' kits. Waving the pungent stick below her nose, the young woman came to with a gasp as the plant did its work.

"Are you hurt?" he asked, reaching out to stop her from getting up as she winced.

"Bruised, but not broken," she said, clearing her throat.

"Let's make sure of that first," he drawled, feeling along each limb before he helped her to sit up. She only winced as he pressed on the arm she had landed on when she fell from her horse. It was scrapped and already turning purple with bruises. He took a canteen from another hovering soldier and had her take a few small sips.

"Simmons, find somewhere to make camp nearby!" he barked before turning back to the mage. "I take it that was a fit your Uncle told me about?"

"Yes, but they're not fits." He waited for her to continue, wetting a cloth to clean the scraped skin that now adorned one arm and her chin. With a sigh she went on, "I get visions. My father was teaching me how to control them when he was died."

"Visions of what exactly?"

"People I know, people I might meet. Places I've been to or never seen before. Sometimes it's the future, sometimes the past."

"And this time?"

"The ocean, ships burning in a harbor. Smoke billowing, ash falling like snow. A hawk circling above."

"Is this happening now or in the past?"

"I don't know. It didn't look like a town I've seen before."

"What can I do to help?" Charles asked.

"Nothing," she said, staring at him in shock. "Seeing something doesn't mean I can change anything. It means nothing."

"Gifts are never given without a reason."

"Gifts?" she said with a snort. "That's what my father used to call it. A God's gift. How is seeing people in pain or dying a gift?"

"You see pleasurable things as well?"

"I saw you in my vision at Breyton," she said, making him flinch before he caught himself.

"Me? In your vision?" he asked, as he bandaged her scrapped arm.

"Yes. You were carrying another soldier away from a battlefield," she intoned. "He called you Captain and died in your arms."

"Three years ago on the Northern border. His name was Phillips, Marcus Phillips. I had just been made Captain in a field promotion."

"I'm sorry."

"It's fine. He was an excellent soldier. He deserves to be remembered by more than just his commanding officer." he blew out a harsh breath. "Everyone deserves to be remembered."

Later that night, Charles came awake with a start as someone shook his shoulder. The mage crouched next to him, her long hair brushing against his neck.

"What?" he snapped, fighting to get his sleep heavy limbs to work.

"Someone's coming," she said, her hand on Charles' shoulder, voice low in his ear. "Ten or more have tripped the perimeter ward."

Silently he roused the rest of the camp. The twang of bows and crossbows broke the waiting silence. The soldiers scrambled to duck behind shields only to watch the arrows strike the now visible ward and fall to the ground.

"Will it let our arrows past?" he asked, eyes taking in the lines of fire the arrows were coming from, trying not to flinch as the front line of soldiers did every time an arrow stopped a hand's breadth from their face, striking the pale silver dome that now encased the camp.

She plucked an arrow from the soldier next to her and laid a hand on the barrier. Both glowed for a moment. "Now they will," she said, sinking to the ground with a hand to her head.

Charles barked, "Ware arrows, fire at will."

"Are you all right?" he asked, sparing her a glance in the darkness.

"Headache," she snapped. "Deal with your soldiers."

The battle was short-lived, and it surprised Charles at how thankful he was of that fact. The raiders retreated and disappeared into the woods, taking their injured with them. Some arrows made it through the warding, but none of the soldiers were injured beyond bruises and scrapes. He was worried about the mage; she'd collapsed back onto her bedroll as soon as the fight was over.

They spent the morning burying the handful of dead raiders and sending out part of the squad to scout for clues where the raiders had headed. They sent another soldier with a message to the nearest guard station warning them about the attack. Charles tried to keep the camp quiet and the soldiers working as the mage slept.

He put off moving camp as long as possible, but the mage was still pale and limp in the saddle as they road to the closest town. The rest of the day was spent calming the town's mayor and fielding reports of other such local attacks with the head of the town watch, arranging for a troop of soldiers from the guard station to scout the area with the local watch and set up a rotating group to guard the town.

Even for such a modest sized town, its isolation left it vulnerable to attack if the raiders grew bold. It looked like the raiders were local toughs, so he had given the descriptions of those killed to the local guard. Their families may wish to know of the deaths. He delivered the proclamation to a local mage and his student, who agreed to head for the castle at the end of the week.

Charles ignored for the moment how much chaos he would have to deal with if the soldiers stayed in town that night. Instead, he concentrated on getting the mage a room and a healer to look at her head. Two blows to the head in less than a week could not be good.

The troops camped just outside of town, but Charles let them visit the tavern and inn if they wanted. Amazingly, the soldiers behaved themselves, and he didn't have to break up any drunken fights or deal with any property damage that night.

By the next morning they were back on the road to the castle. The healer in town had declared the mage fit for travel but cautioned the young woman to rest. Sadly, that was not something the Captain could grant. He had his duty to the army to fulfill, and an injured mage was not enough to prevent that. He could slow their pace for the next two days, however, until the young woman no longer collapsed into her bed roll each night like she was dropping dead.

CHAPTER 4

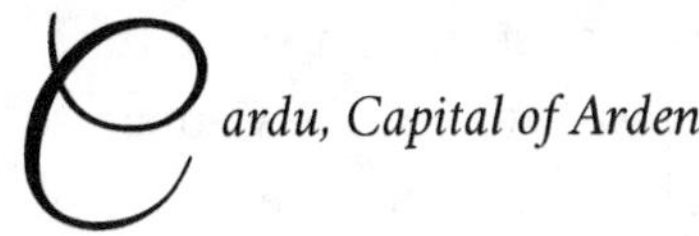

CHARLES STOOD at attention on one side of the room. The King was holding the petitioners court in a nearby audience hall. Normally, he would have turned in his reports upon arrival, but with the complications that had arisen on his trip, he sent a soldier ahead to ask for a private audience.

He pulled himself back into a more rigid stance as the door opened. Charles saluted as King John Roscomb, Queen Marie Roscomb, the King's magical adviser, Lord Darius Fremont, and the King's steward, Lord Rupert Calehill entered the room.

"Please Captain, be seated. I know you are tired after such a lengthy journey," King John said with a smile.

Charles took a chair with a slight smile. He always enjoyed his interactions with the King. He had come to the crown after a brief career in the army both well liked him the public and those in power. Charles got right to the point. "Distribution of the proclamation is going well. All towns within a seven-day ride have been informed, and the next round of messengers is heading out to those beyond. By the end of the month it will be given to every mage in the country."

"Your message mentioned some complications on the return trip?"

"Yes, Sire," he said, taking a cup of tea with a murmur of thanks to the serving maid. "When we arrived in Breyton, we discovered a young female mage who had been injured. It was not clear if they had hurt her in an attack or by her Uncle. I moved her to the next town where there was a healer so they could treat her. She confirmed that most of the young woman's injuries were from abuse. However, the original cause of her collapse was because of what the Mage called 'uncontrolled visions.'"

"Visions? Preposterous!" Lord Rupert said loudly. "You agree, Darius? No one has shown signs of true visions for generations."

"It would have to be investigated, Rupert. I will not dismiss a possible magical gift just because we have not seen it in some time," Lord Darius replied. He leaned forward, gesturing for the Captain to continue. "It is clear she is a powerful mage who needs a new guardian. What was her name?" Lord Darius asked. "Would we know her family?"

"That is the strange part. Although I asked several times, and she told me, I cannot remember her name, nor can any of the other soldiers that traveled with us. Some said they asked multiple times but could not remember the name afterwards. I hoped that a mage could look into this," the soldier said, uncomfortable with the situation.

"How strange. Did she offer any explanation?" The King asked, motioning for a page, "Bring her in, please."

"She said they attacked her as a child by a rogue mage. She was found and in the healing, a spell to prevent her from speaking of the crime was altered."

* * *

BERYL CAME in a few moments later, following the page. She was all but swaying with exhaustion. She wore the grime of road dirt, and horse sweat. Beryl looked anything but ready for a royal audience, yet she steeled her spine and dipped into a low curtsey that would have made her mother proud.

"Please, sit. Captain Marshal has explained your situation, and we are in agreement that you need a new guardian and magical training to control your visions. However, the matter of your name has come up." King John surveyed the girl with a raised eyebrow.

Beryl flushed and hastily said, "Yes, I'm sure I need to explain. When I was five, I got away from my nurse, chasing a cat, I believe. I was attacked and found the next morning." She rolled her sleeves back to expose her scars.

"My father, Mage Zyon Marcian, used a massive amount of magic to save me. In the process he altered the spell cast on me by my attacker. I could not tell people the details of the attack or who attacked me." She paused, "Well, I could tell them, but they forgot once the conversation was over. Also, I could tell no one my name who did not already know me before the spell, nor could anyone else."

"Surely you must go by something? You could pick any name you wished!" the King's Steward retorted. Beryl blushed, forcing herself to face him and with a lift of her chin, correct him.

"No, sir. As soon as I respond to the name as my own, the spell removes it. Common terms work best. Everyone calls me Mage because that is what I am; however, it is not my name, so I can always use it," she said stiffly. Lord Rupert looked affronted at this and opened his mouth to chastise the child, but Darius interrupted him.

"Your father could not break it? Marcian was one of the more powerful mages in his day." He raised his eyebrows in disbelief, glancing at the King and Charles to see what their reactions were. Charles looked amused at the spirit the girl was showing, while the King watched with a guarded expression.

"No, Lord Darius. When he healed me, the spell was accidentally attached to the healing. He was too afraid that he might undo the healing and protection runes he had woven into the wounds."

The older mage blanched at this, "Strong spells cause a complete backlash when removed. There is an excellent chance it would have killed the child," he said to the King.

"The spell must stay then. However, I am not sure we can continue calling you Mage in a castle full of mages." The King frowned in thought before the Queen touched his arm, drawing him close for a murmured comment, "Yes," he said with a smile for her, "we can decide it another day. Both you and the Captain must be tired from your journey. The page outside can show you to a room in the guest wing for now. In three days you will go before a group of Master Mages to be questioned and tested in your craft."

"Thank you, Sire." Beryl said, standing. She paused awkwardly clearing her throat, "Sire, if I may, I have a horse. Who would I need to see about its care? I have some money for its upkeep," she said.

The King floundered for a second over what to call her, and with a slight frown continued. "Mage, for the moment you are a guest of the castle and owe nothing. If they test you and you become an apprentice here, you will be charged as an apprentice would. Your mount's expenses will be included in that." The girl curtsied and thanked the King. Charles led the way out into the entryway, handing Beryl off to the waiting page.

Beryl barely remembered the trip back to the guest room and bed. She changed into the night shirt that had been left out for her and after a cursory wash slid into the bed as a maid started a small fire to chase away the chill.

CHAPTER 5

$\mathcal{B}$eryl had three days of waiting and fretting ahead of her until her testing began. She spent most of the first day in her room organizing her things and trying to plan where she would be headed after the results of her testing were reviewed. None of her options were looking good.

There were too many problems with running away now that she was in the castle. Her curse may help people forget her name, but it didn't force them to forget about her. They would know that a potential mage had come in for testing, even if they could not remember what she was called. If she ran they could label her a rogue mage and hunted if she stayed in the country.

If they registered her as a full mage she would be assigned a job somewhere by the Mage's Counsel. She might still travel depending on where she was assigned, but she would have very little input in where she was posted.

If they apprenticed her, her new Master would have ultimate control of everything she did. He would control her work and studies completely until she passed the tests and became a full mage. They would force her to bow to her Master's whims for up to five years, and after that, if they assigned her to work with them.

None of her options were pleasant. She almost wished she'd simply run as soon as Charles dismissed her to find a horse. It had been tempting, but the chance at an education and legal job had made her stay. She hoped she would not come to regret that decision.

Beryl wandered the streets of Cardu, trying to let the swarming crowds fill her mind instead of worrying about her upcoming tests. She moved with a smooth stride like she had somewhere to be, her feet automatically taking her away from the well-kept stores and homes. Twisting, she caught the hand of a pickpocket trying to lift the coin purse at her belt.

"Pick someone else to tap, boy," she said, taking in the ragged clothes on a boy that might have been eight years old.

"Let me go!" he snarled, twisting in her grasp.

"Learn to spot someone who's watching the street before you earn a broken arm," she snapped, releasing the child and moving away before he could retaliate.

The boy ran off without a backwards glance. He would need to brush up on his skills if he didn't want to lose fingers. The standard punishment for a child pickpocket was the loss of a pinkie finger on the left hand. If he was caught again, they marked the other hand. Once both hands were marked, the criminal was sentenced to prison time, to work in the mines, or to work houses, no matter their age.

She might not steal herself, but she had learned the basics of too many ways to trick and deceive while she traveled with Jared. After all, her playmates had been the children of whores and gamblers who frequented the taverns and inns that Jared worked.

It hadn't been that bad traveling with Jared at first. He did his best, making sure she was at least clothed and fed. She spent most of those past years waiting in rented rooms or hiding in corners of crowded gaming halls. Once she started using magic around him, and he realized she could cast small wards and spells, he started selling her skills when cash was tight.

She could feel some tension in her neck and shoulders ease as she moved into the shadier parts of town. She'd been working toward getting away from Jared for years now, but she had lived with the man for eight years. He had not always been the bitter drunkard that pushed her to sell her magic and body to the highest bidder.

She ducked into a small tavern off the primary thoroughfare, smiling despite herself as the musky smell of stale beer and the organ meat heavy stew the barmaids were doling out hit her nose. They crowded the area around the gaming table and bar, but most of the small tables covering the floor were empty. Beryl sat at a table near the wall where she could watch the rest of the tavern.

During her travels with Jared from tavern to tavern, she learned to gamble with dice for pennies. She hid under the long gaming tables when she was little, learning the jargon and curses that flowed across the table like the cheap beer and pipe smoke that filled every tavern they visited. Coming back to a tavern was like coming home in some small way.

"Care for a draught and something to eat, Lass?" one barmaid asked, pausing in her rounds next to Beryl's table.

"Stew and hard cider if you have it," Beryl said with a slight smile, relaxing back into her chair.

"It'll be out in no time."

"Thanks."

The game seemed like a relaxed one; all the players were laughing and chatting with each other. As her food arrived, she saw the extra cards slipped into one of the gambler's hands; experience had taught her that trick years ago. Apparently, two of the players were coordinating their hands and rigging them when needed.

Beryl didn't let her eyes stay on the game. Old habits had her watching from the corner of her eye, keeping the slow flow of other patrons in her gaze as she ate, letting the bustle and shout of the winning calm her nerves.

She noticed someone take a seat behind her, but she refused to let her calm go simply because she had caught someone's eye. Beryl did her best to ignore the eyes she could gaze at her from behind, but she pressed a turning spell into a small stone in her pocket just in case. It could be activated with a harsh rap against her side.

"Casing the table for the next deal or planning to take names to the Trolls?" a voice asked from just behind her.

"Nothing like that," Beryl said with a wince, shifting to face the young man who had stopped just short of her table. "I just got into town and my Uncle was a gambler."

"Looking for a game?" he pressed with a quick flash of teeth.

"No, just some place to relax where I know the score," She said, cursing her twisted luck. She might need to leave a few coins at the local trickster's shrine if things kept going awry.

"Well, you've got trained eyes even I if I spotted you. Are you interested in joining the local guild?"

"No," she said, fighting to keep the exasperation out of her voice. "My Uncle was the player, I just learned from proximity."

"He's independent, I take it?"

"Yes, we never stayed in one town long enough to join a guild."

"Fair warning; if you try your hand here, you need to join up. Independents aren't tolerated in Cardu."

"Good to know," Beryl said. "But like I said, my Uncle played, not me. I'll let him know if he comes by."

"What's his name? Maybe we can extend an invitation."

"I doubt he would take it even if you did," she said with a sigh. It figured that Jared would get her in trouble even at a distance. "His name's Jared Voss."

"Not anyone I know but I must let the Watchman know. Long as you stay away from the tables there shouldn't be an issue. If not, you'll owe us the usual Guild fees and tithes, plus a fine for playing without Guild protection."

"I'll keep that in mind," she said, trying to suppress her irritation. "Is there a Guild mark I should watch out for?"

"Yes." He grinned while producing a small knife and scratching out a crude shape, a "u" with a lengthy line through the middle. "I'm Troche."

"Beryl," She said, suppressing a frown. She tried to commit his face to memory as he snatched a pastry from a passing barmaid.

So much for a quiet afternoon to relax, she thought with a mental snort. She watched the young man walk away with a frown. He was about the same age as she was, but he slid through the building crowd in the tavern with skill, barely attracting attention. He snatched two wallets as he moved along.

She might as well head back. Beryl handed off payment for her meal and moved through the crowd to the street. It was getting dark, and she did not know the streets well enough to trust them once night fell. If there was one thieves guild in town, there were bound to be more. She would have to keep an ear out and see who were the current top dogs and their competitor. It would not do to offend either group while she was still a newcomer.

She spent most of the last day before her testing in the palace stables grooming Flox. He had somehow found the only mud puddle in the pasture and now looked like a brown, crusty, plow horse. Turning to exchange the stiff brush for a softer one, she jumped; the Stable master was watching her.

"You must have an expert eye to get this one. He's of a good nature." The man gruffly approached Flox and ran his hands along his head and jaw, checking teeth, before giving the gelding a lump of sugar.

"It was more luck than anything," she murmured, turning and starting to groom again. Running a hand down Flox's leg, the Stable master glanced at her.

"More that he lucked out. You have been here two days and been out to check on him every day. Most people wouldn't set foot in a stable yard for weeks after coming in from a lengthy ride. Come, I'll give you a hand taking him back out." Once they had released him, they stood at the fence watching him wander over to his other stable mates. With a sigh, the stable master pushed away from the fence.

"Let's go, I have stalls to muck and you seem in the need of something to do." They spent the rest of the afternoon cleaning stalls and feeding and grooming horses. It kept her too busy to worry about the upcoming tests and too tired not to sleep that night.

. . .

THE MORNING of her testing she could barely eat. She sat wearing her only dress, fussing with how it lay, waiting for the page to arrive. At the first knock she snatched the door open, startling the waiting page.

"Miss, I am to show you to the examiner's room." Mouth too dry to answer, she nodded and gestured him to precede her.

What should have been a brief walk felt unending. These tests would decide if she stayed here at the castle to learn or if they would grant her her mastery and allowed to go out into the world as an adult. She was dreading either outcome.

Beryl couldn't see herself out working on her own; she'd met too many people like Jared to think of moving from town to town as they had. She would have to choose one village or town and hope they wanted a girl who was also a mage. How could she just choose a place, when she had been nowhere on her own?

Also, there was the problem of Jared. Whether they made her an adult or an apprentice, Jared would protest and try to control her or get money out of the arrangement any way he could. It was what he always did.

She realized with a jerk they were walking toward a tall doorway that was the room where she was to be tested. Once they reached the door, the page announced her, and then gestured for her to enter. Before her were four older gentleman seated on a raised platform with a table in front of them.

"Today on this twenty third day of Hare we will test this... Mage before us. Normally we would begin by having you state your name and titles, however in your circumstances I believe we can overlook this. The spell preventing your name from being remembered is cumbersome," he said as thick lines of disappointment marred his features. "Can you explain this spell again?"

Beryl told of the spell and how dangerous it would be to remove it. "I go by common titles that a mage or girl could be called. Perhaps there is a term used by the college or mage's guild that would suffice?"

"Once a mage develops an affinity to one material or stone they are called by the name of the material, such as an Opal Mage. Perhaps you could be called by the name of the stone you favor?" an older man sitting to the right asked. He had white and grey hair clipped close to his head and a clean-shaved face that watched her sternly as she answered.

"I have not had access to many kinds of gems or stones. I have used common pebbles or river rocks," she answered, struggling to keep her tone polite and even.

The first examiner snapped, "Speak up! What was your answer?" She repeated herself forcefully, her cheeks heating with a blush.

"Then the first thing in your training will be to test which stones you respond best to. For now perhaps we can call you Acolyte in class or by the name of the Master you will be apprenticed to," he said, leaning away from her with a look of disgust.

One of the other mages leaned forward, giving her a piercing stare. "Your jewelry is rather unusual for such a young mage. May I ask where you received it?"

"The belt was my father's. They returned it to me upon his death." She touched the chain link that draped low on her hips as she spoke.

"And the others?" he demanded sourly. None of the Mage's Counsel were enjoying having to test a young girl months before the regular testing occurred each year.

"When my grandfather passed away, they sent his belongings to my mother. I was helping her sort through several trunks, and in doing so I found a case with the cuffs and necklace. Because I was young, I tried them on only to be unable to remove them. Father said that the jewelry had chosen me. I've worn them ever since." She replied as calmly as she could, forcing her chin up and her eyes to meet the stare of her questioner.

The men shifted and muttered among themselves. The man who had yet to speak silenced the room with a raised hand. "There have been rumors of jewelry spelled to choose the mage that could weld them, but I did not know of an actual case ever being found." With a shake of his head, he dismissed the topic.

"While this may need further study, we are here to test this young mage. Let us complete this task before we delve into mysteries. Now, one last question, I could find no records of you being tested by a

Mage Finder. Were you tested in your eighth year as is mandated by the crown?" he asked, eying her sternly.

"Yes sir, I was tested by my father as he was a mage." The man frowned at this before turning back to the paperwork in front of him. "Perhaps, in his death, they misplaced the forms. We will have to look into this," he said, shuffling the stack of parchment in front of him.

The testing began immediately. They gave her a simple spell to preform, and the examiners would tut over each effort. They pushed her to do increasingly difficult spells. She started with lighting a candle and continued casting increasingly difficult spells until they asked her to create a ring of protective fire about herself. They pushed until she could not cast the requested spell, and then they would move onto the next spell.

Demonstrations inter-spaced with questions on magical theory and spell crafting rounded out the tests. Often she would accomplish the task in a manner that no one taught and would have to explain how she came to use such a method. It became obvious that there were massive gaps in her education.

While she had a solid grasp on the basics, her formal education had ended at ten when her parents died. She had gone straight from the funeral to her Uncle's care. She learned what she could from the occasional book, but most of her education had been hands on experimenting to see what worked.

Some things she accomplished were outside of her age group, like her mastery of wardings, while in others she was lacking. She could ward a village but not cast the simple light spell that first year apprentices used. She pushed herself to do her best but much too often her answer was, "I do not know, but I can try."

She was excused for over four hours as they discussed her results. Exhausted, she sipped at the cool water a page had offered her. But she could not make herself eat the small sandwiches that had been left for her, no matter how her stomach rumbled. She was just too nervous to even think of touching it. Then, she was called back into the room with the masters.

"Given the lack of theoretical knowledge you exhibited in your testing, it has been decided that you will be schooled in the third year areas. You will also participate in some fourth and fifth year areas of tutelage. As you improve, we will move you into the fifth level with the rest of your peers."

"The lack of control in your visions is very disturbing; you will need someone to work with you on this. Because of these factors we have decided you will be apprenticed to a Master Mage who will also assist you in your higher level skills."

"Your guardian should have sent you to the castle to become an apprentice as soon as you hit your eleventh birthday. As he did not, I am afraid you will spend the first few months catching up on the material you have missed. Your Master will guide you in this."

"Sir, if I may?" she interrupted. "I was told that I could not attend because of the cost of apprenticeship."

"Nonsense," the man blustered, "all apprenticeships are sponsored by the crown, and there are no fees beyond your supplies and those are covered by your Master or your family till you can take your testing in the fifth year. After that you will be charged for any materials, but we will also pay you will a small wage for any work you do. After your testing in the fifth year, we will allow you either take a specialized apprenticeship with a different mage, or you may begin work as a mage of the realm." The man looked offended that she did not have such common knowledge.

Beryl struggled to keep her face blank at this flood of information. She had been lied to so many times over the years. No wonder Jared had not allowed her to become an apprentice—he would have lost his control of her and the steady income she made for him. It was another mark against him on her heart. Eventually, he would have to give an account for those marks and be judged.

* * *

BERYL SAT UNHAPPILY in the small room they had given her. Her new guardian should arrive soon to take her to her new quarters. She was certain no one could be as bad as Jared, but there were still so many ways they could try to control her. After an eternity there was a knock on the door which then opened, revealing a group of pages.

"Miss, we're here to take your belonging to your new quarters. Your Master has asked to be the one to show you your rooms and will be here momentarily."

She gave a nervous smile and thanked the young men, showing them the small pile of baggage. They thanked her, and began moving her bags and heading off down the hall. Suddenly, an older man in robes appeared at the door.

"Hello. I am Lord Darius Fremont. We met earlier when you arrived, if you remember."

"I do, sir. It is a pleasure to meet you, Master Fremont."

"I will be your master for the next three or four years, child. Please call me Darius. Come let me show you to your rooms. I am sure you have had a long day with the testing."

He moved down the hall and through the castle at an easy pace, pointing out various places and works of art or magic as they went. Beryl watched him as she tried to remember if she had been this way yet. The castle was proving to be a maze of corridors and passages.

Darius Fremont was a tall man with a head of close-cropped white hair and beard. He had runes that had been spelled permanently into the skin of his hands, and thin blue bands that wrapped around each wrist. He wore no jewelry except a large silver ring that studded with moon stones, probably his primary magic stone.

Most of the castle was warded or littered with chains of carved runes. Even the glass in the windows had minuscule runes etched into them to prevent ice from forming and to protect from breaking. Darius pointed out the runes that had been carved into the entryway that encircled the entire doorway and ran along the floor on either side of the hall.

"Anytime you see these runes it means you are in the Mage's wing. Every room and hallway in this wing has been warded to prevent spell damage should an experiment or spell working go wrong."

Looking out the corner of her eye, she could see the wards glowing a steady gold. These were powerful wards that had been placed and renewed over and over through group efforts. She could see where each individual line of power wove together to form the golden braid of power that formed each ward.

"These are your rooms. As you are almost sixteen, we gave you your own rooms like we do for the other the older students. My rooms are at the other end of the hall. Knock if there is anything you need. I will leave you to your rest. I remember how draining my own tests were when I was your age. Enjoy your night," He said with a slight smile.

Beryl moved out-of-the-way as the footman brought in her bags. A maid followed them in and turned down the bed; she asked if Beryl would like a bath drawn. She glanced at the retreating back of her new master; only time would tell if he would be an improvement on her last guardian or not. She wasn't sure she liked the kindly air that he was projecting. No one became a confidant of the King by being kind.

After a rather long argument on what was proper and that the servants should draw a lady's baths she got the maid to show her how to use the enchanted facets so that from then on she could draw her own baths if she wanted, proper or not. With that settled, she shooed the maid out of the room. She surveyed her quarters as she closed the door and leaned against it.

The room was twice the size of the small bedroom she'd been in before. To the left of the doorway was a four-posted, single bed; they had drawn the hangings back. A small table and desk sat along the other wall. There were two doors off of the main room. One door lead to the bath which was done in the same grey stone as the rest of the castle with the floor lined with animal skins next to the bed and fireplace. The other door led to the small library, a chilly room that had two massive windows and a fireplace on the wall next to the door that would back up to the fireplace on the wall in her bedroom.

It was more than she had ever planned on having. Before her parent's death, they had lived in a modest sized house where she had a single small room to call her own. With Jared, she had barely had that. Most of the time she slept on the floor. Or, if Jared was feeling generous and flush with cash after a good night at the tables, she might get to sleep on a small, ratty cot.

She headed back into the bedroom and began unpacking her things. She did not have much, but she carefully hung up her dress and folded her pants and shirts, placing them in the drawers under the bureau. She added one more log to the fire before heading to the bath.

Beryl intended to enjoy having constant access to a true bath. It was rare that she'd been able to take a bath more than once a week. The few times they had been to a city large enough to have bath houses she had spent spare minute soaping away the grime.

The bathing room was done in the same grey stone as the rest of the castle she had seen so far, with a large tub that looked like someone had carved it out of one table sized stone. The bath had rune worked pipes that delivered hot and cold water with a touch of the correct rune.

Touching the pipe she pictured the temperature she liked her bathes, just hot enough to feel like it was too hot, yet not hot enough to burn. Steaming water began spilling from the main pipe, filling the tub. Two mage lights glowed in the corners of the windowless room, casting soft shadows on everything. Gathering a bar of herbal soap and a towel, she took a quick bath, unbinding her hair and washing the road grime from her body. Once her hair was toweled dry, she began her exercises.

Every morning, and every night before bed, she did her exercises to stretch and strengthen her arms, legs, and hands that had stiffened in the night or after a long day. The scars on her body hid the actual injuries that she had received when she was attacked. Since her healing, she had been stiff and sore every morning. She learned to push and stretch her muscles each day so she could move to her best ability.

As she did this, she chanted her name and that of her attacker, telling her story over and over lest she forget any detail. She had tried so many ways to tell others about the attack and her attacker. She left notes penned on paper, written in sand, written on walls.

She'd told objects her story over and over, praying someone would overhear and connect that she was talking about herself. Nothing ever came of it. Children were the most likely to be unaffected, but once they told an adult, they dismissed it as lies or imagination with the child forgetting the entire incident soon after. She had tried for years till eventually giving up on everything but her morning and nightly recitation of how she was attacked and the man who did so.

CHAPTER 6

At breakfast the next morning in Lord Darius' study, the main topic had been what to call her. When she explained that she preferred to be called Mage, Master Darius had agreed. Still, he had taken to calling her Apprentice or My Dear by the end of the morning.

That morning Master Darius had barely blinked at her new attire of shirt, faded vest, and pants. She had prepared to argue against wearing dresses, and was ready to defend herself, when the old mage went back to what he was doing without a word.

"My dear, you may wear what you like, unless they call us to court. Then you must dress as befits your station. However, the rest of the time as long as you and your clothes are clean, you may dress as you wish. You will soon hear how "eclectic" a mage I am. Part of my duty as the King's Magical Adviser is to research rumors of both old and new spells and attempt them. Research and spell development are more suited to comfortable clothes than fashionable ones."

Darius himself was wearing grey pants with a pair of soft boots and a loose shirt, all covered with a plain black cloth robe. Nothing about him screamed wealth or prestige the way his robe of yesterday did.

"Now for your schedule," he said pulling out a pipe and setting it unlit between his teeth. With a slight gesture the pipe bowl flamed for a moment before settling down to a thin trail of smoke. Beryl committed the slight motion to memory. It was done with a fire rune, but she would have to see if she could find out more.

"I was thinking for your first week you should catch up on the basics and learning the layout of the castle. Lessons with the other apprentices do not start back for another month, so until then you will have your lessons with me. We will have lessons after breakfast until lunch, and then you will work on a project I assign you for the last half of the day."

"Today I want you to go to the library and make a list of all the subjects you think would interesting to learn and a second list of those you know but about which you would like to learn the theory behind. List all the materials you have used so far in your magic. We need to experiment with different stones and seeing what suits you."

"These are a few books with which you must be familiar: law and how it applies to mages, the various professions of mages, a basic primer of conduct and manners to use while in court or around royalty, and a book on meditation. I want you to review these and later this week we will discuss them." He said handing her the stack, "You will eat in the mage's dining hall for every meal after this. One of the castle pages can show you the way once you finish in the library. They require all apprentices to attend meals there, I am afraid," he said with a slight chuckle.

Beryl fought to keep her reactions to herself. She had never been one to play with children her own age or to make friends easily. She was deemed either too fragile from her injuries or too busy once she was traveling with Jared.

"Now child, each weekend and day of rest I would like you to spend some time in the stables, or helping with the royal hunting dogs or hawks." Looking up at the young woman, he sighed. "You have a question, child?" The girl fidgeted and shifted in her chair, straightening the stack of books with one hand.

"Master Fremont, may I ask why?" she asked, not meeting his eyes.

"You may always ask me anything; no matter the question, I will do my best to answer it. Now, back to the original question. Captain Marshal has told me of your devotion to your horse and the stable master speaks highly of you, which is no insignificant thing." He leaned back watching her for a moment, "Some mages develop attachments to certain kinds of animals and many have familiars that their magic binds to them. So, we must see what animals may be an excellent match for you."

"By working with them you learn their habits and upkeep necessary if one bonds with you and the animals get the care they need and the closeness to you that is needed to form a bond. The more time spent together, the stronger the bond becomes. So strong, in fact, that sometimes a mental bond occurs. Even rarer is the bonding to multiple animals, but it happens; do not stop the work because you may bond to one animal. While you will take lessons and lectures with the other apprentices, you will work on your own projects as well. I will review and guide you, but the work is your own."

* * *

BERYL STEPPED into the large dining hall for lunch, fighting to keep her head up and her lips smiling neutrally. She had spent the morning taking notes from the books Darius provided and jotting down things to research. Darius followed her into the hall and pointed her to a table near the far left wall, before moving to take a seat of his own at the head table.

Most of the tables for the apprentices were empty. She had arrived in the middle of the summer holiday when most of the apprentices returned home to visit with their families. She headed toward one end of the line of tables with a motley group of various ages. Another group of older students sat farther down, but she avoided them on principle from the rich velvet and jewelry the females were wearing.

"Do you mind if I sit here?" She asked, catching the attention of a red-headed boy around her age who was reading a book in between bites.

"No, go right ahead," he muttered going back to his book.

"Thank you," she murmured, taking a seat. Pulling an extra plate from the center of the table, she served herself a small helping of vegetables and sliced chicken.

"Here," the girl across from her said, passing the rolls, "Ignore Lucas, he doesn't have time for us mere mortals. He's studying for a test his Master set him. I'm Rose, by the way."

"Beryl," she said with a smile, "Do they set tests for the apprentices often?"

"I have to present my progress once a month to Master Portsmouth, but it is more so he can see what I need help with or to give me an extra project. Lucas is hoping to be tested by the Historian's Guild at the end of the year, so his Master is pushing him. If he passes, they will allow him to get runic tattoos," Rose said, looking envious.

"Are you the new Apprentice Master Fremont took on? I'm Tor," asked a small apprentice seated by Rose.

"Yes, I'm Beryl."

"It's a pleasure to meet you," The young girl said shyly, ducking back to her meal.

"Do you know what year they will place you with yet?" Rose asked, pushing a red lock of hair back into the thick mass of curls running down her back.

"I will start with some classes in third and fourth year, but they might move me higher later in the year."

"Rose, is your hand doing better?" Tor asked, tugging at the older girl's sleeve to reveal a white bandage around her wrist.

"Yes, it's much better," the young woman said with a blush.

"Rose is the best at fire spells," Tor said with a hint of worship of the older student in her voice.

"My Master had me trying a new Runic combination, and I don't have it quiet right yet. The spell backfired on me," she said, again brushing back a few loose tendrils of her frizzy curls. Beryl noted with a smothered grin that the tips of her hair had been singed.

"Sorry, I have to run. Pleasure to meet you, Beryl, I'm Varik." A dark haired lanky boy on the other side of Tor called out as he grabbed a last roll and stood.

"Varik works at a local blacksmith here learning how to spell the metal as it's hammered," Rose said as the muscular boy moved away at a jog.

"Do apprentices learn a craft like that?" Beryl replied.

"Only if they want to or if their Master thinks they should. Master Portsmouth thinks I should learn glass blowing in my fifth year."

"That could be interesting," Beryl said. "I've only ever worked with stone. It looks like I will be spending the next few weeks seeing if any other materials work for me."

"Yeah, that's all I did my first year. I kept melting every sample my Master gave me." Rose said laughing.

"I've heard that fire talents are like that, though. At least with stone the worst that can happen is it breaking? Right?"

"Yeah, fire is a strange element. It's needy, like a spoiled child demanding your attention. What is stone like for you?"

"Cool and steady. Like it knows it will endure anything you could do to it." Beryl intoned.

"I work best with wood and water," Tor put in. "It's kind of like that; willing to change but staying the same. Water doesn't like to hold on to a spell for long, but wood will take it and pull it along with it as it grows."

"How strange, I've never tried to cast on water," Beryl said, picking at her meal.

The next few days went slowly for Beryl. She worked in the library, trying to memorize what she could to prepare herself for when she had to attend lectures. Those would start the following week when the rest of the apprentices returned.

She ate her meals with Rose and Tor, while the others came and went as their schedules and Masters allowed. They all spoke with one another and shared tidbits of their days at dinner and lunch, but none of them could be called friends. Beryl was wondering if she could be friends with anyone. Everyone seemed to be determined to keep his or her distance from the strange mage who did not have a name.

* * *

CAPTAIN MARSHAL SPENT the week since he returned to the Capital getting his squad back into a normal routine. They assigned patrols of the city and work details along with morning training sessions. He heard that the young Mage was going through testing.

The only testing he was aware of that Mages went through was at the end of their apprenticeship. Mages died during testing that could go on for days. It made his chest hurt to contemplate the woman going through unknown tests and trials just to attend lessons she should have received years ago.

Striding into the training yard outside his squad's barracks, he joined the line of soldiers going through stretches before they started sword drills. The sword master leading the morning drills barked out a command. Straightening, he fell into line with the other soldiers.

Four squads and their Captains filled the yard. Each soldier moved in time with the others to the barked commands, their wooden training swords weighted with bands and cores of iron, pulling at their muscles. His body continued the well-worn path of motions as his mind twisted and turned.

All too soon the drill ended, and he headed to his barracks to finish cleaning and fixing his armor. He'd been a soldier for too long to trust that the peace would last. Even in times of peace, an army still had battles and wars to win.

"Hey, Marshal! Good to see you back."

"Hendricks, good to see you. I heard things have at least been quiet while I was gone."

"If you ignore the normal bar fights and such that the town patrols are managing, it's as quiet as Cardu ever gets."

"True." Charles said with a snort, digging out his cleaning supplies.

"Heard you had a bit of an unusual run," Roy Hendricks said, tugging out his own kit to clean his boots. "Bringing back strays now?"

"I would have been in the stocks if I'd left an underage mage to be abused by her relative."

"I heard she's not under age. She was what, fifteen?"

"Around there."

"Marrying age, and she was still trucking around with an abusive Uncle?"

"Not everyone thinks with their crotch, Hendricks. I'm just glad she didn't go rogue."

"Don't even joke about that. Burr." The other man shivered in mock terror. "I heard from Barnes about the cleanup they had to do in Debus after the last rogue. He destroyed everything around him, including himself. Burned to ash so fine that nothing will grow. Even animals shun the place now."

"Thankfully, she does not seem the type," Charles said with a tight laugh. "She warded the camps at night and kept the camp safe during a night attack."

"Really?"

"Yes, excellent head on her shoulders."

"Good thing. I don't think this country can take many more rogues without half the towns rioting."

"Is it getting that bad? I thought the anti-magic groups were still just small-time crooks looking for some quick coin and a bit of violence."

"Word is that they are getting organized. Nothing too big yet, but it's something to monitor."

"Wonderful," Charles murmured under his breath.

* * *

THE ONLY THING feared in the kingdom more than war was rogue mages. A rogue mage that attacked his own country or joined with outsiders to attack his homeland using spells and they had taught to him by the mages in his homeland was terrifying to many. To prevent this, every mage of the realm must go through testing to see at what power level they were and once they finished their fifth year of training their loyalty to the realm and crown were tested. His mage could go through this right now.

If the anti-magic fanatics were growing in number and power, then the delicate peace holding the country together could be shattered. Magic was an unknown to most of the population, with the King and Mage's Counsel controlling where Arden's mages were posted and what it allowed them work on. Few commoners saw any kind of magic beyond the hedge mages, who were not powerful enough to do more than simple healing spells and crude protection charms.

Anti-mage sentiment was already rampant since past rulers had used their powers as a preventative to riots and discord. What chance did a common man have against a person who could call down fire from the skies or cause the earth to swallow entire forests? It did not help that many of the mages came from wealthy or noble families, thanks to generations of arranged marriages. This was the way to ensure magical children.

It was becoming a resentment of both the wealthy nobility and the mages position outside of the normal laws. Mages were a law unto themselves and could only be tried by the Mage's Counsel or the King himself. The general opinion seemed to be that they bought their way out of trouble and into higher positions and titles.

Charles could only hope that the resentment wouldn't fester into outright hatred while Arden was still scrambling to reinforce their borders and coastlines against raiders. The country could not protect itself against outside threats while the population fought amongst themselves. It looked like he would be busy in the coming years if things did not settle down soon.

* * *

"Good afternoon, Mage," the Queen said with a slight smile. She had taken a liking to the quiet girl who'd joined the junior apprentices at the castle. Her story was making the rounds of the nobles, and a good deal felt pity for the orphan girl who did not even have a name.

The Queen, however, was reminded of herself as a child, growing up in the courts of Glastonbury in the West. They had viewed her since her birth as a bargaining chip to bind two countries together. Either ignored or overly tested by her parents and teachers, she had learned to be quiet and polite to avoid the confrontations that always occurred when political power was involved.

While rules here in the East were much more relaxed for women, in the West women were viewed as property, to be moved about, used, and sold as needed. Women had no rights beyond what their husbands gave them. They could not have their own money or businesses.

Thankfully, Gastonbury was a small country that had little political influence. They had hoped to increase that influence by marrying her into a foreign house. However, it had earned them few rewards beyond some alternative trading routes and a treaty between the two countries to prevent war.

"Good afternoon, my Queen," Mage replied with a curtsy.

"May I ask what you were looking at on that wall?" the Queen asked, pausing beside the young woman.

"Master Darius asked me to observe the wards on some castle walls and attempt to identify them. The wards are tangled here, and I was trying to see which spells or wards were causing the tangle," the young mage replied with a slight blush.

"Ah, I am afraid I do not have any magical talent. I must take your word for it. Can you tell me what it looks like?" The queen's ladies-in-waiting, and guards stood to the side politely ignoring the conversation.

"If you like I can show you, my queen?" the mage said in an uncertain tone.

"Please do so then," she said nodding to the Mage and taking a few steps back. She had seen a young mage still in training get caught in magical backlash once and had no wish to lose her eyebrows if the spell was miss-cast.

Turning back to the wall, the mage placed one hand on it, bowing her head and closing her eyes. One lady-in-waiting stepped forward to say something to the queen only to stop with a gasp. The wall was glowing; lines of color swirled and twisted through the rough stone of the wall.

Pale blue lines marched along every seam, while a net like golden thread covered the stones. Random lines of red, green, and purple swirled throughout the stones. Sitting in the center of the wall was a tangle, as the mage had said, the size of a medium shield. Opening her eyes, she stepped away from the wall but left her hand in place.

"Is this what you see all the time, Mage?" the Queen asked in a shaky voice.

"No, but we can feel the spells and wards. It is like walking through spider webs when you cross one, and they are all over the castle," she said with a slight shudder.

"What do the colors mean, Mage?" Lady Vivian, one lady-in-waiting, asked.

"The blue is a fastening spell that helps hold the mortar and stones together. The golden net is a protection spell that helps prevent the stones from breaking if they are struck or heated. The red, green, and purple are threads of wardings that have been done to the castle. The red is an alarm spell, but for what I cannot say. The green is a cleaning or freshening ward used to freshen the air or to prevent dust. The purple is the ward that confuses me."

"And the tangle?" the Queen prompted.

"The spells are fighting each other. You see how the green and red have wrapped around the purple, pulling it to the center of the wall." Reaching out the mage ran her free hand along one such spot, causing the lights to move, making one lady-in-waiting stifle a shriek, before covering her mouth and turning away in embarrassment. "Once I know what the purple does, I can ask if Master Fremont would let me attempt to untangle them."

"How would you move them?" one of the other ladies asked.

"Most wards in stone don't want to move, but these are so tangled they want to go where they should be. See how they will flow about with just a touch?" she said, running her fingertips along one twist in the tangle. "This was how they got so tangled. Once a small tangle was formed, the strands would move when anyone with a bit of magic touched the wall, trying to right themselves." The glow was fading from the wall, allowing the stones to return to a regular grey stone wall.

"How interesting! Once you begin you must inform me of how the work goes. Thank you for the lesson, Mage." The Queen gave a slight smile to the girl.

"You welcome my Queen," she said curtsying. Leaving the young mage to her work, the Queen gestured for her ladies to accompany her, and they headed once more down the hallway with a soft murmur of voices.

CHAPTER 7

$\mathcal{B}$eryl wandered through one of the palace gardens on her way back from the library. Lessons with the other apprentices were resuming tomorrow, and the halls were filling with people as the apprentices and their Masters returned to the castle.

She had spent her morning with Darius, working on identifying which materials her magic reacted to best and doing mediation exercises to control her visions. He was working with her to control the visions so she could sit down or brace herself when they began. Eventually, they hoped to prevent the visions until she triggered them herself.

Beryl felt one begin, a low ache building behind her eyes and her hands tingling, she hurried to a low wall. She planned to brace herself if it got too bad, but she barely took a breath before she was swept away so completely that the wall, the ground, and her whole body seemed to disappear, leaving only the vision.

She was running through a dark and dying forest chasing after something. Something was behind her, crashing after her like a monster from a nightmare. Branches slashed her face and hands as she threw herself forward. There was a glint of something in front of her before the ground dropped out from under her.

She came back to herself, lying on the ground near the wall. Someone was shaking her and demanding that she wake up because if she was dead he was not responsible. He was just getting to a rant about silly girl faints when she brought up her hands to stop the shaking and sat up.

"Are you all right? You just fell; you didn't break anything, did you?" The boy stood there all but wringing his hands, glancing around for help like someone would appear from thin air to take this 'girl' off his hands.

"No I'm fine." To prove it, she stood up, holding onto the wall and starting to brush off her shirt.

Looking up she saw a boy who looked about fifteen with black unruly hair, he had pale skin that had been covered in a dusting of freckles where the sun had access. His brown eyes glittered with concern and worry as he watched her get up. He wore the grey and blue uniform of the castle pages, though his was wrinkled and the cuffs ink spotted.

"I'm Robert. I'm a runner after lessons in the castle. You sure you're all right, you're awfully pale." He shuffled his feet, watching her with a frown.

"Yes, I'm fine. I'm Master Fremont's apprentice, everyone calls me Mage."

The boy took a step back for a moment as if waiting for her to turn into a frog. "Oh, so you're the girl. We were all surprised when Master Fremont took a girl for an apprentice."

That made her stop and look at him, "Why, because I am a girl?"

"Well, yeah, there aren't too many girl apprentices at all, and most of them just want to get married. They fawn about and learn how to do their hair and faces with magic, useless stuff like how to use magic to put ribbons in their hair." He made a face, disgusted at the wiles of women. He looked her up and down, taking in the patched vest and worn clothes. "Though you don't seem like them. They're too concerned about getting dirty to do much. Where were you going dressed like that?" he said, watching her with a wary look.

"I was going to head to the stables," she said with a shake of her head. "You know, if you have some time you could help." She forced her shoulders back and tried to ignore how her head ached and her heart raced, still coming down from the panic the visions caused.

"With what, mucking stalls?" Robert asked with a grimace.

"No, I have a horse I have to exercise today. I thought if you were not doing anything you could ride one of the other horses at the stable."

The boy glanced at the sun and grinned, "Sure, it's close to dinner time, anyway."

Beryl shook her head and laughed, the last of her headache fading, forgotten, gesturing for him to come along. It was barely after lunch and hours till supper. She hoped Robert would not get into too much trouble for skipping out on his duties for half a day. Soon Robert and a dark bay were trotting laps around the pasture as she trotted and cantered Flox in figure eights. They rode until both horses and riders were sweating and ready to head in for dinner.

That night at dinner Beryl was speaking with Rose about her latest attempt to cast a complex fire rune when a messenger came up and handed her a note. Opening it, she found a message from Darius asking her to meet him in his work room after dinner. Looking up, she saw that half the hall was watching her. Pocketing the note, she picked up her cup and took a sip before looking at the rest of the table.

Meeting their questioning gazes, she relented and said, "It was from Master Fremont, I have to meet with him after dinner."

"Are you in trouble or something?" Tor asked looking worried. The girl seemed to always be in trouble for something with her Master. Somehow, Mage doubted that the quiet girl was one to get into mischief, yet the girl always seemed to be assigned to do kitchen duty or extra spell practice at all hours of the day.

"I doubt it; he just wants to go over something with me. Probably one of the spell designs he asked me to work on." The rest of dinner was tense, and Mage left early to go find Darius and see what was amiss.

"I heard from one of the castle pages you had a vision earlier today.

I wanted to make sure you were all right." Darius said after gesturing her to sit down with him next to his work table. Wonderful, she thought with a sigh, Robert was already spreading gossip around about her.

"Sorry, I'd forgotten about it. I'm fine; I fell but didn't hurt myself. Once the vision was over I got up and went to the stables to ride. I was heading there when it happened." she added.

"Do you remember what it was about?" Darius asked, filling his pipe and puffing to get it going.

"Not really, everything was blurry. I was running through the woods, and people were crashing through the trees behind me, chasing me. I never saw what I was chasing or who was chasing me. It was all just motion and fear." she said, turning pale as she remembered the fear that had been pumping through her.

"Have you been doing your meditation exercises each night?" he asked, rising to head to his book shelves.

"Yes, and the visions are getting better, easier to ride out." She said sinking into the comfortable chair, watching as Darius searched the shelves before pulling one book down and returning to the table.

"Good, I want you to continue the exercises but now when you are having a vision I want you to step back from it, to control what you are seeing or doing. To slow the flow of the vision around you till you are standing in a frozen space in time. This should allow you to see what is happening."

"There haven't been many mages with the gift of visions, and there are none that I know of, that are alive now, but from the books I have been able to find this is what visionaries in the past have described as their methods. I want you to go to the mage library and try to find a few books on the lives of other mages known to have visions. I would like to compare your visions to those of others in the past, so look at the recorded visions as well and see if you can find any similarities," He said handing her the enormous volume and shooing her on to her task.

. . .

BERYL HAD BEEN WANDERING the grounds for some time when a young woman stopped her. "Need some help?" she asked, giving her a slight smile.

The girl was tall with black hair pulled into a fraying braid that hung to her hips. She wore a muddied tunic and breeches with a thick leather vest. I tucked large gloves into her belt, pulling her tunic heavily to one side.

"Yes I am trying to find Master Ion, the hawk master. I was told the falconry was near here."

"It is. I am headed there myself if you want to walk with me," she said with a ready grin.

"That would be grand. I was about to give up and head back. I'm Master Fremont's apprentice."

"Ah, the one without a name. I'm Salendra, but please call me Sal. I'm Master Ion's apprentice, the Hawk Master. Is it nice not having a name? I would love to get rid of mine."

Sal chatted the whole way, barely breathing. Beryl learned how to get to the falconry, how Sal liked Master Ion and the hawks, which was her favorite hawk, and a myriad of other things. However, once they reached Master Ion and the hawks, Sal was silent and intense, helping her master as he explained the basics of hawk anatomy, care, and training.

Master Ion was a stern looking man whose bushy brows and beard hid his expression. He was dressed like his apprentice, though cleaner in is tunic and vest with arm guards. He surveyed his new student with a frown, taking in the scarred hands and wrists.

"So have you ever dealt with any birds?" He asked, as he fed a bit of meat to a small hawk sitting hooded on a stand.

"Only sparrows" she said with a swallow, eying the fierce birds in the surrounding cages. These birds were nothing like sparrows.

"The only thing in common between sparrow and hawks is feathers and heartbeat. A bird's heart beats fast, too much stress and a bird can fall over dead, and their heart gives out." He said eying the way the girl was watching the bird near her. "They look fierce and mean, but once you know how to deal with them they can show you affection in their own ways. Still they're not pets, my birds. We raise them to hunt and kill. It is what they know to do, their nature to do. You cannot fault them for not having a softer nature then what the gods gave them."

"No, sir."

"You will come here three times a week until your Master decides that you will not bond with a bird. Until then you will learn how to exercise, feed, and care for the hawks here."

"Yes, Master Ion. I look forward to it."

"I hope you do, Apprentice. I won't go any easier on you just because you're a mage." The man growled, gesturing for Sal to step forward. "Salendra, show the Mage around and start her on feeding one of the older hawks."

"Yes, Master Ion." She said with a quick nod, tugging Beryl away with her. Once they were farther away, Beryl touched Sal's sleeve to slow her down.

"Is Master Ion always like that?"

"What, the temper? He just doesn't enjoy having to deal with the Mage Apprentices. Many come for just a few weeks before their Masters call them away. They learn only the utter basics, and even if they find a bondmate, they never return or let Master Ion check on their charges."

"They couldn't be abusing their bondmates, Sal. They're bound to each other. If one hurts the other will feel it."

"Only if the bond is deep enough, according to Master Ion. If the Mage still sees the animal as only an animal and nothing more, the bond doesn't deepen and they won't feel when the animal is hurt or mistreated."

"But why would they even bond if they don't want the animal?"

"I don't understand it myself. There was an apprentice who graduated a few years ago who bonded to a hawk. Master Ion raised a massive fuss because the idiot was leaving the bird caged at all times. I never understood why the hawk wasn't just taken away and given to someone who would care for it."

"They were bonded. Nothing can break a bond except death,"

Beryl said with a sigh, hoping that whatever she bonded with will share more than just a surface bonding.

"The poor thing. Well, at least you seem willing to care for whatever you bond with. Do you know what you want to try for?"

"I don't know. My Uncle never let me have any pets, but I could see how a dog or cat could be useful."

"And fun," Sal said with a grin. "The hawks don't play, but you can tell they enjoy doing the lure work and rabbit hunts. I wouldn't mind a dog, but my parents don't want one."

"Bondmates are more than pets if the books are right. They say it's like finding a lost part of your soul."

"Sounds like the children's stories where the women are locked away waiting on their perfect husband to find them."

"I never liked those stories," Beryl said with a grimace. She'd seen all too often just how mean and controlling men could be.

They spent the rest of the afternoon in the Hawk mews learning how to care and clean up after the birds. She was filthy by the end, but she had earned Sal's grudging respect for not complaining as she cleaned the stinking straw from the cages.

* * *

THE FOLLOWING week Beryl's lessons began, and she was already having issues. She was studying both in the afternoons and late into the night to try catch up on the theory she had missed while traveling with Jared. Beryl needed to learn the correct way of casting the spells she had been casting for years in her own way. She was forced to memorize new runes and casting methods that seemed clunky and impossible compared to her own ways. It was all giving her a massive headache.

She took to stealing away in the late afternoon to ride Flox through the forest trails and nearby fields to release some of her stress. Her work with the hawks was going well, but she didn't feel any genuine connection to any of the birds. She wasn't even sure she wanted a bondmate. To be bound to something for the rest of your life or until the animal died? To have it in your head and heart?

She could barely remember having a stable home and parents. She'd spent most of her life with Jared on the road, learning how to ward and watching as back corner deals were made and money exchanged. She knew her way around a bar better than most adults, yet here she was taking lessons a few hallways away from the Royal apartments.

Her lessons were painful; she was either too advanced or woefully behind. In her lessons with the third years she was too advanced. The teacher was already talking about moving her in with the fourth years if she did well on the practical at the end of the month. In her two fourth year lessons she was fairing much better, but none of the students had warmed up to her. She was treated almost like a cursed object that no one wanted to touch or talk to.

They only included in groups during class time if the Master Mage teaching the lesson assigned her to one. Trying to join in on the other established groups in the classes had not gone well. In her one fifth year lessons on wards, they ignored her for every lesson.

After she had tried to talk to a few of the quieter apprentices her things had been stolen or accidentally damaged with supposedly misfired spells or ink smeared palms. All while the more popular and wealthy apprentices looked on in glee. Once you were a fifth year, you stayed there till you could pass the end-of-year practical and were judged ready for the testing by your Master so she would deal with their attentions for a while to come.

The class had apprentices from age fifteen to eighteen in it with groups of every age going to take the testing at the end of the year. The testing for fifth years was two-part, one being a practical test and another being a test of magical strength. No one would speak of the second test, only saying it measured your strength as a mage.

Her work was sabotaged and destroyed at every turn in many of her classes. The other apprentices resented that she could skip several years of training and just step into the fourth and fifth year lessons.

After her fifth project was covered accidentally in ink, she started carrying all her work in her bag.

When oatmeal and mud made its way into her bag, she spent the rest of the week warding her possessions. Her shoulder bag was now warded to not open unless she released the ward with a specific rune. Her inkwells were spelled shatterproof, and her fountain pens etched with runes of protection and strength.

She thought she'd protected her things well enough, but it only led the bullies to taunt her in person. The long minutes between lessons, and before the Masters arrived to teach became a kind of hell. There wasn't a morning or afternoon where she wasn't shoved in the hallways or tormented until the lesson started. Today was no exception.

"Well, if it isn't No Name. Why anyone would want to live without a name is beyond me. I'd have killed myself years ago," one of the fifth years simpered to her seat mate in a loud voice.

"Well, what else would you expect of an orphan. Have you seen the rags she's wearing? It's a disgrace her Master hasn't provided her with better."

"You'd think the Masters would prevent such peasants from the apprenticeships. My father would certainly never have allowed it. I must mention it to him; perhaps the Mages Council can add a new rule to block such a thing from happening again."

They fell silent when the Master came in and started his lecture. Beryl tried to keep her mind on her notes, but the words kept circling her mind. Was Master Fremont ashamed of his new apprentice? She didn't think so; the eccentric older mage didn't seem to put much stock into gossip or how a person came into their positions or power.

She went about her lessons, eating a quick lunch before running to the library for a book she needed for her research that night. She raced into the lecture just as the Master was taking the lectern. He gave her an unimpressed look as she took her seat.

"Mage, you will stay behind after the lecture," he said with a frown.

"Yes, Master Lens," Beryl blurted, pulling out her parchment and starting to take notes as the lecture began.

She blushed as every eye in the room seemed to watch her gather

her things. Someone had inked the runes for confusion, ignorance, and fragility along one side of the wooden table top she noted trying to keep her attention on the lecture. Thankfully there was no power to the runes, they were just meant to hurt, not do any actual physical damage like the properly cast runes would have she thought with a sigh, rubbing at one rune to smear the ink.

The rest of the lecture passed in a blur as Beryl fought against her anger. Marietta kept sending her smug looks, so she had to be the one behind the runes; if not the actual one to place them. She was above such menial work herself.

Robert would have called her one of the ribbon heads, an apprentice more concerned with garnering a wonderful marriage than learning true magic. Her group of sycophants ruled the fifth year's apprentices with Marietta at the head, the spiteful presence behind every taunt and slight they doled out. They were all the daughters of powerful men and wealthy families, isolated from the common classes and their problems.

Marietta seemed determined to force Beryl away from her classmates any way she could. The latest rumor going through the students was that her curse was contagious and anyone touching or being near her would lose their own names. Beryl had dealt with bullies before, but they had never forced her to stay in one place long enough for anything to escalate beyond name calling and the occasional fight. Marietta's father would see her expelled if it came to blows, and the other Mage's would see her stripped of her magic if she used it against another apprentice.

There was no suitable way for her to react, so she had remained silent to the abuse. Somehow that only seemed to make it worse. The random comments and sly looks were driving her crazy. She longed to lash out or scream at the idiot girls trying to ruin her life. Didn't they realize how good they had it?

She made her way to a remote garden after dinner was in disrepair to catch up with Sal and Robert. Beryl had introduced Salendra and Robert one day after running into Robert while Salendra and she were talking after a lesson with the hawk master. Soon, the three of them could be found talking or walking the grounds trying to find something to do on most of their rest days.

Salendra hoped to become a hawk Mistress herself and was very interested in hunting and tracking, which she happily explained to Robert and Beryl. Feeling a tightening in her chest, Mage asked where she was learning to track and live off the land. It turned out that Sal was taking informal lessons from one of the King's huntsmen about twice a month.

"Do you think he could teach all of us?" she asked fiddling with one of the gem studded bracelets hidden under her shirt cuffs.

"He might, but you will be a mage, why would you need to know tracking?" Sal was looking at her strangely.

"I think it might be useful. Can you ask for me?" she pressed, trying to breathe around the panic building under her skin.

"Yes, I meet with him next week, maybe you both can come with me and ask him then."

"That would be great," she said with a relieved smile. Robert changed the subject a moment later.

The tightness in her chest loosened and receded as they continued to talk of general things and the gossip that was going around the castle. Beryl hadn't told her new friends about her visions or the tightness in her chest that often foretold something important.

She'd learned over the years to pay attention to it and to not tell anyone. Too many people would start making the sign of Bain at her passing, hoping to ward off the rotten luck associated with the negative aspects of life. As Ruth was the guardian of the light, Bain was the guardian of the dark. While Ruth was life and healing, Bain was the death of crops and the turning of the season to winter.

While priests and priestesses of Ruth were healers, those of Bain were scholars, teaching the children of most villages how to read and write. They portrayed Bain as an antlered man depicted as a black silhouette. Neither Ruth nor Bain were ever depicted with faces, however Ruth was always shown in brightly colored robes.

They'd been run out of one village after the village elder declared her a demon when she had a vision in the town square one morning.

They'd barely been allowed to gather their things before they were being escorted out to the main road by several brawny local toughs. Jared had cursed and howled their ignorance for the rest of the month, while it had forced them to use the little savings he had to get to the next size-able town.

CHAPTER 8

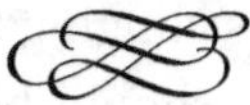

Beryl's lessons in mage craft with the fourth years were getting better. Thanks to months of constant work, she was no longer constantly behind in the theory. The instructor, Mage Winters, drew the room's attention with a sharp rap on the podium.

"Today's class will be held in the main gallery if everyone will follow me."

Standing up, Beryl slid her things into a shoulder bag and pulled her cloak back on as she followed the rest of the group to the Royal Gallery. It was a collection of massive rooms and hallways that were lined with suits of armor, jeweled artifacts, and massive paintings and tapestries.

"Today we will recharge the mage lights that line the gallery. As a project, each of you will learn how to make both a light orb and the mage lights used in the gallery. We will help recharge the orbs in the castle libraries later this week. For those of you who have yet to go to the Mage library, I suggest you familiarize yourself with it. You are to research how to craft the light orbs on your own. I expect a paper on how you accomplished this, along with a functioning orb, to be turned into me before your next rest day."

They spent the rest of the lesson learning the runes that worked to recharge the orbs by pulling magic from the caster. Luckily the orbs only had to be charged once a year. By the end of the lesson, every apprentice was exhausted. All the apprentices were in fourth and fifth year were expected to help charge the mage lights, and it was with knowing grins that the fifth years greeted the four years at dinner.

"Look at the poor weaklings!" Marcus sneered, one of the male mages that Marietta was always clinging to.

"No mage worth his magic should be tired out by such a simple task," she agreed with a smirk, sipping at her goblet.

"Leave them be," Rose snapped. "I remember you being just as tired last year when we had to charge half the lights in the gallery."

"And you melted one," Marietta said with a sneer. "How are you lesson going, Rose, dear? Set your hair on fire yet again?"

"Leave them be, Rose," Beryl said tugging her away from the table where Marietta's group sat and towards the younger group with whom they normally sat.

"She has no right to be such a bitch. She thinks she's so much better than everyone when she'd been the same way last year, drooling into her soup." Rose said with a grimace, nudging a nodding Tor who was drooping over her sparsely filled plate.

"She just likes to cause pain. Some people seem born to want to hurt others any way they can," Beryl murmured, serving herself some chicken and rice with a sigh.

"Wake up, Tor. You need to eat at least a little," Rose murmured, shaking the small girl's elbow.

"All right," Tor said with a sigh, starting to nibble sleepily at her meal. "Why aren't you worn out, Mage? Those light orbs are horrible."

"I'm used to it, Tor. When I traveled with my Uncle, I would ward most of a village every few days. After a while you get used to the drain and learn how to work around it."

"I'll make sure Tor gets to bed," Rose said with a sigh, when the smaller girl put her head down on the table. "Didn't you need to head to the library?"

"I think Master Fremont has the books I need in his study. I'll ask him in the morning," Beryl said with a sigh, helping Rose tug Tor to her feet.

Mage surveyed the exhausted younger students around her with a frown. Several had fallen asleep over their dinners in the hall, while the missing seats marked those who had skipped dinner to stagger to their rooms and collapse.

Beryl ignored the knowing looks as she forced herself to finish eating. She knew from experience that anyone casting that much magic over an extended amount of time grew tired, no matter his or her age. Coupled with learning the new spell, they had wasted energy and time on repeat attempts before they had lit each orb.

The assignment to make an orb wasn't a hardship for Beryl as she had already read up on this when she had first seen the orbs. She wondered if the orbs could do other things and made a mental note to ask Darius about this later. How the glass orbs were recharged was like how you recharged a spell stone, however it used different runes.

Beryl couldn't understand why mages made so many runes that did the same thing. There were sixteen runes for fire, four of which cast the spell for a small flame to burn. She had found that most mages didn't use chained runes because of the need to balance the runes in order for them to be stable. A fire rune had to be balanced with a rune that symbolized its opposite, such as water, so that they could store the spell in a stone or cast into a ward. This was a very delicate balancing act that required the mage to constantly change his chains.

No chain would work every time, as everything from the stars, weather, tools used, and time of day could affect the way the chains would react. Mage's gift of warding was that she had an innate sense of what runes they should pair with each other. To her there was no need to do more than learn the runes and their meanings, while most mages who used chained runes also had to memorize how each rune reacted with various variables.

This was one thing that they seemed to like to test the students on in lessons. It forced her to write out small chains of runes on each test so she could see how it might react to the proposed situation. Her teacher, Mage Laima, had realized this and began giving her extra work to see just how far she could push this gift.

When she had complained to Darius about the extra work, he had smiled and said he would speak to the teacher. The next day Mage Laima had given her a stack of books on the mages of the last century and asked for a report on them and how she compared in her talents to them. Beryl took them with a sigh; it looked like she would have a busy weekend.

As she read, it surprised her to see that several of them had few talents as a child, perhaps only one true gift. It was through the honing of this gift that they discovered their other abilities and became great mages. it also was through a massive amount of hard work. Few of them did not have to push their gifts to expand them, and even then they needed a drive to do well or complete some goal.

When her teacher gave her another set of exercises and a book of ancient runes to learn, she took them and tried to apply herself to all her work and not resent the time it took away from her other projects. Finally she cornered Mage Laima and told her of the other work she was doing and asked if she could combine the study of the various runes and rune chains into a project, so she could continue to work on the other areas she was interested in. She agreed and suggested that Mage work on using the ancient runes in different spells to see how they worked with their modern counterparts.

* * *

THE NEXT REST day Beryl went to town with Robert and Sal to see the vendors. Once a month the town shops set up a small outside fair that sold food and goods in one of the main courtyards of the town. Sal said the mages sometimes came and cast spells for the children or enchanted the fountains to shoot colored water or flower petals, and most of the vendors would give small samples of the fresh foods available to those who asked.

What she wanted to see was the exotic bird dealer who sometimes brought his wares into town. However, all Robert wanted to see was the weapons dealer that would come and occasionally demonstrate each weapon and show how sharp the swords were by tossing an apple and cutting it in mid-air. Once they made it to the courtyard, they were sad to see that there were no mages or bird sellers there. They watched a woman clad in scarves and her partner dance for coins for a few minutes before moving on.

Pooling their money, each bought a steamed bun with meat and candied fruit. Juggling the hot buns they wondered the shops gazing at the ornate saddles and silk robes that were being offered and the simple cotton cloth tunics and trousers that most people wore every day.

The best part was watching the people. Everyone seemed to dress in their best clothes for the fair and happily parading themselves about. The three laughed themselves silly over a woman whose hair had been piled on her head with stuffed birds poking their heads out of her nest of hair.

"I bet she wouldn't know what to do if she had an actual bird in her hair!" Sal crowed.

"Would you?" Beryl said with a laugh. "No one likes live animals in their hair."

With a slight grin, Beryl eyed several pick pockets and thieves working the crowds and steered Robert and Salendra clear of their paths. The two were stunningly naïve for city dwellers. She let herself relax and enjoy the sunny day. As the day wore on, the tensions that had been filling the town seemed forgotten.

They had given all the apprentices the day off of their duties for the afternoon so they could enjoy the festival. Beryl trailed behind the other two, trying to enjoy the games and music. Watching their joyful faces, she felt so much older than the year that sat between them. Salendra and Robert were happy to play at being children, dragging Beryl to a small booth selling tiny colored fish in cups if you could toss a ring and knock down several pins. She didn't bother to tell them they rigged the game with the center pin set on a dowel so it would never move or weighted so it would not tip over.

When Robert and Salendra headed back to the castle for dinner, she stayed and wandered as the storytellers and gaming booths were closed for the night, leaving room for a rougher sort of clientele to arrive. Out into the twilight came the beer sellers and the gaming tables, the courtesans and the prostitutes.

"Took you long enough," Beryl said with a slight grin, sipping at her drink as a slim form dropped to a seat next to her. "I spotted you hours ago."

"I wasn't sure you'd want me to meet the noble born you were with," Troche said with a grin, pushing his dark shoulder length hair away from his face.

"Noble born?"

"Castle bred," he said, pulling a face of disgust.

"They're the children of castle servants, not the same as someone with noble blood," she said with a sigh, eying the thief with a frown.

"And you're a mage slumming about the unsavory parts of town. Word travels fast when an unknown, untrained mage shows up out of thin air," he said with a snort.

"Apprentice Mage."

"Still, it's never a bad thing to know people in prominent places."

"That only works if they have some influence. I have none," Beryl pointed out with a slight frown.

"But you will, and I'm willing to bank a friendship on a future investment."

"And why would a mage spend her precious time with a gutter rat?" she asked with a smirk, hoping to tweak his pride.

"Because you miss it," Troche pointed out with an answering smirk, "You might not have been a rat yourself, but you lived on the rough side if you lived with your Uncle."

"I doubt I will have time to come into town often," she pointed out with a sigh. "Not a very worthwhile investment of your time."

"Then I'm just going to make it worth it, won't I?" he said with a cheeky grin, stealing her mug and taking a sip. "Would you be willing to come watch a card game? I know of a tavern near here that the guild members frequent. It makes for a fast and mostly trick free table."

Beryl watched him for a long moment before agreeing, leaving her mug on a barrel for some else to finish.

"I can't stay too late. I have to work in the falconry in the morning."

"A mage learning to handle hawks? Is your master cracked?"

"My Master thinks I'll gain a bonded animal and is trying to expose me to as many as possible," she said with a laugh. "I'm waiting for the order to have to clean the stables of the King's prized chargers."

She followed along a pace behind Troche as he led her through the crowd to a side street. A short while later found them seated near the fire in a large tavern, watching the card games going on around them. Troche splurged and bought them both tankards of ale and slabs of bread smeared with a thick, fruity jam.

"Are most of the players in your guild?" she asked softly, letting the general roar of the crowded tavern swallow her words.

"Most, not all." He agreed, nodded at a nearby table . "Those are outside traders playing against one of our better card handlers. Watch his hands. How they never seem to stop moving? It's next to impossible to see his card slips."

"Adding to the deck?"

"Mostly, look at the next table, that's several of the high ups in the Guild. They'll call each other on the cheats if they see it. I've seen them restart play a dozen times in an hour when a player cheats out of habit."

"Do you game?" Beryl asked.

"I prefer the dice games. I've a deft hand at throwing sevens," he boasted with a grin as he finished his bread.

"We used to game with stones in the taverns while the adults played cards. First to skip had to buy the group a treat."

"Did you play often?"

"We traveled too much for anyone to trust me at the games. I was never in town long enough to find a group to play with much."

"I bet at every town you entered the locals doffs tried to fleece you," he said with a grin.

"Pretty much, until I got good at avoiding them," she agreed. "I learned that I was best served by avoiding the local children once they found out I was a mage. Got beat enough for just having magic that I learned to run fast."

"Surely not that bad? You had played with some, you said."

"Only in the towns where I didn't do warding. If I'd cast wards then they knew I was a mage and different. Why would they want to play with a girl who was strange?"

"So you were alone a lot?"

"Yeah, I learned to watch the tables and to entertain myself; it's how I learned to spot the pickpockets and gamblers in a room."

"About the same for me," he said draining his mug, "No one wants a gutter rat for a playmate growing up but other rats. Only the guild members ever seemed to get out, so I knew that if I wanted to move up, I needed to clean up myself, so I did. Got apprenticed to Master James and have been on the upward bound ever since."

"Up is the only way to go when the gutter's behind you." Mage agreed, sipping at her own ale while Troche waved for a refill.

"Surely you were never that low, you're a mage!" Troche scoffed, shifting on the stone hearth.

"My uncle was a drunk and a gambler, Troche. The last few years he started using Bright weed. We'd go from flush and living the high life to begging for change on the corner day by day. It all depended on his game and habits. If he was flush he'd drink it away again in a few days. If he was on the weed, we'd be kicked out of the gaming dens and off to pawn what little we could until we could reach the next town. Magic doesn't mean that life gets any easier."

"Huh, so you can't magic your way out of being poor."

"Not without someone paying me for the magic."

"Pity," he said handing over his mug to be refilled.

"Yeah," Beryl said, finishing the last of her ale so the barmaid could refill her mug.

"So you don't game at all?"

"Not beyond friendly games, I don't need the money that bad. Not right now, anyway," she said with a grin.

"Come on. Let's see if we can get on a table. Some lower tables play for tokens, so there's no money lost."

"Teaching games?"

"Something like that. Care to play?"

"For an hour or two, I still have to get back, eventually."

"I'll make a night owl out of you yet," Troche teased with a grin, leading her to a back room where most of the players were junior guild members.

Beryl relaxed into the chair she was shown and watched as they dealt the cards. She could afford to forget about magic and bullies for a few hours. She gathered up her pile of cards and glanced over the table. Troche gave her a shark's grin that she returned. This would be fun.

CHAPTER 9

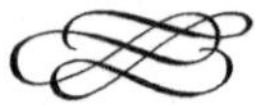

*B*eryl was heading toward the stables when a low whistle drew her attention toward a small doorway used by the castle servants. Troche stood hidden in the shadows, flashing her a slight smile before disappearing inside. They chased each other through the castle and out into alleys and backstreets of town. It was a game they had played several times since they first met.

She grinned and tagged the young man on his shoulder as he walked past her hiding spot. They were both breathless and giggling when Troche finally pulled her to his side. They hurried, catching their breath but not dawdling. It was never a good idea to linger in the rougher parts of town.

"We might have a problem, Mage," Troche said frowning as he gestured for her to follow.

"How so?" she asked. She ducked down the small alley and lengthened her stride to keep up with the taller thief. "Are you still sour you lost our last card game?"

"I still say you were cheating, but this is bigger than that."

"You should know better than to play against someone who grew up under a gaming table, Troche," she pointed out with a grin tugging at her sleeves to make sure it covered her bracelets. The last thing they needed was for some thug to see a gleam of metal and gemstones and get greedy.

"Will you shut up a minute and listen?" Troche snapped, pushing her to a stop against a wet brick wall. "And stop flashing those damn cuffs, you will get us both roughed up, guild or not."

"Fine. What?" she asked with a huff of annoyance, still tugging down her sleeves. "Where are we headed anyway?"

"My Master wants to meet you. A bloke called Vesp is calling in a debt from your Uncle. He heard you were in town when I told my Master."

"And he wants me to repay Jared's debt?" Beryl asked, falling into step next to him as he moved.

"Yeah, you need to meet with him and the Nail to negotiate the terms."

"I don't have any coin to give, Troche. I don't even earn more than pocket money as an apprentice until I reach my fifth year."

"Then your Uncle will have to come and pay the fine, or they will hound you until you do."

"Jared's a drunk and a liar. He may have done his best to raise me when my parent's died, but he's never seen me as anything other than a means to a little more coin. He won't honor the debt," she said, her tone bitter.

"Which is why we will talk to Master James. He'll know how to fix this."

"I can't leave, Troche." Beryl said, tugging him to a stop. "If I run, I'll be branded a rogue mage."

"So you won't run. I would miss your horrible sense of humor anyway," he said with a cheeky grin. "Don't worry. Master James is second to Nails. He has some sway; it'll work out."

They walked in silence for a while, Troche leading her deeper into parts of town were strange to her.

"When are you going to explain the gems, anyway?" he asked.

"I told you," she said with a sigh.

"Yeah, they're 'mage cuffs'," he said, making a face and gesturing with his hands. "I've seen the mages that get hired to ward houses and businesses around town. They don't have as many gems as you do, and they're fat and stinking rich. How does a broke apprentice like you get gems like that?"

"They're a family heirloom. They belonged to my grandfather."

"And?"

"And what?"

"You never take them off. Even when running around with me where it could be a problem."

"They don't come off, okay? They locked the first time I put them on and haven't come off since."

"Want me to pick it?" he offered with a frown, glancing at her wrists and the thin collar that wrapped her throat.

"Mage cuffs, Troche. There are no locks," she pointed out with a sigh. "Even my father couldn't remove them and he was a powerful mage."

"Why would anyone create something that could never be taken off? Especially a piece of jewelry? That's just crazy."

"They're mage jewelry, Troche. When have mages ever made sense? Anyway, the cuffs and collar do unlock."

"When?"

"When the mage wearing them dies," she said giving him a tight smile. "Lead on, Master Thief. Let's go meet with your Master and hope he has a better idea than selling my cuffs."

"Grand; You get stuck wearing enough gold and silver to buy a small port and can never take it off while being penniless and working yourself ragged as an apprentice mage. I thought being a mage was supposed to be a marvelous thing?"

"So they would have you think," she said with a smirk.

Troche lead them to a rundown tavern, bypassing the sparsely filled tables, making his way to a back office. He knocked and entered, pulling Beryl in after him. A fit looking middle aged man wearing a green silk vest sat reviewing several ledgers. He ignored them, taking a moment to tidy his desk before he turned to gaze at the two teenagers in his office.

"For once you are on time," he said with a huff. "Come urchin, introduce me to this mage you have befriended."

"Master James, this is Mage. She's apprenticed to Master Mage Fremont."

"Yes, the mage with no name, whose Uncle is a gambler with outstanding debts," he said looking her over with a frown.

"I cannot help who my Uncle is, sir."

"Nor can anyone help related to them by blood. They must, however, still deal with the complications that relation may bring about," the man said with a sniff. "I need to know how we can help each other, young Mage. What can you offer to cover your debt?"

"I have very little beyond my skills as a mage, sir. I've no real coin and will not earn any for at least another year of my apprenticeship."

"And your skills as a thief?"

"I've never worked as a thief," Beryl said flatly.

"But Troche has sung your praises. Born to the gaming table with a handful of dice, was it?" He asked. Troche flashed a wry grin as he poured tea for the three of them.

"I only said she had a deft hand, sir. Not that she would be suited to do the work."

"Not everything in the guild is done in the shadows and not every hand dealt is a rigged one. I may have a way to defer your debt until you can pay them back, but it will mean some work," he said, checking a pocket watch before tucking the silver case away.

"What would you have me do?" Beryl asked.

"That will have to be discussed later. We have an appointment with the Guild Leader, Vadna. Smarten yourselves up and come along."

Smarten themselves up? Beryl glanced from Troche's sweaty, wrinkled clothes down to her own patched shirt and scuffed boots. She had dressed for a late afternoon running through the bad parts of town, not an audience. She tugged the tie from her frizzing braid and finger combed out her long hair to lie along her back in soft waves, hoping that would be enough.

They headed to the docks, Master James leading them to a dark and rundown warehouse in the warehouse district. One rhythmic knock and a password later they were led through a maze of corridors and into a large open room. A woman clothed in mismatched silks, and coppery red boots sat on a raised dais. She watched them approach, one hand stroking the small dog in her lap.

"Master James, always a pleasure to have you in our court," the woman said with a crimson smile, flashing silver teeth.

"Always a pleasure to be in your presence, Vadna, the Nail," he said giving a courtly bow.

"What have you brought to entertain us today, Master James?"

"I have both an introduction and a request. Allow me to introduce Mage apprentice to Master Mage Fremont and niece to Jared Voss."

"Excellent! Come forward girl!"

"It is a pleasure to meet you, Ma'am," Beryl said with a small curtsy. It never hurt to be polite, and she'd heard rumors of the ruthless Nail, who earned her status by nailing her competition to the sides of the dockside pilings with iron spikes.

"I'm afraid we have a bit of a quandary, you and me, Mage," she said, teasing the dog in her lap gently. "Your Uncle owes us a debt—a debt that you now owe. We need to decide what currency you will pay with. What would you prefer, my dear Mage? Coin or blood?"

"If I may, Vadna, I have an alternative arrangement that may suit everyone," Master James interjected, edging forward to stand just before Beryl.

"Enlighten me, James, but do it quickly," Vadna snapped, running her sharp red nails through the fur of her pup, ignoring how the insignificant thing shivered at her touch.

"I propose we allow the girl to join the guild as an apprentice. Paying her debt in coin or blood would gain nothing for the guild in the long run. If we harm a mage apprentice and it gets back to the guard, we could have a trouble on our hands. If we let her join us, however, we gain the use of a mage to assist us for years to come."

"And who would take her on? I doubt the other Masters would teach a Mage. They are not known for their stealth and subtly."

"I would take that hardship if you allow it," he said with another low bow.

"Then you will assume her debt until we judge it as paid in full and any punishments she incurs."

"Of course," James said, giving a slight bow and gesturing for Beryl and Troche to do the same before he drew them away from the throne.

"Master James," Troche whispered once they were out of the guild hall.

"Quiet until we are back at the Inn," he hissed, grabbing Troche's elbow and tugging him along.

Master James pulled Troche along faster, forcing Beryl to jog to keep up. He only stopped once they were back in his office with the door shut behind them. He opened a side door and gestured for them to follow, revealing a comfortable looking sitting room. He poured himself a glass of something much smoother than Jared's normal rot gut alcohol and slumped into a chair by the unlit fireplace.

"All right. We have things to discuss. You needed to say something, Mage?"

"I'm already apprenticed to Master Fremont. I can't be an apprentice to two masters," Beryl snapped. She was barely managing her time with Troche now, with a second apprenticeship she would not even have time to sleep.

"Master Fremont has been known to use the services of the Guild from time to time. You won't have many duties for us at first. I see you following Troche in his lessons for the next month."

"I don't enjoy stealing," she said bluntly. "I never helped my Uncle with the gaming tables if I could help it."

"No one likes to steal, Mage. Only the weak take what they cannot earn. Once we have a use for your skills, they may require you to ward a building or two for the Guild, but most of your tasks will be simple. You will take or receive messages or compact packages and pass on information to your other Master as we need. Would you consent to becoming our runner when the need happens?"

"I don't see how I have much choice in the matter."

"Everyone has a choice, Mage, even if it is just to endure what you must. I'll inform Master Fremont later this week. Don't mention the change in your relationship with the Guild until then."

"I will tell him if you don't by the end of the week," Beryl snapped stubbornly.

"And there is the steel I've been waiting to see. I think we'll learn much from each other, Mage. Troche, see your new sister home and take the rest of the night off. I'll send Troche for you when I'm ready to start your apprenticeship. Until then, Mistress Mage," he said with a grin, waving them out.

"Well that went well," Beryl snarled once they were back on the street.

"Considering we still have all our limbs and no one died, I'd say it was a rousing success," Troche said. He tugged her off balance, and out of the furious pace she had been setting.

"I can't be apprenticed to another master, Troche. I'm barely keeping up with my lessons in the castle now."

"You're finding time to go running about with me," Troche pointed out, pulling out a handful of dried fruit and offering her some. "We'll just work your lessons for the Guild into that."

"You're to calm about this. You could've died as easily as me or lost your Master tonight, Troche."

"I've lost Masters before," Troche said leading her through back-streets she yet to travel. "I lost my first two masters in the Guild to Vadna. She scares me, for truth, but Master James is an agreeable man under it all. He stands up for the guild members under his care. If he says you have a place, then you're as safe as any of us can make you."

"So I just need to keep away from Vadna?"

"Not just her. There's a few rotters in the bunch, but Vadna will forget you once she finds a new toy to play with. Master James will have you lying low for a few months doing odd jobs, and then he can give you the real training like what I'm doing."

"What's the real training then?"

"Nope, I can't say until Master James makes it official and all. You'll just have to wait."

"Wonderful," she grumped, stealing another dried cherry.

"See, I'm telling you, deft hands. You'd make a grand picker."

"I'd rather do something of use," she said with a huff. "I enjoy making things and fixing wards, Troche. Stealing feels too much like I'm breaking things apart."

"Then we'll just have to figure out ways you can help the guild without stealing. I'm sure there's something."

"You're much too optimistic for a thief, Troche."

"And you're too sour for someone who can do magic. I mean, come on, who doesn't want to wave your hand and make things happen?"

"I don't know what it's like not to do magic; I've been casting spells since I was a small child."

"And I've been a pickpocket for just as long. We'll just have to figure out a way to get both to work together."

"You know Mages take an oath to never harm the King or the country when we become Master Mages, right? I'm sure stealing from its citizens is considered harming the country."

"Yeah, but you have a few years until that, right? We'll find a loophole before that becomes an issue."

"You're crazy."

"Without a doubt," he said with a grin. "I'm off to hit the tables before they close. I'll see you this rest day, probably."

"See you then," Beryl said with a sigh.

Just when she thought she was getting her life back under control, things like this happened. There was not much she could do about it for now. She spent the rest of the night curled tight in her bed, worrying over every potential way this could blow up in her face.

CHAPTER 10

Two days later Master Fremont calmly informed her he was aware of her arrangement with Master James, and as long as it did not affect her work as his apprentice, he would ignore the second apprenticeship.

"But sir!"

"I will not speak of it farther, Mage. I expect your report on Blood wards on my desk by the end of the week."

"Yes, Master Fremont," she said, watching as he went back to lighting his pipe.

"Darius, my dear," he reminded her gently. "Now, get the tea started while I gather the books I want you to read for next week's lessons. I think you're ready to work with agates."

"Yes, Master Darius," she said with a sigh. She was used to dealing with things herself; she would just have to make the additional apprenticeship work with her mage studies.

Beryl returned to her attempts to cast on a chunk of crystal, flinching as the spell hit the stone. Once a week Darius presented her with a new stone to work with. Some worked as easily as her road and river stones. Most of the others only worked for certain spells or didn't work at all, exploding in a shower of dust and stone.

Only a few stones worked in generally the same way for all mages. They used granite for buildings to create stable wards and protections. Granite and other hard stones would hold a spell tight within themselves, and this caused spells cast on them to last much longer than those cast on softer stones. This also meant that spells set into granite were next to impossible to remove without damaging the spell or destroying the stone.

So far she was showing a knack for working with the harder stones like granite and marble. This might stem from her ability to ward; it was impossible to say. Small garnets and lesser gemstones like yellow citrons and smoky quartz worked well for protection spells.

So far, she hadn't been able to find a stone that worked better for her than the river stones and pebbles she'd always worked with. With a sound like breaking glass, the crystal shattered into a pile of fragments with a sharp snap. Apparently, working with crystal and glass would not be easy, she mused with a groan.

Darius was inquiring in town to see if any of the local jewelers would let her watch or even apprentice to learn the trade during the next summer. She was reading books on how to work magic into metal or to even sculpt and mold metal with magic. The work that she seemed to lean toward was more the making of small items like jewelry or small statues made of stone and metals. However, there were very few books to help her in pursuing this.

Most of the records seemed from mages who crafted enormous stone statues or made full size metal swords and shields. There was nothing on the small scale she was looking for. For now, she was hunting for books or records about it while trying to apply they could do what the other large-scale works of magic on a smaller scale. It was very slow, looking like it would take years of practice.

* * *

"Bain's bollocks," Beryl cursed, taking in her mud covered cloak that an hour ago had been clean and dry.

The older apprentices had taken an instant dislike to her when she joined the fifth year's lessons. They delighted in trying to destroy her work in the lessons or humiliating her with snide comments and taunts. It didn't help that she was excelling in her projects in lessons, drawing praise from several of the Masters who taught their lessons

With another curse she pressed a hand against the runes stitched into the hem of her cloak, pushing magic into the fabric. In a soft wash of golden light, it purged the mud and water from the material in a wave of heat. Beryl had spelled all her clothes with runes of protection and purity to prevent any stain and even to prevent them from burning. It had helped often in the last few weeks as several of the fifth year students seemed determined to get her to quit the apprenticeship. She was harassed in and out of the lessons; her things were stolen from her tables or covered in ink.

The thick wool still smelled musty, but at least the material was dry and warm in the corridors. She pulled it on and headed out of the lesson rooms, trying to ignore the waiting bullies who watched her leave with sharp eyes. She was working on several projects along with her school work, and it meant many trips down the castle corridors to the library and its cold vaults. The last thing she needed was to head there with a wet cloak.

The one project that was showing the most promise was her use of ancient runes. She'd discovered that many of them were much more stable than the modern runes in use. They took more energy to cast, but they anchored the spells, allowing them to be stored longer and to have a larger effect when triggered.

She hunted the library each day for ancient texts on runes that were no longer used and befriended several of the librarians. They kept their eyes out for any texts that she might use, passing them on as they uncovered them in their own research in the vaults beneath the castle. The library was renowned for its massive underground corridors full of magical relics and spell books.

The one thing the other apprentices always poked at was her lack of a name, saying that she'd been cursed so by her family as they did not want her, or cursed because she was such a poor mage that they had disowned her. She did her best to ignore the torment, but her anger at their thoughtless cruelty was growing. Beryl longed to corner one brat in a side street and teach her just how painful a true beating could be. She doubted the brat had ever felt the side of a hand growing up.

One of the upper years had thought it hilarious to tip a bowl of gruel along her side that very morning. She stood and left the dining hall, ignoring the gasps and laughter that trailed behind her. A spell and a quick wash in a nearby bath had her clean and on time to lessons, which left the upper year students gaping. She did her best to ignore the taunts and not react to the treatment she received from the other apprentices, but it was getting harder every day; she could not let them force her into a fight. She refused to get sent away from the school.

All she had to look forward to if she was sent away was going straight back to Uncle Jared or to some remote town where she would be expected to marry the first man who asked her. No, the best thing was to ride this year out and make sure they asked her to stay. She would become a royal mage and show everyone how wrong they had been to deride her. She just needed to endure it another year, and then she would be back out on the road working.

She ran to the town to train at her thief lessons or just to wander the town many afternoons. It got her away from the castle and the constant bulling as well, which was all the incentive she needed. She often ran into Troche on these trips, and they would spend a few hours at the gaming tables watching and occasionally placing small bets on the outcomes.

Today she headed to the town's temple to Ruth. Her mother had been a devote follower of Ruth, keeping a small alter in the entry way of their home. Since her death, Mage had rarely visited the temples or to do more than an absent morning prayer to the healer god.

The temple of Ruth was a massive stone building that covered a city block. They divided the temple into three parts: the temple proper (where the faithful prayed and worshiped), the healing wards and the library, and the rooms of the priest who lived and worked in the temple. Temples dedicated to Ruth were devoted to light, healing, and growth, as these were the three fundamental aspects of the goddess.

The temple was full of windows, built around a central garden that had a stone statue of Ruth in the center. The main hall of the temple where everyone came to pray and reflect, was a long hall with doors leading off to compact rooms that held padded benches and desks that faced a mural of Ruth so that the follower could pray in private. Priests waited to offer advice from the books of the revered or historical works on the martyrs.

The chief place to worship was at the end of the hall. An enormous bronze statue of Ruth showed her kneeling with a female deer on one side and an orb representing the sun in the other hand raised like it was a light globe. Braziers of incense burned along with herbs and candles around the statue. Those who wished to alert the god or goddess to a need would light a candle and pray while the incense wafted their prayer to the goddess.

There were dozens of gods. However, Ruth and Bain were often viewed as the two major gods, supreme above the others. There were rumors that many considered profane—that Ruth and Bain were ancient mages who stopped a great war, leading to their eventual worship. Occasionally, someone would come forward claiming to have found documents or proof of this; however, it had always been dismissed as a fraud.

Beryl didn't like owing anyone something if she could repay it, so she went to the temple to see if there was any way she could repay the kindness they had shown her in healing her on her travels with the Captain. After speaking with one acolyte, they took her to the temple priestess. She explained how she wished to help, offering to ward the temple if they wished. The priestess smiled and took her hand.

"Child, one thing we agree on is that every act, even one done in kindness must be paid back in kind, whether in this life or after. I think the best way to help would be to learn. Since your gift was a healing, I believe that you should look into learning some healing. Now, I am not saying you must become a daughter of Ruth," she said with a smile when Beryl went to protest. "Just that you could learn some basic magical and non-magical healing. So that next time someone near you is injured, you will help them. That is what we ask of all our children, that each blessing given to them is passed on to those who may also need it. Now, let us go to Healer Jenna and see when she will have time to teach you."

"Thank you, Healer."

"Ruth thanks you for your giving spirit, child."

Beryl spent the afternoon helping to make healing salves in the infirmary. It surprised her to see several marked members of the thieves' guild in the ward for various injuries. A small blue trident marked on the webbing between their thumb and fingers of their right hands. She would have to ask Troche later if the guild didn't have someone who cared for the injured.

A week later Beryl chased Troche through the city. Her first actual test was to catch the nimble thief, and Troche was proving his guild status by leading her through every back alley and muddy lane in the town. Scrambling up a low wall, she fought to keep her breath steady as she lurched after her quarry.

Hours later she staggered after Troche back into Master James' study, slumping onto the rug next to the fire with a curse. She was covered head to toe in mud and soaked to the skin thanks to misjudging a step along a wall and tumbling into a small pond.

* * *

"How did she do, Troche?" Master James asked, puffing at his pipe as he worked on several ledgers at his desk.

"Kept up ok, but you'd have thought I had a herd of horses chasing me. We need to work on running silent. She climbs well but scraped her hands up good. At least she could ignore the pain and keep going," Troche said, handing Beryl a cup of tea and several biscuits while he took his own to a pile of pillows in one corner.

"Humph, show me your hands, girl. We cannot let you go back to the castle injured," James said, tugging out a small kit of bandages and ointments from his desk.

"I know how to treat scrapes," Beryl snapped, "and don't call me girl!"

"Mage, then," The man snapped back. "Let me see your hands. Your hands are your livelihood in the guild. You may fall back on your magic if you're injured, but most of us have only ourselves to do the work needed. We remove the injured from the guild if they aren't able to work."

"Permanently?"

"No, those who are too injured to work are sent to relatives or to stations where they can work such as in the brothels or the local inns working the kitchens or stables."

Beryl let him clean the scraps along her knuckles and wrists. The worst was where the scars on her palms had split. They did that whenever she over used her hands. She was used to it and ignored the glances Troche was stealing of her wounds.

"The scars on your hands are from an old injury?" James asked as he applied a healing balm and started winding a light bandage around one palm.

"Yes, I was attacked as a child by a rogue mage."

"And the injuries don't hamper your movement?"

"I do stretches in the morning and at night. My hands ache in the cold or bad weather, but I can still work."

"From now on you will wear gloves when you're working with Troche. You said you know how to treat scrapes. What other healing do you know?"

"I've started helping the healers in the Temple of Ruth. I'm learning how to make simple balms and healing runes."

"Good, continue with that. I will see if we can get you more lessons in healing, it wouldn't hurt to have a second healer for the guild."

"I saw a few of the guild marked at the temple being treated," she said, unsure if James would answer her questions.

"Those that don't have serious injuries are sent to the temple or left to treat the wounds themselves if they don't have the coin."

"Why send them away if you have a healer in the guild?"

"Why waste a healer's strength and ability on a few scrapes and bruises? Our healer is part of the Nail's household. He won't heal unless she orders it."

"So only those she favors are treated?"

"Vadna is stingy with her favor. Only her current favorites are worthy of her attention and those change weekly. Until she steps down or is removed from power, we are at her mercy."

"Are the others hoping to replace her any better?"

"Some are better, some are worse. Right now she has an iron grip on the guild. It would take something massive to shake up her rule, but that's not something we can expect to happen tonight. For now, once you have finished your tea, you may go. Come back the next rest day in the afternoon. I'll have your next lesson ready for you."

"Don't you mean test?"

"When is anything not a test?" he said with a snort, "Finish your tea, brats."

"Yes, Master James," Troche sing-songed from his sprawl, making Beryl chuckle at his cheek.

"Brats, the lot of you."

* * *

HER WORK with the hawks was still not going well, but after a rather awful lesson, Salandra had told her about a cat in the kitchens who had given birth. The cook was giving the kittens away; perhaps she could try cats instead. So that afternoon found her winding her way deep into the castle in search of the kitchens. It took a servant pointing out a hidden doorway invisible behind a tapestry.

All the doors to the servant's passageways and quarters were hidden this way. The kitchens, storerooms, and laundry were hidden on a lower level of the castle. The only light came from narrow windows near the ceiling. To compensate, there were roaring fires and lamps burning in the rooms were in use. The kittens and their mother sat on a pile of blankets in an unused corner of the room. Once the mage stepped in to the kitchen, the head cook stopped her.

"I was hoping to see the kittens," Beryl mumbled, trying to appear young and cute. Confidence had its place, but seeming harmless could pave a way just as easily. The cook looked her over with a frown yet still waved her in.

"Go on child, just stay out from under everyone's feet."

"Yes, Ma'am," Beryl blurted, ducking past the cook and moving toward the back of the kitchens where the storage rooms were located.

As the kitchen staff continued their dinner preparations, the young mage sat and offered a hand for the mother cat to sniff. Once she'd been allowed to scratch the mother's jaw and stroke her head lightly, she allowed her to see the kittens themselves. They were several weeks old; old enough to venture away from the mother a small way.

The kittens tumbled and chased each other about the floor. There were eight kittens in total. A white and a calico slept curled next to their mother while a black nursed. The others tumbled and bounced each other across the floor as the staff stepped around them. The rest of the cats varied in shades of black, grey, and white with only one bright orange puff that seemed determined to be a mischief maker.

Beryl jumped out of her skin as she felt claws hook into the back of her tunic and climbed up her spine, coming to a rest on her shoulder. Sitting there peering at her was a grey tabby kitten with golden eyes. After inspecting her hair, mage collar, and chin, the kitten settled down and started purring in her ear.

"See you found a friend," a cook said with a grin, coming up behind her. Starting hard enough to jar the kitten which squeaked a protest before settling back down with a grumble Beryl turned to see one cook grinning down on her.

"He's yours if you like him, but I warn you, he's one that's into everything. He fell in the middle of a pie last week," she said with a laugh.

A few hours later she was showing the cat to Master Fremont.

"A fine brawny lad, he will make a good familiar, I think." Handing the kitten back he asked, "How does your magic feel when you're holding him, Mage?"

"It's strange, it almost feels like it is fluttering or stretching," she said, while pressing a hand against her breastbone. Darius drew a small glass orb from his belt pouch and began rolling it between his hands, a habit he had when thinking.

"That is the connection forming. Once your magic stabilizes, you will see what abilities your familiar has. Have you read the books I gave you?" he asked, glancing at her.

"Yes, but the abilities of each pair seem so random. A man who had a bobcat bondmate could see in the dark while another who had a dog could tell when people lied to him." Untangling the cat from her hair, she set him in front of a saucer of finely cut chicken which he began to gobble.

"It is rather random, I'm afraid. One theory is that each familiar is making up for a lack the mage has herself, but it is not always clear why certain abilities manifest themselves. One thing that is constant is that you will know your bondmate at all times, and both of you will know if the other is in danger or in need of the other. Some close pairs even develop mind to mind speech. We will just have to wait and see how your bond develops."

"Now what were you going to tell me about this ball? It is a suitable piece of magic." Placing his glass orb back in his pouch, he picked up the leather ball and gave it a shake. A musical chime played with a small glow of runes. With a flick of his hand, he sent the ball bouncing across the table and onto the floor with the kitten right behind it. As the kitten raced about chasing the ball, she explained.

"I would have made a collar for him and had set everything out but once I got started I wound up with a leather ball instead. I don't even remember making it, it was strange." With a laugh, Darius watched the kitten batting the ball around a chair leg.

"That's the bond, I am afraid. When it's first forming it's like wild magic. It grabs what it needs and forces things along so both bondmates are happy. Have you decided on a name for this rapscallion?"

Beryl blushed and ducked her head. "Yes, but I was hoping I would think of something better."

"Again, the magic and both partners need to choose the name. It may not be up to you."

Red faced the girl burst out, "But I can't name a mage's cat, Rune!" At the sound of his name the cat turned and bounded to its partner. Quickly climbing into his bondmate's lap, he purred and rub against her hands.

"I'm afraid he seems to like his name and once named it cannot be changed easily. One agreeable thing is while the bond is forming bondmates cannot be separated for long, and he'll be allowed to attend lessons with you and your other duties."

Beryl blanched. "They won't let me bring a cat with me to the falconry or to see the hunting dogs."

"Ask whoever is training you to let you see the ones most attached to you and see how they react to the cat. They cannot bond to you if they cannot tolerate your other bondmate. That will need to be put off a few weeks until the bond settles."

"The hawk master does not think I will bond with a hawk and has arranged for me to meet a friend of his who raises common and exotic birds in a month. I'll bring him with me then."

"I'm afraid for the first few months it's more that you will bring him everywhere. The bond is fragile once it's formed and can take up to a year to stabilize." Darius pulled a strip of ribbon from one pocket and teased the kitten.

Days passed and ever since gaining Rune, Beryl felt that things were taking a turn for the better; at least until she started lessons back. Darius had warned her that an out of control familiar was not tolerated. If Rune couldn't behave in class, then Beryl wouldn't be allowed to attend lessons until she could prove he was under control to her teacher.

The first lesson with Rune was a fifth year lesson that met twice a week. Several of the older students in class had bondmates of their own; she hoped they would be mature and not bother her or Rune.

She had spent part of the night and that morning explaining to Rune he needed to behave, but she was not sure if he understood.

The bond was still new, and though she got the occasional feeling or image from Rune, he was still a kitten, and she wasn't sure how much he understood of what it meant to have a bondmate or to behave in a certain way. Taking off her cloak and hanging it by the door, Rune remained where he was sitting on her shoulder, hidden by the fall of her hair. When Master Bardic came in, he looked surprised to see her back so soon.

"Mage, I see you are back. How is your bondmate adjusting?" he asked with a kind smile.

"Very well, sir," she said, straightening in her chair and refusing to look at the others who whispered and muttered.

"What bondmate?" Marietta turned in her seat and sneered. "Did you bond with a slug?" Flipping her blond hair, she scoffed, "I think she made up her bondmate, after all what animal would bond with a waste like her."

"Marietta, that was unnecessary," Master Bardic said, looking sternly at Marietta. "Mage, if your bondmate is willing perhaps he could be shown to the class. He will have to get used to being in public anyway,"

Reaching up, Beryl stroked Rune's small head. Cupping her hand, she sent that it was his decision if he wanted to come down or not. The small cat was anything but timid when put to the test. Stepping out into her hand he allowed himself to be lowered onto the table where everyone could see him. Blinking his bright gold eyes, he observed the class, sitting as tall as a tiny grey kitten could. He was proud of his bondmate and would not let her down.

Marietta scoffed, "You might have done better with a slug. That's the smallest cat I've ever seen." This led to a round of laughter from several members of Marietta's group of sycophants.

Master Bardic snapped, "Marietta, I will inform your Master of your behavior in this class. As you do not yet have a bondmate of your own, perhaps you need a refresher of the standards of behavior and laws about having a bondmate. I expect a two scroll essay on bondmates to be handed into me by the next rest day. As for the rest of you, I want everyone to write a one-page essay on the laws concerning bondmates in this realm and in two others to be handed in by rest day after next." Giving the rest of the class a glare, he walked to the podium to begin the day's lesson.

The rest of the day went well, except for Rune learning that ink didn't dry immediately after she wrote something, leaving several paw shaped smudges across one of Beryl's papers and Rune with black feet for a day or two. For now Marietta avoided another confrontation with Beryl and her new bondmate, but Beryl knew that it would have to happen eventually. She just hoped that she could make it to the next summer break before she wound up decking the blonde snit.

She'd never been so happy to head out into town as that afternoon. Beryl strolled through the streets, happy to be out of the castle for at least a few hours. She still wasn't used to being stuck in one place for so long and being stuck in her rooms for two weeks had left her almost climbing the walls.

"Where did you get away to? I've been wondering if you skipped out?" Troche called out, dropping from his seat on the wall above her to land grinning at her feet several days later.

"No, Master Fremont grounded me until the bond settled," Beryl said with a grin, tugging at her hood. They had confined her to the castle for two weeks until Darius had decided that their bond was stable enough for her to go out.

"Bond?"

"This is Rune, my bondmate," she said, holding out a hand so that Rune could climb out from his hiding spot inside her cloak.

"I take it he's more than a pet?" Troche asked, stroking the small cat and laughing at the loud purr that he produced.

"He's my bondmate. We... it's like being bound by magic. Where I go, he goes. Eventually, we'll be able to speak to one another and maybe even see through each other's eyes."

"He goes everywhere with you?"

"Once the bond settles, we should be able to be separate for a while but... it's like leaving part of yourself behind, Troche. Could you take off an arm and leave it somewhere without a worry?"

"So, you're dependent, one on the other?"

"Yes, it scares me a bit how important he is to me. I've never owned much growing up with Jared. They never allowed me to have pets, or even friends, and suddenly I have this person in my head and heart refusing to let me go."

"It could be an enjoyable thing too, right? At least now you'll always have someone to watch out for you? I'd always wanted a brother or something growing up; someone to have my back when I needed it. Now you have one that no one can take away."

"True. What did Master James have us doing tonight? Darius said that I needed to come find you today."

"So, it's true that James and Darius are friends, then?"

"No idea. Darius never seems to leave the castle, so I'm not sure how they could be."

"Maybe they grew up together or something. They could've met like we did."

"I know little about Darius' past beyond what he studied as an apprentice. If Master James grew up here, they might have known each other."

"James grew up in the guild. He told me once that he'd been through eleven Guild Masters."

"Then they could have known each other. It doesn't matter, I guess," Beryl said while picking up Rune and tugging Troche over to a street vendor. Buying two meat buns and a small bag of roasted nuts, she gave Troche a bun. They chatted about the general gossip around town as they made their way to James' office. Troche polished off his half of the nuts as he knocked.

"Come in, come in!" Master James called out, gesturing them inside once the door was open. "We have a busy night ahead of us, children. The Nail would like a demonstration of your abilities, Mage."

"She wants me to ward something?"

"Two somethings. She wants you to ward a small building against fire and to ward this box against theft."

"I've never warded something against theft. I can hide it. But then no one but another mage could find the box," Beryl said slowly, eying the small object with a frown.

"Then you have an extra project. Tonight, you must ward the building, however. Is there anything you will need?"

"No, it depends how long you want the wards to last. If the building's wood, I can carve runes which will last a few months or maybe a year. Or, I can lay copper or metal inlays which will last for a few years without recharging. If the building is stone, the wards will last much longer."

"This is a wooden building with a stone foundation," Master James said, gathering up his coat. "Come along, we need to get this finished tonight. How long does it take you to ward a building, Mage?"

"Anywhere from an hour to a full day. It depends on the size and the wards I have to cast."

"Then we better get started. Keep up, children."

"Yes, Master James." They sing-songed behind his back, giggling when he stomped out of the inn and into the street.

When they reached the building, it was a little more than a small run down shed. The thing was hardly standing on its own, even without warding. Beryl looked at the leaning structure with disbelief, while Troche cracked up from where he leaned against the enormous stone warehouse next door.

"You cannot be serious," she sputtered as her hands pulled out her knife and roll of copper wire. Rune jumped to the ground and wandered over to sit with Troche while she worked.

"Have you gained a pet, Mage?" Master James asked, watching as she marked out the runes that would power the wards.

"A bondmate," Troche called out while teasing the kitten with a bit of string. "His name's Rune."

"This is our first outing outside of the castle, and he was curious to meet Troche," Beryl muttered as she carved out the next string of runes, eyes on her work. "How much protection does the Nail want? A stiff wind could bring this thing down, warded or not."

"As much as you wish to place. I believe she wishes to see what you are capable of doing."

In other words, don't show them everything, Beryl mused as she strengthened the building and set wards to prevent fire damage. It would keep the building standing for a while, but if someone was determined, they could still tear it down once the wards gave way.

Three hours later she called the job complete and gathered Rune back up into her cloak. The kitten was exhausted from playing with Troche and collapsed into his mage's arms. Master James inspected her work before handing her a small jewelry box.

"This is the item to be warded against theft. You have until next rest day to either produce it or admit it's beyond your skills."

"Yes, Master James," she said with a sigh, tucking the box away in her bag.

"Get back to the castle, Mage. It would not do to have the watch notice you out late in the city. Troche, I have a task for you tonight, come with me."

The next morning, Beryl sought Master Darius before he went down to breakfast. He gestured her into his workroom while calling a servant for tea and a light breakfast. She explained about the box and how she'd been asked to ward it so it couldn't be stolen.

"I'm not sure I want to supply a guild of thieves with boxes protected against theft. What would they be storing in them?" she asked.

"Not every action the guild takes is illegal, Mage. They may try to protect their clients from being stolen from themselves. If they are supplying the protections, then they could charge for the use of them. Renting out such a box for transporting items would be a sound strategy. I see no harm in crafting small boxes like this one; it's only if the boxes become larger, or if they ask you to make the items in bulk, that I could see a problem."

"But I don't know how they will use them. They could do anything with them."

"As could any of the other people who have commissioned objects from the Mage's Counsel. We cannot control how the items we craft are used, Mage, any more than a sword smith can be blamed for the lives his blades take."

"But if I know they will use something I made to do harm, doesn't that go against the mage's vows?"

"You have made no vows to King and Country, Mage. However, if you feel like the Guild is asking you to do something that goes against your personal morals then you can tell both myself and Master James. We'll figure out a way to assist you in your tasks or to see the task given to another." Beryl nodded, but she was still unhappy.

"You need to learn to lean on others, Mage. As your Master, it is my duty to assist you where I can. You need to accept that help when it's needed."

"Yes, Master Fremont."

"Darius, please. Now, this box you are to ward. Have you considered how you want to accomplish the task?"

"I'm not sure how to prevent someone from just stealing the box. I can ward it so only certain people can open the box, or only someone with a pass phrase, but that doesn't stop someone from just picking up the box and running with it."

"Certain wards can harm those who try to touch certain objects or to prevent spying by incapacitating those who handle an object. It depends on whether you want to harm the thief or just the one trying to open the box."

"And if I don't want to do either?"

"Then you have a dilemma on your hands, child."

"Thanks, Darius," Beryl said with a huff, glaring at the offending box.

"If I may, you might wish to practice on several simple boxes before you attempt warding the actual item."

"Yes, I'll pick up several this afternoon in town," Beryl said, cuddling Rune to her as she considered how complicated this project was becoming.

* * *

RUNE WENT EVERYWHERE WITH HER, either riding on her shoulder or running along the ground to keep up. The one problem she had encountered was how she was to carry Rune when she was horseback riding. He refused to be left on the ground while she rode, even if it was only small circles in the pasture. Finally, she left for town to shop for some way to carry the small cat.

Beryl was thinking of adding a pocket to her cloak so he could ride there but wasn't sure it would work. She wandered through three different tailors' shops before coming to one that seemed to have cloaks and coats of every color. She approached the owner, a sturdy looking woman who had worked the shop ever since she married her husband and now worked it after his death in the king's army.

She laughed to see how small the cat was as she listened to the young Mage, but she agreed that there must be some way to carry him while astride a horse. After a bit of searching, she came out of a back room with a long green coat. They made it of thick wool that had been treated to be water proof and was split along the back to allow it to be worn while riding.

"These were in style a few years ago among the nobles; it's called a great coat. No one wears them anymore but it may work for you," She said pulling it up onto the counter, "See the deep pockets on the outside. It also has pockets on the inside to carry small packages, letters, or a purse where the rain cannot get to them. I know it is too early in the year for the wool, but I can make you one in a lighter fabric and include it for no charge if you buy the wool. I've been trying to clear these out of my stock for almost a year now, and I'm down to the last few."

The green wool coat was expensive, but it would be perfect for what she needed. The coats had to be measured and fitted, so she asked that a few extra pockets be added. They would allow her to have Rune sitting on the inside or outside of the coat, depending on how the weather was, and store anything she needed to carry.

The lighter coat was to be cut from a soft pale blue cloth. They would line it with a courser linen cloth to help absorb horse sweat and such, but the mage hoped to stitch cleansing and wear prevention runes in to the material to help with this. When she came to pick up the coats later that week, she was astonished to be given three coats instead of two.

"My littlest one is eleven and is attending the mage's lessons in the castle. When I told her of your cat, she asked if she could help. She became convinced you needed a suede coat, so we made one for you. She gets these notions in her head sometimes, but they can come true, so we follow them. I hope you don't mind." With a wince the woman added, "I'm afraid I need to charge you for the leather, however I will give you a good discount. I would let you have it, but the price of leather is so high right now."

Mage reassured the woman. "It's fine. I think I have enough, I understand about the knowing of things others do not, and if your daughter thinks I need it, then I'll buy it. It is a beautiful coat," she said with a slight smile, stroking the supple leather.

"Oh, I will tell her how much you liked it. She did the edging and embroidery herself," the woman beamed, "She has such a steady hand with a needle. Her talent seems to be stitching runes and working with cloth so she may have worked some magic into the coat. I'm afraid I don't have the gift so I couldn't say what she has or hasn't done."

The leather was a dark tan that looked like honey right when it comes off the comb. They lined the inside with soft grey linen that also edged the cuffs and collar of the coat. It didn't have a hood and was shorter than the other coats, stopping at mid-thigh. The girl had embroidered flowers and vines along the collar, cuffs, and lapel in a black grey thread that almost looked violet in the light. It still had the same cut as the other coat, including the extra pockets inside. However, the outside pockets were for one's hands, but a larger, third pocket had been added for Rune.

They had padded the shoulders of the coat with a second layer of leather that was a touch lighter than the rest of the coat and also had a slight line of embroidered vines coiled near the neck. Tilting her head,

Mage looked at the embroidery, observing the soft glow of magic coating the thread. It was a subtle but strongly cast bit of work for a mage so young.

It was not a spell she recognized, but it didn't have the aura of a spell that would cause harm. It glowed soft lavender. Touching the thread, the well of comfort that enveloped her surprised her. She felt energized and ready to move. Moving her hand off the thread, the feeling faded after a moment.

"Tell your daughter that the spell is amazing. I may have to get her to teach it to me," she said with a grin. "I was planning to stitch some runes into the inner lining of each coat, but hers put mine to shame."

"Oh, she will be pleased, thank you miss."

She left the shop wearing the light blue coat with Rune riding in the front pocket; she carried the other two coats with her. The next day, she wore the coat to the barn and tested it out with Flox. Rune discovered how bumpy riding could be but was happy at the scents and view he had on horseback. Both were happy that they could continue to be together.

Flox had taken to the small cat immediately, letting him sit on his wide back and bask in the sun as he slept in the paddock. Whenever she went to the stables, Beryl said hello to the stable master, stopping to see if the stable boys had heard anything interesting. The nobles ignored the servants and errand boys that worked around them, which lead to a massive gossip chain that ran throughout the castle. A servant of the court often could tell you more than any noble who lived there. Information was never an inappropriate thing to possess.

Beryl had spent most of her spare time that week working on the boxes the Thieve's Guild wanted warded. Her work tables were covered in small wooden boxes by the time she got the correct combination of spells and wards to prevent the box from being stolen yet allow its owner to handle the box. Darius had been impressed and asked to show one of the test boxes to the Counsel to see if they might allow such items to be crafted and sold by the apprentices.

That night Beryl took the finished box to Master James to arrange a meeting with the Nail. Two hours later she was being escorted back into the warehouse lair of the current Guild leader with Rune hidden deep in the hood of her cloak. She did not want to see him hurt, because they forced her to play court with such a blood-thirsty woman.

"Master James, have your mage explain her creation."

"Of course, Madame. If you please, Mage."

"I warded the box to prevent damage from blows or fire. When activated, any person except the person who activated the runes will be knocked unconscious should they touch the box," Beryl said, She stepped forward with the box held out at arm's length.

"A demonstration if you please. Activate it. Master Dart, come take the box," The Nail called out, gesturing for someone to the side to step forward.

Beryl set the box down, nicking a fingertip and pressed a drop of blood onto the copper plate on the lid. Dart strode up with a sneer and snatched it off the ground. A moment later he collapsed to the ground unconscious.

The watchers around the room collapsed in laughter. Vadna was the loudest, with her high-pitched cackle. Beryl picked up the box and deactivated the ward. Carrying it to the throne, she held it out to Vadna who snatched it with a frown.

"How is it activated?" she asked, turning the box this way and that.

"Place a drop of blood on the copper plate. To deactivate it, do the same."

"Well done, Master James. You've trained your new apprentice well."

"Thank you, Madame. Is there another task you wish of us?"

Vadna waved them away irritably as she examined her new treasure in one red-nailed hand. They bowed and retreated from the warehouse. Beryl was silent until they were back safely seated in Master James' rooms.

"You did very well, Mage," he said, pouring them each a cup of tea.

"I don't enjoy crafting objects like that for her to misuse," Beryl said, breaking a biscuit in half so that Rune had something to nibble.

"And I don't enjoy giving a Guild Master such as Vadna objects of power, but you came up with an elegant solution on your own. A box that renders anyone who touches it unconscious. You could have crafted such an item to burn, disfigure, or even kill at a touch, and yet, you did not." He said, sipping at his drink while he watched her fuss over her bondmate.

"Was this a test?" she asked, watching Rune gnaw on his treat.

"From Vadna? No, she wished for something magical to play with."

"But you took it as a test."

"Every challenge in our lives is a test, Mage. Most people ignore the results."

"And if I do not wish to be tested?"

"Then you should give up your magic and live the life of a normal farmer or innkeeper. Chose a life that will never force you to interact with the law makers or breakers of our small slice of the world."

"I did not choose to be here!"

"Then you need to accept your lot in life or change it, Mage. You cannot have it both ways. You cannot be powerful and expect the other powers around you to be ignorant of that fact. Power attracts power, child. As long as you are capable of being used others will try to do so. You need to be strong enough to refuse or to temper that power as you did with Vadna tonight."

"I'm not stronger than anyone else. I'm just an apprentice."

"Tell me, Mage. Who are the most powerful people here in Cardu?"

"Vadna controls the underground and black market of Cardu."

"Yes, and her current rival Marcus controls all the illicit shipping and transport by ship. Who else?"

"The King and his army control Arden and its borders. He has the mages at his disposal to use as he needs."

"And yet the King hasn't issued a direct order to the Mage's Council since his coronation. He makes requests such as to send mages if the country goes to war, but the Council does the actual posting of various mages. The Council controls which magical items are available for sale, it allows which mages sell their services as warders, and what spells they can offer to the regular population. Even the prices of what they sell are set by the Council."

"But the King has final say on a Mage's actions."

"A right he has never used. As far as the Mage's Council is concerned, the King has no power over them, because he chooses not to use the power his position grants him. Who else?"

"I don't know."

"You are apprenticed to one. Lord Fremont is a powerful mage and a direct advisor to the crown. He has lands and political power of his own that make him a minor noble, and he has a seat on the Mage's Council allowing him to have a hand in every decision that is made in Arden. Who else?"

"I don't know. Why would you say Darius is powerful? He doesn't seem to use his friendship with the King to his advantage or his position on the Council to change any of the laws they create."

"Not all power is flashy, Mage."

Beryl sighed and nodded, sipping at her tea. She had said as much to Captain Marshal while they traveled to Cardu. It sounded like she wasn't seeing the power plays at work in Arden like she thought she was. If Darius was a person of influence, then so was Master James.

It seemed like she was just being passed from hand to hand to be used by whoever had the most power at that moment. She would need to figure out a way to change that. She had not gotten away from Jared only to be abused and controlled by other masters.

CHAPTER 11

*H*er lessons with Darius continued most afternoons when she was not working on a project for her classes, or if Darius wasn't needed in court to advise the King. They were still working with different materials, trying to see what she was most suited to use. Darius was also showing her new spells and ways to combine runes to change the effects of her spells.

The way a rune was drawn could change the complete meaning of that rune, but the intent placed behind the rune was the most important thing. A rune to summon a bird could summon other animals if the intent was strong enough, but a rune customized for the intended task always worked faster and stronger than one that did something different.

Some runes fought over what you were trying to do with them. A mage who didn't have at least a small affinity to fire couldn't use any rune that called for fire. Mage was showing an affinity to runes that controlled both earth and water, which might explain her preference for using river stones for her spells.

Some spells used only a single anchor rune to hold the spell in place until they activated it. This was what was generally used in the stones used by mages. A mage concentrated on a specific spell and forced raw magic into the stone before sealing the stone with a rune of activation. A rune drawn on its surface or a word spoken by the mage who crafted the spell could then activate the stone.

Beryl had taken to casting various spells that might prove useful on a handful of river pebbles and keeping them in her pockets so they would always be at the ready. The one thing that was forbidden was to use magic as a weapon against another person, if they were another mage. Those that were caught had their magic stripped from them, and they would be exiled from the realm.

The spells Mage cast on her rocks were everyday spells like a spell to start a fire or to cause a stone to glow like a light orb. Nothing that could be considered a weapon, but minor things would be helpful if they caught her in a tight spot. Every advantage she could get might as well be at hand.

Too many years with her Uncle running from one dangerous situation to another had taught her to be ready for just about anything. She had been hurt too many times on the road when someone caught her unaware to not be armed in some fashion. Between Jared's casual violence and the hungry eyes of the drunken gamblers, she had learned when to hide and when to run at an early age. She refused to go back to being a helpless victim again.

* * *

It surprised Charles to see the young mage walking through the market several months after he had brought the injured mage to the capital. With her grey cloak drawn about her shoulders and long braid falling down her back, she could have been any young woman buying bread and vegetables for her table. It shattered the illusion when a grey head popped out of the basket on her arm. With a chuckle, the mage picked up the cat and set it on one shoulder. Charles caught up with her as she was turning to inspect the rows of inks and papers set up in front of a book seller.

"Long time no see, Mistress Mage. How are you adjusting to life in the castle?" Turning to face him, the young woman's face broke into a smile.

"Good morning, Captain Marshal. How are you this morning?" she asked, brushing a loose strand of hair behind one ear.

"Well enough and you, Mistress Mage?" he asked, tendering her a brief bow with a wide grin.

Laughing, she responded, "Well enough, I think. Have you heard I gained a bondmate? This is Rune." Charles grinned at the small grey tabby. This was a tiny cat, even for a kitten.

"Good day to you, Master Rune." He greeted the cat with a grin and another bow. Turning to Beryl, he inquired, "And I thought we'd agreed that you would call me Charles?"

"Of course. I'm glad to see you again, Charles," Beryl said, letting Rune scramble up her sleeve so he could look the Captain over. The cat gave a chirrup of greeting and sniffed the captain's hand before going back to his perusal of the crowded streets.

"What are you shopping for today?" he asked, scratching behind the kitten's ears.

"I needed to pick up a few books and some other things. I think Master Darius is determined that I spend all my allowance on books," she said with a rueful laugh.

She had started another stash of coins, but it was slow to grow with how much she was having to spend on books. Turning, she led the way into the bookshop. Hearing the door open, the owner strode out from the back room and grinned when he saw who it was.

"Ah, Apprentice; I have your order." Ducking behind a counter, he emerged with a stack of books, which he set before the mage.

"Hello Roel. How goes business today?" she asked, setting her basket down on the counter.

"Good, good, nothing to complain about. Hello Rune, and no playing in the inks today, you!" He shook a finger at the cat which caused the Captain to laugh. Rune looked affronted and gave a soft chirp before turning back to his perusal of the books on the table. Jumping down, he wandered among them, sniffing the occasional one before leaping up into the store window to watch people walk by.

"Roel, can I introduce you to Captain Marshal?"

"Pleasure to meet you, Sir." The captain replied.

"And you Captain. Could I interest you in anything today, as a friend of such a good customer, I would give you a good price?" he said with a grin.

"Not today. I leave on a rotation of patrol in two days and would not have time to do any book justice for quite some time."

"How much do I owe you, Roel?"

"Your finder's fee more than covered it, my dear. Are you looking for anything else?"

"Not at the moment, but I'm sure I'll see you again by the next rest day."

After saying their goodbyes to Roel, they collecting Rune on the way out into the market.

"So, where are you headed on patrol this time, finding more wayward mages to kidnap?" she asked with a grin. She enjoyed teasing him, maybe a bit too much, but he seemed to enjoy the banter.

"No, this should just be a quick run to escort provisions to the border. They're adding more soldiers, and they have attacked the supply trains several times in the last few months."

The press of potential war was starting to being by everyone. There was a near constant flow of soldiers training and heading out to the border to reinforce the troops stationed there. There was also talk of more warships being built farther south.

Arden was an enormous country that only shared borders with two other countries. Bourdain in the west was friendly with Arden, but it was currently at war with Dandridge; Arden's neighbor to the north. It was expected that soon Arden would have to also enter the war as Dandridge was encroaching upon Arden's borders to log wood for their war efforts.

Across the sea, there were several other countries from a massive continent with three countries and several island nations. Most were friendly with Arden, however one seemed bent on constant minor attacks against Arden. So far they hadn't been able to prove that

Orlean caused the attacks was a sparse country of ice and rock that sat off the eastern coast of Arden.

With no other close neighboring lands, they had gone to war with themselves, tearing the country apart and destroying much of its resources. Now there was talk of raiding parties hitting the coast of Arden and sometimes ever farther inland, to steal goods and treasures. The King of Orlean continued to deny that these attacks were caused by his men or people and that he did not know of who they were.

Charles said goodbye to the Mage with a fond grin and headed back to the barracks. He needed to make sure his small squad was packed and ready to move in the morning. At least this would be a brief trip; less than a month if he was lucky with the road and weather.

* * *

BERYL WAS on her way to the library when she remembered that she needed to ask Darius about a book she wished to borrow from his personal collection. Turning back, she was just off one of the main hallways when she heard Darius' voice down an unlit corridor. The room was deserted and unused; however, a light glowed beneath the edge of a door on the far wall.

She didn't want to bother Darius if he was in conference with the King or speaking about something important with one of the mage's council. Pressing against the wall next to the door, she tried to hear if Darius was busy but froze when the conversation made sense.

"Sir, the web has found little evidence, but I can tell you that we caught the King of Orlean boasting of the attacks in the last month." An unknown voice replied in response to some soft question from Darius, "He didn't say he ordered them, but it sounds as if he's the one funding the raiders, giving them the money to buy weapons and boats to continue to harass us. Most of the reports I've been getting are gossip. They say that we deserve to be attacked if we cannot protect our own boarders. It also sounds like some nobles from Bourdain and

Dandridge are agreeing with him. They may pressure their monarchies to assist in any war effort that Orlean begins."

"How goes recruitment? Have you found any others that may be up to training?" This voice that sounded too much like King John for Beryl to be comfortable. She edged back but Rune leaned in against her leg, he was a ball of curiosity, and he wanted to know what they would say.

"I have a few possible names among the fifth years, but I would like to wait until after their testing. I have recruited several more messengers and a handful of soldiers are to be stationed in the north. I am still looking for a person to station at the Orlean court. It has to be someone able to be visible and able to take part in the day-to-day court life. I have a few already stationed there, however they're posing as maids and servants. They can't get into many of the court functions where we need someone. We will just have to keep looking." The voices trailed off to a murmur as the conversation continued.

Backing away from the door, Beryl flinched as the spells that layered the wood came to light. If she'd touched the door, she would have been burned and stuck to the burning wood until they ended the spell. She quickly scooped up Rune so he would touch nothing.

Frowning, she turned away; she needed to think about what she'd heard. It sounded like the King had spies in other courts, and that Darius was the one in charge of them. She couldn't fault the King in placing spies where he knew there may be a threat to Arden; however, she was surprised to find out that Darius was involved in it. It made a kind of sense, however, since he was known to the Thieves' Guild and Master James.

He seemed like an old mage who was happily puttering amongst his books; however, she knew he was extremely intelligent. Apparently, he also was good at wearing masks to hide his true abilities. It was a talent the girl herself used to an extent. If one looked small and harmless, the worst blows tended not to fall. She knew all about wearing masks after years with Jared and still wore them during the day to deal with the torments of the other apprentices. She would have to monitor Darius and see if there was any way that she could help him.

Beryl's lessons were continuing, but what made her love being an apprentice was Darius letting her work on projects on her own. She'd spent so many years teaching herself how to craft spells and work out problems that the structure of being lectured with the other apprentices was stifling. Darius, however, tried to give her two free mornings each week to research and experiment.

She also used the time to learn her way around the castle, taking Rune on trips to find out where the dark unused hall went and how to get to different parts of the castle without ever hitting one of the main halls. In the process she found things, from a small library that was rotting itself back into dust to armor and implements used by mages that were left sitting in storage and forgotten.

She'd asked one of the librarian mages if they knew about the small library and led a trio of them to investigate. They lamented over the condition of the books and began moving them an armload at a time to the main library to be restored and placed on the shelves or in the vaults.

She asked Darius about the storage she found, and if she could use any of the items in the room. He agreed on the condition that she showed it to him first, and soon even he was amazed at the various things that had disappeared into the storerooms of the castle. It became a favorite pastime of Mage and Rune to investigate the storeroom on rainy days when they were not needed in town, Rune happily chasing mice and climbed the old boxes and crates.

Robert was taking lessons to learn how to be a scribe, because it was what his mother wanted for him. But he wanted to be a soldier in the king's army. He was trying to convince a member of the king's guard to train him and had brought Beryl along for moral support. The man they saw was on duty on the castle battlements when they found him. the soldier sighed, visibly annoyed, as he watched Robert approach.

"Boy, you are too young to join the army and too young to train. I've told you this a dozen times."

"I'm not too young to train, I'm fourteen! King John himself started training when he was ten!"

"Yes, but you're not the King. He had the gold to pay for a tutor. You do not!" The mage interrupted before the two could continue an argument that clearly had been going on for weeks.

"What can he do that would help for when he joins, not training, but other things?" Beryl asked, wanting to at least get something productive out of the time they had wasted tracking the man down.

The soldier frowned at this before nodding and grudgingly saying, "You can run, get in better shape. Learn to shoot a bow or how to live off the land, how to read a map and how to travel by reading one. You don't have to know all the drill and such, you learn that in the first year, but if you know how to survive if you get separated from your troops, or how to bandage wounds, then you will do twice as good as most grunts." Robert opened his mouth to argue again, but Mage grabbed him and thanking the soldier pulled him away. Once they were far enough away that the soldier could not hear, she released him.

"Are you crazy? Antagonizing him will not get him to help you in any way; all it does is make him mad and make him remember you when you get to training so he can treat you like dirt. Weren't you listening to what he said about running and such?"

"Yes, but how is that going to help? We're already learning some of that with Salendra."

"Yes, and now all you need to do is work harder at it. Start running on your free afternoons, practice with the bow more, and get your teacher to show you how to draw maps in your lessons. Then you can get someone to show you how to heal a bit, like one of Ruth's priests. You do all that and work hard at it, and by the time you are sixteen and can join the army, they'll beg for you to join them." The boy glowered and slouched along as they walked back through the castle.

"Sounds like a lot of effort for something I won't use once I become a soldier," he said sulking.

"Robert, why would he suggest it if you don't use it? Ask Captain Marshal if he uses it if you like? I'm sure he knows how to read a map, shoot a bow and all the other things. Anyway, who said it would be easy? Learning magic is hard, so why should learning to be a soldier be any different."

"You think I could ask the captain?" he asked as she walked away.

"Yes. I'll take you to see him next rest day; I'm certain he'll tell you the same thing."

So, Salendra's archery teacher, Pol, taught the three friends to track, read maps, and live off the land. The older man clearly thought they all were mad, but he was willing enough to teach the three children for the handful of coppers they paid him once a week.

CHAPTER 12

$\mathcal{D}$arius had convinced a local blacksmith called Marit to allow Beryl to work in his shop. Compared to her workrooms, the blacksmith's foundry was dim, hot, and cramped. Marit's two apprentices pumped the bellows and hauled rods of black iron back and forth, their shirts dark with sweat and soot.

Marit refused to let her handle any of the actual work beyond trying to cast runes onto the finished products. Nearly everything she'd read said that the metal needed to be infused with a spell while still hot; iron once cooled would not accept a spell. She'd been trying to fix runes into cold iron nails for weeks now with no results, but she wasn't allowed anywhere near the forge.

His apprentices were not helpful at all, scornful as they were of the presence of a girl, much less a Mage, in their forge. They did everything they could to make her life more difficult. She had to ward the small table they allowed her to work at after they covered her desk and chair in metal fragments and filled the drawers with sawdust. Earning her a dressing down from Marit for being so slovenly.

Rune disliked being in the forge. He jumped every time they pumped the bellows to make the fire surge and roar. The constant clang of the hammers striking metal and anvil hurt his ears. He spent his time crouched in a miserable ball, ears pinned to his head, waiting for his Mage to finish. His jumps of alarm and panic at various noises twitched along the bond, making both of them nervous and stressed.

Twisted and shattered nails littered her work area. Holding a new nail by a small pair of tongs, she began again, cursing the thing under her breath. Snarling, she tossed the first rune that came to mind. The rune for fire struck the nail, heating it red hot. With a gasp, she dropped the nail and watched at it smoked against the wooden desk for a moment before knocking it to the floor.

Wrapping the tongs in a cloth, she picked up the cooling nail. Concentrating on just heating the nail, she spoke the rune for fire again. This time when the nail heated to red hot, she blurted the rune for strength and the chain of runes to repel water and prevent rust. The runes carved themselves into the nail, glowing blue for a moment before sinking into the metal. Inspecting the cooling metal, she grinned. She needed a bucket of water.

She felt the eyes of the other apprentices on her as she gathered her supplies. Soon Rune was peering into the shallow metal basin she had filled with water. She moved him out of the way and picked up a new nail. Heating the nail, she cast the runes needed before thrusting it into the water with a hiss of steam. Drawing it out, she dried it on a rag and inspected her work.

The nail glowed a soft blue in the corner of her vision. The strange part was the nail itself. Its edges were now a shiny silver instead of the black iron it was before. They pulled the nail from her hand. Marit inspected it, then turned to another box and pulled out a steel arrowhead.

"Do this next," he said tossing the nail back on her table and walking back to the anvil. "Why are you standing there? The bellows, boy!" he snapped at his apprentice. The boy began pumping the bellows while the other lad continued to stack the wood he was carrying. Placing the arrowhead in her tongs, she repeated the process. The steel gained a bluish edge to the metal once they quenched it.

A month later she was upgraded to working on chain-mail and daggers, now that she was showing some progress. She was just closing up when a soft whistle caused her to turn around with a grin. Troche stepped out of the shadows with a matching smile.

"Been too busy to visit, Miss Mage?"

"Too busy to breathe, Mr. Thief. Does Master James need me?" Beryl asked with a grin as Rune meowed his hello from her shoulder.

"I'm afraid so," Troche said with a grimace. "I think the Nail might have another project for you. James has been closeted away in meetings with people from all over the countryside the last few weeks. Something big is brewing."

Beryl gathered her things and followed Troche deeper into the city. With the growing rumors of war, and increased anti-magic groups forming around the country, tensions were high. Darius was spending most of his days in counsel with the King and his other advisors. They had left Beryl to her own devises after lessons for the past few weeks while he worked late into the night.

The northern borders were seeing a resurgence in raiding parties and the eastern coastal towns were dealing with anti-magic protests and attacks on local mages. The King had ordered reinforcements to the northern garrisons, but the coastal mages were needed to control incoming storms and would not be recalled.

There were not enough mages to send more, and the Mages Council did not want to rile the population by sending out more soldiers to protect their mages. Magic was only used to fortify the forts and to heal the injured; the rest of the time the troops had to fight and die while the mages waited safely behind fortified walls. Magic had been banned from the battle field for generations now, but occasionally a mage would be forced to defend himself with his magic. The two known cases in the last five years had resulted in the person's death attacking the mage and the council ordering the binding of the mage's magic.

Beryl couldn't imagine having her magic bound. She wasn't as bad as many mages who used their magic throughout their daily lives in everything from lighting candles to the everyday objects they used like ink pens that never ran dry or pots and pans that cleaned themselves at a touch. She could live a normal life without it, but it would mean the death of her bondmate if she was ever bound, something she was not willing to chance.

Her visions were becoming stronger as the unrest grew. The small groups of Anti-magic believers were even growing in the Capital, a known haven for Mages and magical families. The leaders had been attempting to get a meeting with the King, even disrupting his weekly petitioner's court in attempts to get him to address their demands.

Several small skirmishes between anti-magic protestors and the palace guards had led to a strict curfew around the castle for the apprentices. Today was the first day in nearly two weeks that Beryl had done more than scurry between her lessons in the castle and her time at the forge. They had put all her other lessons on hold at Darius' insistence until the city calmed down.

They had put the apprentices in the castle to work making all kinds of objects and items that would be sold at an upcoming fair next month. She knew they meant it to keep the young mages too busy to notice their restrictions, but she had been running with Troche three nights a week for months now, and the lack of movement was leaving her jittery and foul tempered. Beryl suspected that Darius had only allowed her to continue her lessons at the forge, because he knew that if he didn't give her some physical outlet, she would find one on her own.

"Ah, Mage. Good timing," James said, standing with a grimace when they arrived. Grabbing up his coat, he urged them back out with a firm hand. "We have a busy night ahead of us, and I want to be finished before the guards catch us out. That will be your task, Troche. Keep an eye out."

"Yes, Master James. Where are we headed?"

"All over, I'm afraid. I have a list of buildings, shops, and homes that need to be warded by the end of the week, Mage."

"I won't be able to ward many if they are large homes, Master James."

"I am aware, Mage. Tonight, I think we will focus on the businesses and leave the others for tomorrow. Come, we must hurry."

"Has something changed that the Nail needs this done so fast?" Beryl asked as she jogged to keep up with the taller man.

"Marcus, a rival of the Nail, is pushing back against her shipping interests and has threatened several businesses we use as drop points for messages. I would see the shops protected in case this turns ugly."

"You think it will?" Troche asked, keeping just behind his hurrying master.

"Yes, several of the Guild have already been attacked for encroaching on Marcus' territory. He's claimed several areas the Nail thought her own, and she's not pleased at all."

"Roth and Blain are still in the healer's care," Troche added with a sigh.

"Do I need to go to the healers to assist after this?" Beryl asked. She'd been working at the Temple as an assistant healer once a week and had noticed the increase in injured Guild members coming to the healer's halls, but not a whisper as to the cause had reached her.

"No, Mage, you are to focus on the wardings. We need as much of the Guild's assets and members protected as we can. If we can protect the shops and safe houses, we will fare much better if this devolves any farther."

"You think war?" Troche asked, his voice hesitant as they entered the middle class shopping district.

"The Nail is not discrete in her rage, Troche. She has no subtly to her. She'll attack with the mindless anger of a wounded dog that will die before he releases his hold."

"And if it takes half the city with it?" Mage asked, already pulling out her tools as James gestured to the small shop before them.

"Then we will have to deal with the fall out once the fires die down."

"She's done this before?"

"Not to this level. Marcus has sent assassins to attack her three times now. She must answer in kind or be seen as weak."

"Will Marcus hire mages?"

"There is no way to tell if he will or not. I don't think he has the resources for it, but I could be wrong."

Beryl worked as quickly as she could while keeping the wards strong and resistant to tampering. It was looking to be a long night. Rune went with Troche to keep watch while she warded shop after shop. She trembled with fatigue and strain when James finally called a stop.

Gathering Rune to her chest, she let Troche guide her back to the castle. Over the rest of the week, the cycle continued. She would finish her lessons and tasks in the castle only to run to meet Troche in the city and be led to the next place to protect. Beryl tried to ignore the times Troche arrived covered in cuts and bruises from fights with the Marcus' men. She treated his wounds when he would allow it but everyone in the Guild was looking warn thin. Something had to break soon; she was just not expecting to be the catalyst.

BERYL WAS WALKING along one of the back corridors of the castle on the way to the library with a stack of books when she was grabbed from behind. Rune yowled and screamed as the mage twisted and fought. Stamping down, she caught the attacker's foot, making him howl. Biting at the hand across her mouth, she thrashed in the man's hold. Rune leaped on to his back, raking his claws down the attacker's neck and head.

Tossing her away with a cry of pain, Beryl's fell into a tapestry. She fell into space as the fabric gave way, sending her tumbling down a flight of stairs that had been hidden behind it. Struggling to clear the ringing from her head, she began half crawling, half climbing back up the stairs as the screams of her bonded echoed along the walls in tandem with the cries of her attacker.

The shouts of men and heavy thud of running boots heralded the castle guards arriving to investigate the commotion. Beryl emerged into the light just as two castle guards grabbed her attacker and slammed him back into the far wall. Rune stopped his attack, running to his bondmate once they contained the threat.

Sweeping him into her arms, she murmured reassurances as she began checking the still growling cat to make sure he was not injured. The guards began dragging the struggling, injured attacker away, who was still cursing and bellowing. As they passed by a torch, it shocked her to see Jared's face covered in stripes of blood before they carried him away from her.

Beryl was shown to the small healer's hall in the castle and bundled into a bed to wait on the guard and her Master. She sat frozen and numb, curled around Rune. She had known that Jared would catch up with her, but she had never imagined he would attack her here.

"Apprentice, can I see your hands? It looks like you took quiet a fall." Beryl uncurled a bit but pulled her hand away when the Healer tried to take it.

"Rune first. Make sure he's okay, first," she insisted, pushing the loose hair from her tangled braid away from her face and holding out the small cat to be examined.

"Of course. He's such a lovely bondmate and so fierce I hear," the healer said with a gentle smile. "Will you let me examine you, Rune?" He meowed in response, letting the healer feel his limbs and sides.

"He'll be tired and bruised but nothing is broken. You however, Mage, have several nasty bruises that I need to see to. May I look at your arms? Your wrist is bruised, and I want to make sure you did not take any blows to the head or ribs," the healer said, getting up and pulling a screen around the bed. "Can you take off your cloak and tunic? I will be as quick as I can."

Beryl stood and untangled her cloak from the blankets. The healer took it and laid it over a nearby chair. Her tunic, gloves, and breast band joined the pile.

"The scarring is old," the healer said hesitantly, examining the twisting scars that branched across her chest, arms, and hands.

"Yes, they hurt me as a child," Beryl. Everything felt distant and blunted as she watched the healer work.

"A few scrapes and bruises. You've bruised your ribs, and they will hurt for a week or two as they heal. I have a cream that should help with the pain and stiffness." She cleaned the scrapes along her arms and hands, applying the salve to Beryl's ribs and helping her back into her tunic.

"You will have a nice bruise on your cheek and neck for the next week or two. Any trouble swallowing or speaking?"

"No, I hit my head when I fell, and my wrist aches."

"Yes, you have a nice bump. Any dizziness or nausea?"

"No."

"The best thing you can do is rest for the next few days. I will speak to your master when he arrives and see if you can have the next week out of lessons to heal. The wrist is just sprained. Let me gather some bandages, and we will wrap it for support. Once your master arrives, you should be able to return to your rooms. For now, rest," she said, pulling the screen away and moving to a cabinet to get the bandages.

"Thank you, Healer."

Once Beryl's wrist was bandaged, they left her alone. Pulling Rune back against her chest, she let his steady humming purr lull her. She couldn't believe Jared had even attempted this. He'd tried to kidnap her from the castle only a few hallways away from the Royal Quarters. It made no sense; had he planned to steal her away in the middle of the day? Counting on her to just trundle along after him like a pet?

Darius and a member of the Guard came in some time later. Darius hurried to her bed, while the Guard conferred with the healer. The healer gave him several sheets of notes and gestured toward Beryl as they spoke. Beryl assumed she was giving him a statement and the list of injuries she'd suffered.

"My dear, I'm glad to see you're not severely injured. What was that man thinking," Darius said with a shake of his head, "Are you in any pain?"

"No, I'm all right, Darius. Just a few bruises and a sprained wrist."

"The guardsman will need to take your statement, child. Once that is done we can return to the Mage quarters. I may see about warding your rooms to prevent people meaning harm from entry. It's a tricky ward, but maybe once they heal you you can assist me."

"I would like that, Darius."

"Good, good. Ah, Guardsman Trey. I would like to take my apprentice back to her rooms to rest once they take her statement."

"That would be fine, Master Fremont. I just have a few questions, Apprentice. Your relative has already incriminated himself once we captured him. First off, can you identify your attacker?"

"Yes." Beryl said with a sigh, "His name is Jared Voss. He's my uncle."

"And you lived with him before becoming an apprentice?"

"Yes," she said, flexing her hands and using the pain to ground herself as the man made notes in a bound book.

"Very good. Now where were you headed when he approached you?"

"I was on the way to the library. Oh, I had some books with me. I dropped them when he grabbed me from behind."

"Don't worry, I'll make sure someone gathers them and gets them to the library." Darius reassured her.

"And this was your uncle?"

"Yes, I didn't recognize him until the guards pulled him away."

"Did he alert you before he attacked you?"

"No, he just grabbed me. He put one hand over my mouth so I couldn't scream, but Rune was yelling as loud as he could." Rune purred and rubbed his head against his mage's hands.

"Yes, he's what brought the guards. For such a small beast, he can be rather loud," the guard said with a chuckle.

"Rune clawed at Jared, and I bit at the hand over my mouth. He tossed me away, and I fell down one of the servant stairways. The guards had arrived by the time I climbed back up."

"I don't know what he was thinking, trying to attack a mage in the capital city," the guard said shaking his head. "I'll need you to write up a statement to submit for the trial, but that can wait a day or two."

"What will happen to Jared now?" Beryl asked. She was not sure if she wanted to know yet.

"We will hold him until the trial, which should be in the next month. Attacking a mage, even an apprentice, is a serious charge; I doubt he'll get less than five years of hard labor."

Beryl thanked the guard, her mind lost in a fog. What had he been thinking? She couldn't just run from her apprenticeship, and the Nail would have caught up with Jared if he'd stayed in town. She followed Darius to her rooms and let him get her settled in bed. They spent the rest of the week holed up in the mage's wing working on different projects. Darius seemed determined to keep her too busy to think about the attack.

As soon as they let her out of the castle, Beryl made her way to Master James' office to see if there was any work she could do. She needed to move. The attack had just reinforced her need to be a step ahead of trouble, and she could only do that if she knew what was going on.

"Come in, Mage. Would you care for tea?"

"Yes, thank you and a cup for Rune if you have extra," she said, shedding her coat and letting Rune bounce down to explore.

"Here you are. Let's go keep Troche company before he destroys another of my books," he said, leading her into the hidden study behind his office. Troche glanced up at her from his bed of pillows with a grin belaying the bruises that cover his face, "Mage."

"What in the world happened to you?" She asked, hurrying forward and pressing a small healing rune to the puffy black eye that dominated one side of his face.

"Ran into some trouble tracking down a rumor. I'm all right, Mage. The arm is the worst," he said with a shrug, wincing when it tweaked his ribs. "Healers think it will be a few weeks until I can get the wrap off. Takes me off the streets for another week at least," he said with a huff.

"More like two, brat," James said with a huff passing out cups and putting Rune's on the floor, cooled with more milk than most of them would drink.

"Who did it?" Beryl asked, as Rune lapped from his cup.

"Marcus' thugs," Troche said, wincing as she moved on to the next bruise.

"Have we have caught them?"

"Yes and soundly thrashed by the Nail's own already. You're blood thirsty for a mage, girl," James said with a sigh. "Save some magic for your own injuries, Mage. You're still black and blue enough to warrant a second glance from the Guard."

"I just don't enjoy seeing friends hurt." Beryl said with a huff, pulling her hand away from Troche's cheek and revealing a mostly healed bruise.

"Well, we don't enjoy seeing our mage hurt either. Troche was loitering in their territory on my request," he said with a huff. "We needed to make sure your attack had nothing to do with the Guild's unrest."

"It was my Uncle. He had nothing to do with the Guild," she said, trying to ignore how Rune abandoned his cup and moved to press against her side in an offer of comfort.

"No, he didn't, at least not until Marcus paid him to get you out of the guild and away from town."

"What? He wouldn't..."

"I'm afraid he did, Mage. They paid him a significant sum, which was recovered from his rooms when the Guard searched them."

"One guard told me he'd blamed me in his interrogation. He'd demanded repayment for having lost my services," she said sipping at her cup hoping it would warm her.

"Not very bright of him; you were working as an illegal warder since you didn't have the Mage Council's blessing."

"He'd started using bright weed more often this last year and was getting farther into debt when I left him."

"Foul drug," James said with a sigh, smoking bright weed clouded the mind of the user and gained them a crippling addiction. "They ban bright weed use in Cardu. If he had any in his possession, he could be sent to the mines even if he had not harmed a mage."

"They're saying I might have to speak at the trial." Beryl said worrying at the end of her braid.

"When will it be?"

"At the end of the month."

"Are you up to continuing our work or do you need more time to rest, Mage?"

"I've rested until I was ready to jump out a window to get away from the castle, Master James. I want to work."

"I've two more safe houses for you to protect. I want you to remember where these are. If you get caught out in the streets and need a bolt hole, these would be the best place for you to use."

"All right."

"Will you be well enough to go on your own? I don't have anyone available right now to keep an eye out."

"Master, I'm not laid up!" Troche said, levering himself upright with a wince he tried to hide.

"You will stay there, brat, until I say you can move! You take another hit to those ribs right now, and you'll be at the healer's hall for a month if not dead in a ditch," James spat, pushing Troche back into the pillows. He moved back to his desk and jotted out directions to both houses.

"Here, head back here if you finish early. Sofia should wait for you at the Bell."

"Brothel?"

"A comfort house for the wealthy. You've seen a few of the girls if you've gone to any events with your master. They turn up at the castle more than you would think. Often on the arms of wealthy Mage's Council members," he said with a snort, "Be careful on the streets, Mage. Things are not safe right now and they have marked you as a piece in play."

"Do you think I could learn to protect myself?"

"I don't see why not, but ask Darius before we train you. You'd do better with some official lessons before we teach you the way a thief fights."

"All right, I'll come back when I finish. See you, Troche," she said with a grin, taking the note from Master James.

"Keep her safe, Rune," Troche said with a grin. Rune chirped in agreement as he settled on his mage's shoulder.

Beryl made her way through the streets as quickly as she dared. The Bellwether House was an extensive building on the other side of town, close to the castle grounds and only a few streets over from the wealthier side of town. The building was painted white and lit with mage lamps, giving it a cheery, welcoming feel. Knocking on the servant's door, she handed over the sealed note from James and was quickly brought to the Madame's office.

"Ah, Mage, James warned me you would come," Sofia said turning to taking in the young woman before her. "Goodness! Are you sure you want to do this today?"

"The bruises are old, Madame. I'm well able to work."

"As you wish, I want as much of the building warded as you can. What can you do for me, Mage?"

"I can ward the building against fire, and the doors and windows to prevent breakage. I will also ward your office, if you wish."

"And the girl's rooms, if you please. We get rough guests who refuse to observe our rules occasionally. We use two body guards, but I would feel better if we warded the rooms."

"Warding everything will take several hours. I'll start with the inside if you don't mind."

"Do my office first; I would like to see how you work before the girls' rooms are warded."

"Of course," Beryl said, pulling off her coat and setting Rune down. "How permanent do you want everything?"

"What do you mean? And why do you have a cat?"

"This is my bondmate, Rune. He's bound to me," Beryl said, pulling out a leather tool kit and a coil of wire. "I can carve the main runes into the wood and fill them with copper. It strengthens the wards but makes them more noticeable. If you are planning to hide the warding, I won't be able to do so."

"I don't care who knows that we've been warded. I'll crow it from the rooftops if it keeps my girls safe," Sofia said fiercely.

Beryl nodded and started warding the door to the room. She spelled the locks and doorjamb as well before kneeling down and sealing the spells together with a wash of silver light. Scooping Rune into her arms, she turned to face the Madame who gestured her out and closed the door behind them, activating the wards.

"Roe, test the wards please," she said, calling out to the size-able man waiting at the end of the hall. The man prowled forward as they moved back, and he started trying to force the door. With each impact the wards flared, lighting the hallway with a wash of silver light.

"Thank you, Roe. That should do," she said, stopping the man after several minutes showed no change in the sturdy wooden door. "Let me show you up to the girl's rooms."

Beryl spent the next two hours warding the personal quarters of the pleasure women. She did her best to ignore the looks of distaste she got from most of the women. Mages were not looked on kindly here. Beryl tried not to take it personally. Many of the wealthy mage's who used these women's services would not have been kind to any woman they interacted with. They were much like the wealthy apprentices she dealt with, confident in their place in society and their untouchable nature because of that place.

Finishing up the outside wards, she said goodbye to Madame Sofia and made her way to the next house on her list. This was another brothel, yet business was booming. The first floor was full of men and women dancing and drinking as a group of musicians played in one corner. Another room gave a roar of approval as someone won a hand of cards. Tightly dressed men and women dealing the cards and dice with flirtatious smiles staffed several small gaming tables.

"Welcome to the Weeping Willow. What's your pleasure for the night?" a young man asked, looking Beryl up and down with a slight frown.

"I'm here to see Madame Talia," Beryl said with a tight smile, handing over her note.

"Take a seat. Sure I cannot tempt you with a game?" he asked with a practiced leer.

"No, thank you," Beryl said firmly, she had no patience for such unfeeling passions.

Rune eyed the young man with a snort of disgust. He reeked of sex and cheap oils. They ignored him until he flounced off to show the next person through the door to the gaming tables, handing off her note to another. Beryl watched the game for a few minutes but could detect no cheating from the players, although the dealers flipped a card or two to keep the game going well for the customers. It was strange to see a normal game without blatant cheating on all sides; she'd been playing with Troche and his friends too much.

"Please come this way," a junior maid said, gesturing for her to follow, "Madame Talia will see you now."

"Thank you." Beryl murmured, following the girl to a tastefully decorated sitting room. After a few moments, a velvet gowned woman came in, glancing over at Mage with a mask like smile before taking a seat across from her.

"Thank you for coming, Mage. I understand you've had some problems of late?"

"Nothing that would affect my work, Madame. What do you wish to have warded?"

"As much as possible," the woman said, standing and starting to straighten up minor items around the room. "I have light wards on the building already, but they have warned me that we'll need much stronger wards in the weeks to come."

"I can ward the building, doors, and windows against fire and breakage. Do you want any other areas warded inside the house?" Beryl asked, trying not to fidget as the Madame moved around the room.

"Not right now," she said, waving off the offer. "We're not being threatened, and I have several body guards to watch the girls while they work downstairs."

"Very well, if you have no objections, I'll get started."

"Do. Please let me know if you need anything while you work," she said already moving to leave the room.

"Thank you, Madame," Beryl said, with a tight smile quickly leaving and starting to ward the outside of the building.

She worked late into the night. Once the last customer was shooed into his carriage, she quickly completed the spell work on the front door, sagging in exhaustion for a moment before she could pull herself together.

She wished she'd been able to use a turning spell to avoid notice while she cast, but the spell failed if she was casting other magic while using it. She sent a note to Master James though a young local thief she caught loitering on a corner on her way back explaining that she was heading to the castle and would see them in a few days.

Rune ranged ahead, sending back impressions and scents back along the bond. Beryl did not keep up with the curious cat. She was exhausted from the wardings and more than ready for her bed.

They stuck to the back alleys and side roads that Troche was forcing her to learn on their night runs to avoid the patrolling guards. The curfew was still in effect, and she didn't want to explain to the Mage's Council why an apprentice mage was out of the castle this late. The last thing she needed was for the Council to look into her abilities and training.

A shaft of fear along their bond froze Beryl in place. Rune was scared, terrified. Scattered images of fire and thundering feet filled her mind. She shook off the images, bolting down the alley, "Rune!" He couldn't be that far ahead.

She pushed her way past fleeing men and women into chaos. A small market place was packed with bodies fleeing and fighting in a mass of fists and bodies. The bond between them snapped tight, Beryl's vision doubling as she saw the market around her and the sea of shifting boots and legs where Rune was trapped against a wall.

Beryl fought her way forward, ignoring the fists and elbows that struck her, the legs and feet that kicked and tripped as she pushed her way through the crush. Windows and bottles shattered as the buildings to one side of the market went up in flames. She shuddered in relief when Troche dropped from somewhere above Rune and scooped him up.

Troche would keep him safe, she thought, gasping as she fought her way forward. She ducked a thrown bottle, but a sudden elbow to the cheek sent her reeling against the bodies behind her. She flailed and staggered, fighting to keep her feet. Falling here would be a death sentence.

Beryl couldn't suppress a shout as Troche shoved Rune behind him onto a crate as the man in front of him drew a knife. She was still half the length of the square away and could only incrementally fight her way forward as the two men twisted and slashed at each other in the small space available.

Suddenly the crowds surged with a roar, carrying her away from Rune and Troche as a building collapsed in a wash of smoke and screams. She fought to get free from the press of bodies as sharp spikes of fear came from her bondmate. Choking on the smoke and ash, she shoved and hit. She could see Troche fighting with the larger man, kicking and feinting with his own dagger but not gaining any ground.

There! She pushed her way to the wall and started edging her way along it to where Troche and Rune crouched, sheltered next to some broken boxes. Thank Ruth, they were safe. She dropped next to them, catching Rune when he sprang, pressing himself shaking against her chest.

"Thank Ruth. Are you hurt?" She projected love and affection at the small cat as they cowered in the small corner. A bottle shattered at her feet, spraying them with bits of broken glass. The crowd was thinning as the fires spread, leaving the injured and those trying to fight the fires.

"Troche, come on. We need to move," Beryl said, nudging the young man where he curled against the wall.

"Troche?"

She pulled him away from the stone wall and lurched to catch his limp form as it collapsed. Blood soaked his cloak and shirt, slicking her hands as she frantically searched for the wounds. Pressing against a nasty slash on his stomach, Beryl poured magic into the limp form, pleading under her breath to every deity she could name. But the magic slid through his still form like sand, sinking into the earth below them both.

* * *

"THE COUNCIL IS NOT happy that an apprentice was out of the castle after curfew, during such violence, but I have taken the blame for it. They believe I sent you out on an errand," Darius said, tucking his apprentice into her bed, making sure her bondmate was right next to her, skin to skin.

Beryl watched in a daze as her Master moved around her room. She'd curled around Troche's body until a healer forced her away as they spread through the area helping the injured. Rune huddled against her, shaking as the healers guided her to a bed in a nearby Inn. There she waited, wrapped in tears and blankets, until Darius came to collect her.

"It upset captain Marshal to find you had been in the market during the riot. He insisted on carrying you back to the Healer's Hall here at the castle. My dear, are you going to look at me?"

Beryl blinked up at him for a moment, "Troche died," she said, her voice wavering.

"And Troche was your friend?" he asked, taking a seat next to her on the bed.

"Yes, he's Master James' apprentice," she said clutching at Rune as he purred nearly inaudibly against her.

"Ah, I am sorry that you had to go through such a trial."

"I've seen people die before, Darius. People died when they could not pay their debts after a card game or in brawls over a bad pair of dice," she said with a sniff. "He jumped down and saved Rune. I couldn't get to him, and he kept him safe. It's my fault."

"No child. It is not your fault."

"But Darius,"

"No, you did not force him to save Rune. He made that choice. He put himself into a dangerous situation to keep your bondmate safe. You cannot cheapen his act of compassion and bravery by taking the blame for his injuries. You did not hold the knife, my dear, and you did not force him to jump." Darius said, "I will speak with Master James and see if there will be a remembrance night for him. Do you know which god he followed?"

"Eshu, he was a follower of Eshu."

"Eshu, god of the crossroads," Darius said with a sigh, "Fitting for a young entrepreneur." Darius smiled and stroked the young woman's hair. "He will be cremated and his ashes spread on the road as Eshu demands. Master James will know how he would have wanted it done. Get some rest, child. I'll have the servants bring you in some dinner."

"Thank you, Darius," Beryl said with a sigh, shifting down in bed so she could meet Rune's eyes. The small cat butted his head against her forehead, starting up a soft purr.

"Here. Safe." Rune seemed to say along the bond, and Beryl cuddled him closer, stroking gently in response.

They still had each other thanks to Troche. He had saved both Rune and Beryl, even if he'd lost his life in the effort. She could not regret that her bondmate was here and uninjured.

The rest of the week passed slowly. Beryl went to her lessons and did the work assigned to her. She spent the hours in silence, her bondmate curled close. Thankfully, the other apprentices left her alone to her grief; she wasn't sure she would not have tried to punch the smirks off of the upper years' faces if they had tried anything.

At the end of the week, Darius escorted her to the memorial night for Troche, which was being held in the Inn that hid Master James' office. He had been quiet but supportive of Beryl since the riot. She knew that the Mages Council had been riding the older mage about his apprentice's involvement, but so far they had not questioned her.

They passed by the market, and she tried to ignore the burnt out hulks of the businesses she had not warded. Only the handful of warded stores and businesses had withstood the flames and destruction. The thick scent of burnt timbers still hung in the air; Beryl quickened her steps to put the place behind her.

* * *

"MAGE, DARIUS, PLEASE TAKE A SEAT," Master James said with a small, sad smile. He ushered them into a side room before turning to the next group coming through the door.

Beryl recognized some milling crowd from her errands and traveling about town with Troche. Rune sent a wash of affection along the bond as her breath hitched; Troche would have been chuffed to see so many people here to remember him. Darius steered her into a chair by the fire wandered off into the size-able room.

Beryl had no intention of talking to anyone. Her bones had turned to stone, and her chest felt hollow enough for Rune to fit tight against her heart. She watched the people talk and laugh around her and could not understand how anyone could be happy; her friend was gone and would never return. She had lost yet another person in her life. Everyone seemed doomed to leave her.

"Everyone, everyone a moment please," James said, gesturing for several servers to hand out cups. "We are here to celebrate the memory of a young man who was taken from use too soon, Troche Rivencroft. He served as a runner for the Trident Merchant Guild since his fifth year and at eight became my apprentice. For the last six years we've worked and lived together, and I will mourn his loss." James stuttered to a stop and wiped at his eyes before he could continue, voice broken. "I remember Troche."

"I remember Troche." was echoed from the rest of the room.

Beryl took a mug when it was handed to her. Hot mulled wine filled the cup, warming her hands and scenting the surrounding air with spices. Rune shifted to her lap and purred, leaning against her as he watched the rest of the room.

"Troche was a follower of Eshu," a priest in a black robe said, stepping forward from his place near the door. "Eshu, god of the cross-roads, god of change and luck, is celebrated on the road by those who travel. We ask that each person who wishes, take a pouch from the table by the door when you leave. We ask that you help spread Troche's ashes as you travel so that his soul may travel the roads he could not in this life." With a nod, the priest stepped back allowing the next person to step forward.

"I remember Troche." the adolescent boy said awkwardly. "He saved me from a group of toughs last year when I got lost on an errand."

"I remember Troche." The refrain ran around the room as each person stepped forward to remember a time where Troche had touched their lives. Some stories were funny, such as when he was running along the docks and fell into the water after a misstep. Most of them were stories about Troche's impact on each person.

"I remember Troche," Beryl said, standing up and lifting Rune to her shoulder. "He was my friend and taught me many things. He saved Rune in the riot, and I can never stop being grateful for that."

With a sniff she moved to the door, ignoring the next person to step forward with a story. She picked up a pouch, tucking it away in her bag. Darius gave their condolences to James a last time before leading her back to the castle and her rooms.

"Do you need anything, my dear?"

"No, Darius. Thank you for going with me," she said, wiping at her eyes.

"As your Master, dear, it is my responsibility to do what I can," Darius said with a slight smile. "Please come get me if you need anything, Mage, no matter the hour."

"I will, thank you, Darius."

"Have a good night, my dear."

CHAPTER 13

*H*er life returned to its previous routine. Fights continued to break out in different quarters of the capital. The war between the Thieves' Guild and its rival burst into flame with Troche's death.

Beryl's rest days consisted of warding more buildings for Master James and running quick messages about town. So far, they had excluded her from the threats and violence, but she knew it could not last forever. The Guild was in chaos, and something had to give.

"Thank you for your work today, Mage. You can head to the castle; I'd rather you were indoors before dark," Master James said, receiving the last letter.

"I thought I would go to the healers. There seem to be a lot of guild members injured, and I wanted to help."

"That is kind of you, Mage, but I would rather you be safe in the castle tonight."

"Very well," she said, gathering her coat. "Can I ask, why haven't you asked me to ward the Guild hall?"

"That is being done by another mage. Don't worry so. The Guild never stays down long. We will rally."

"All right," she said with a huff. "I'll go."

"Be careful out there," he said with a slight smile. "You will be busy enough next week, child. I'll send word when you're needed."

Beryl walked back to the castle, keeping an eye out but spending most of the walk worrying about the upcoming trial for her Uncle. She was required to attend the trial in case they needed her to speak in defense of her actions. A trial could go on for days, but Darius was confident that it would be over quickly.

Her work at the forge had been placed on hold until someone could be found to allow her to work with smaller metal objects. With Master James cutting back what he allowed her to do and limiting her time outside of the castle after dark, she suddenly had too much time on her hands. Too much time to think and remember.

The town was rebuilding from the fires, and the rains of the last few days had washed away the smells from the fire. Still, she avoided the markets as she made her way back to the castle, keeping Rune safe in her arms. They walked back in silence, content to take comfort in each other.

Back in her rooms, Beryl sat cradling Rune to her chest. Freeing one hand, she stroked the black ash colored stripes that marked his back and legs, marking the top of his head with a four-barred stripe. They reminded her of her own scars that striped her back, arms and chest.

She saw much of herself in this small cat. Eternally curious, he sent her a constant stream of half felt sensations and smells. It was strange to know you are seated holding a cat and to feel you are the cat being held. One thing she knew was Rune would die for her as she would die for him. She would just have to see about making it harder for either of them to get hurt like that again. She did not know what she would do if she lost this small cat that had become one half of her soul.

Later that week she was sitting with Darius in his study when a thought hit her, "Darius, did you ever have a familiar?" she asked.

Darius looked up blinking at the sudden question before smiling and answering, "Yes, I did," he said leaning back and tugging his beard. "When I was around your age, I bonded to a crow, Bastic, I called him.

He was such a thief, always finding shiny things and hiding them away. I was all the time having to find his stash and raid it for jewelry or silver that had gone missing. He was such a naughty bird. He was with me till my 38th winter, and then he passed on."

"You didn't want to get another familiar?" she asked.

"No," he said, shaking his head with a sigh. "When a bond-mate dies, it's like losing a part of yourself. Most bondmates have a life much longer than their regular animal cousins, but even so it is not as long as a mage's life. Those that bond late, or whose mages died young, almost never outlive the mage by more than a few days. I believe there was a case of twin mages who when one died, its bond-mate bonded to the other twin. But it still is rare for the animal to survive a mage. In fact, most mages do not survive the killing of a bondmate. In past wars the easiest way to stop a mage's attack was to kill his bondmate."

Darius set about refilling his pipe as Beryl fell silent. That was her greatest fear. That she would lose Rune or would die and leave Rune to grieve. Neither was an acceptable solution. There had to be a way to protect both members of a bond, she just had to find it.

"But such times of war are past us; do not look so worried. I'm sure you and Rune will have a long and happy life together." Yet not even Darius' kind reassurances could lift the tightness from her chest and the sense of wrongness that his statement brought.

"Darius, would you object if I began learning how to defend myself?" Beryl asked the next morning. She stood tall, waiting for the argument she was sure would occur. Darius set his pipe to the side and sat back, observing his apprentice for a moment before he replied.

"After your Uncle's behavior, I can see how you may believe you need it. However, I do not approve." He continued, noticing her downcast gaze. "I did not say I would forbid it, I just said I do not approve. You may find a teacher and learn how to defend yourself, Mage. I ask that no matter what you learn, you never use it against someone who has not tried to strike you first."

"You can learn defense. However, if you use your skills to attack anyone while an apprentice, they will force you out of the castle and your powers stripped from you. The crown does not deal lightly with violence against its mages or mages who harm the populace." The older mage stared sternly down on the girl, only relenting when she assured him that this would never be the case.

* * *

BERYL MADE her way to the barracks on the far side of the castle grounds once Darius had agreed to allow her to go back into town. At the door, she was stopped by a junior soldier standing guard duty.

"I need to speak with Captain Marshal."

"And who are you?"

"Beryl Marcian," she said with a sigh, "He knows me as Mage."

"Please have a seat. I'll see if he has time to see you." He showed her to a bench to one side of the door while he went to find the captain.

Several soldiers walking by noticed her, their gaze turning shocked as Rune popped out of her cloak and bounced down to the ground. He looked up at her and gave a grating cry, sending her the scents of leather and sweat drifting from the exercise yard. He was happy that they were no longer restricted to the castle.

A handful of soldiers were there wearing plain grey loose pants and shirts as they sparred. Two were fighting with wooden staves, while another two sparred with leather wrapped swords. Ten others were trickling through the motions of various blocks and moves without shield or sword. These were the ones she watched.

She didn't think she had the upper body strength to use a sword, and her old injuries and scars had a tendency to spasm if she was carrying anything heavy for a lengthy period. She was used to it and often could continue what she was doing, but sudden shooting pain could be deadly in a sword fight. No, she wanted something to defend herself with; something that she could throw or use to keep another person's hands away.

Beryl knew that most fights were not the brawls she had seen growing up, and she knew how to get away from someone grabbing a wrist. But she wanted, no, needed to know more. She had to keep herself and her bondmate safe. She couldn't lose someone else.

Charles came out the door and smiled when he saw the young woman waiting for him. She was sitting on the low bench outside of the door speaking to her familiar in an inaudible voice. Her hair was pulled back in a severe braid, and she wore a brown leather coat that brought out the color in her cheeks and eyes. The small was planting his feet on her knees while arching his back, pulling a smile from the girl.

As the man stepped forward, he could see the fading bruises on her cheek from the riot. Between the riot and her uncle, the woman was not having a wonderful year. Add in the fact of her uncle's upcoming trial, and she had to be stressed.

The trial was to start in a few days, but he doubted anyone was looking forward to it. The man was an idiot to think he could just walk into the capital, into the King's castle at that, and take one of the apprenticed mages. He was lucky that the mage had refused to speak against him or charge him with her injuries, or he would have been sentenced to death.

Charles realized with a jerk why she was so adamant in her refusal to testify; she was refusing to send a man who was one of her last close relatives to his death. Stopping just behind the girl, he cleared his throat. The cat gave a grating cry and pounced on his boots before winding himself around his legs. The woman looked up and smiled at him, her grey eyes clear even if the edges were pinched with exhaustion.

* * *

"Good morning, Charles." Beryl offered with a tired smile.

"Morning, Mage. To what do I owe the pleasure of your company this morning?"

"Do you mind if we walk while we talk?" she asked, eying the various soldiers trying to be unobtrusive as they strained to hear what an apprenticed mage would have to say to their captain.

"Yes, that would be fine." He gestured her on.

Scooping up Rune and placing him in one pocket, to the laughter of several soldiers, they walked to the gate and followed the path that lead to the town wall; a massive thing here in the capital made of stone as high as a man was tall. After a few moments of walking, she turned to look at him.

"Honestly, I wanted to ask a favor of you if I may," she said fiddling with a loose bit of stone.

"And what would that favor entail?" he asked, even as she laughed, delighted in his response.

"What?" he demanded. She shook her head with a grin.

"I like that you did not immediately agree. Most people would say yes and then spend the next hour trying to get out of that answer."

"I like to know what I'm getting into before I agree to anything," he responded.

"Yes, and I like that about you." She took Rune out of her pocket and set him to chase bugs and motes of dust as they walked. "I want to learn to defend myself." She held up a hand to stop his protest. "I've already spoken to Darius, and he agrees. I just need the name of someone who may teach me. I spoke with the man teaching my friend Robert, and he refused to teach a girl. He says I have no need of the training. I disagree." She waited, watching his reaction to her words.

"Frankly, I'm not sure I agree with you either."

"Will you at least let me explain my reasons?" she asked, watching in silence as he sighed and turned to gaze at the sky for a long moment.

"Yes, but I withhold the right to still say no."

"As I withhold the right to find someone else to teach me," she countered with a stubborn look.

With an exasperated huff, he growled, "Mage."

"You said you would let me explain," she retorted, standing there, arms crossed, glaring at him with stubbornness showing in every line of her body.

"Very well," he said with a sigh, "Explain, please." He turned to continue along the path, the young mage at his elbow, and her cat trotting along next to them.

"I need to be trained." Here, she held up a hand to stop his protest before he could make it. "And don't tell me that women cannot be trained. I know well and good you showed your sisters how to stop a man from touching them if they didn't want it!"

"That's not the same as what you are asking, is it?"

"I want to know more, but I'll need it more than your sisters," she stated, eyes dark with memories and pain.

"How do you know you'll need it," he paused a sinking feeling filling his stomach, "your visions?"

"Yes." She turned and walked over to a stone and sat down, scooping up Rune and cuddling him. "Rune and I have discussed it, and he's too small to protect me. We got lucky that Jared tried what he did while I was in the castle. What if I had been out here, or outside of the castle walls, where the soldiers could not help me like in the riot? What if no one had been there to help Rune? I need to both protect myself and Rune if something else happens, and it will," she watches him with those too old eyes. "I know that it will. The best I can do is to be ready for when it happens. I have to try, don't you see?"

"You're certain you need it? I can't see you wielding a sword and shield," he said, eyeing the thin girl. She was small for her age and of an average height.

That brought a quirk back to her lips as she stroked Rune, "Nor do I. I want to learn how to use my hands and maybe a dagger to avoid the people with swords and shields. I want to live long enough to run away." Looking up at him she asked, "Do you know of anyone who might teach me that?"

He sat down next to her with a sigh. "There will not be many who would teach a girl. I will have to ask around. I know of one who may, but if he does, he will work you harder than you have ever been pushed. He expects the best out of his students, and once you start you cannot say it was too hard and quit. You would have to see it though till he says you are trained. Are you willing to agree to that?"

"Yes, I knew it would be hard," she said grinning up at him with relief and determination.

"Very well, I will contact him. His name is Durn. He is a former captain of the king's guard. He is hard but fair, and you will learn a lot, but you will also curse his name by the end of every day," he said fondly.

"Did he train you?" she asked.

"Yes, I did not know it but he was grooming me as his replacement. He trained and pushed me harder than anyone else in our troop, and I grew to hate him for a time. Then on a mission I took an arrow in the leg that had been meant for him. After that, he started teaching me strategies used in fighting and in war. We became friends, and when he retired, he got them to name me as his replacement. Said the only way he could leave was if he knew the guard was in expert hands. He lives on the outskirts of town to the west. If he agrees, I will take you with me the next rest day. After that it is up to you."

"Thank you, Captain," she said with a cheeky grin.

"Don't thank me yet. Trust me, in a few weeks you will curse the day you asked me," he said with a grin.

* * *

AFTER HEARING the stories of how mages and their bondmates were used in wars, Beryl had gone to the library in the palace to research the histories. What she had found were the things of nightmares. Brennan, one mage who worked in the library and archives, had looked at her with concern when she asked which books would tell her about that time. Thin and blond, Brennan looked like someone who should be a princess or lady instead of a mage toiling in a library repairing books.

Once one spoke with her, it was obvious why she did what she did. Brennan loved to learn and read. She was happiest when she could find what someone was looking for and help them learn something new. Whenever Beryl went to the library, Brennan had a new tidbit to share about some obscure spell or story that she had found. Brennan's mage marks were blue runes etched into either temple and a single blue rune etched in the hollow of her throat.

After her request, Brennan had looked at Beryl and Rune perched on her shoulder for a long moment before nodding and leading her to a side door behind her desk. Reaching into a pouch attached to her belt, she removed a light orb, igniting it as she went through the door.

They went down a gentle sloping spiral hallway, before coming to a massive locked wooden door. Pressing her hand against one door, Brennan chanted softly under her breath. The runes carved into the wood glowed, casting flickering shadows on Brennan. With a low grinding sound, the door swung out of the way.

"We're about to enter the archives. I must ask that you and your familiar touch nothing without asking me for permission first. We have spelled many of the books and scrolls to prevent those who should not be handling them from doing so."

The young mage agreed with Rune chirping his agreement. Once in the room they passed rows and rows of shelves and book stands holding massive tomes. Some rested on tables or in glass display cases. Every bit of wood or stone in sight had runes carved into it, preservation spells, cleaning spells, spells to refresh the air, spells to keep the temperature constant and to remove the moisture from the air. Even with the spells to circulate the air, the room smelled of the oil used to polish the wood and the vanilla smell of old paper and leather.

Leading them to a back table, she bade them sit while she found the books they needed. The wooden table was covered with tiny carved runes along its edge, most of which Mage had never seen. Running her finger along the line of runes, Mage listened to the images and scents Rune sent her as he explored the table top.

He alerted her from her study when Brennan came back with a stack of books and a few sheets of paper. Setting everything down, she turned and fetched a quill and inkwell from the desk across the hall. Returning, she sat next to Beryl. Spreading them out she laid them out, explaining the spells used to open the two volumes that were locked.

"Why are they locked?" she asked, restraining her impulse to touch the worn leather bindings.

"Most mages want to forget about this part of our history. They wanted to burn these books and destroy all memory of them, but they are part of our history and they should be remembered. The archivists and librarians threatened to lock the libraries and to hide away the books if they tried to destroy them." Reaching out, she lifted the first book, placing it in front of them.

"Just because the times were bloody and dark does not mean that lessons cannot be learned from what happened." Drawing the opening runes with a finger across the cover, Brennan opened the book. "Those wars were very violent; the countries they lived in used mages to defend or to attack other countries. We crafted many wicked spells during this time. As the number of mages dwindled, the Kings and rulers became more desperate for them. They began kidnapping mages and holding their families and familiars captive to control the mages and force them to cast the spells the king's wished against the mages own homelands." Turning to look at the young woman and her cat she asked, "Will you be all right reading about this down here, Mage? I have to go back to my desk in the main library. I will come back at lunch time and get you then if that is okay."

Beryl forced a smile, "Yes, that should be fine. I can cast a light spell and make my way out if I finish before that."

"Actually, the archive doors will not open unless they key you into them. How about I come check back with you in a while, and if you are finished, we can head up then, but if not I can come get you at lunch?"

The last thing she wanted to do was be locked in the archives with no way to escape while reading about bloody battles and kings torturing mages, but she forced a smile and said, "That should work fine, thank you Brennan."

"Ruth and Larkon bless, Mage," she said before turning and heading back up to the main library. Larkon was the patron god of learning and books. Most librarians and archivists were also acolytes at his temples, working as scribes and teachers of reading and writing for the community.

Turning back to the books, Beryl began reading about the mage wars that had happened in Arden's past. The stories were as bloody as she had heard. What caught her eye were the stories about bondmates and mages who survived being captured and won their freedom or to trick their captures into releasing them. These kinds of stories were few, but it happened and that was enough for her.

One such story told of a woman they had captured with a bird familiar, and they forced her to send storms against her homeland. One day she demanded to see the bird to ensure that it was alive. When the bird was brought to her in its small cage, she snatched the cage and crouched near the floor with her body protecting the cage.

Calling on her gift, she caused a storm to hit the tower she was held in with lightning over and over. It brought the castle to the ground, struck by lightening until it was nothing but rubble and her captures were dead. It injured her in the collapse, yet she escaped and return to her homeland.

Another scrap of a story that was so old it could barely be read, spoke of a spell that a mage crafted that caused the expansion of the bond a bondmate shared until the animal could cast magic of a sort and escape its cage, however there was no mention of what the spell was called or how it was cast.

She found little else besides a few references of mages who tricked or bought their way out of captivity by using their family's wealth. That would do her no good. While having a way for her bondmate to cast his own spells would be nice, there were no clues on how to proceed, and she was not about to harm Rune in an attempt that might lead nowhere. In a little while when Brennan came back she was ready to give up and told the woman so.

"You give up too easily," she laughed. "I take days or even weeks sometimes to find what I am looking for in the archives. I'll keep an eye out and see if I can find anything. I'll let you know."

"Thank you, Brennan." The librarian mage smiled at her and gave Rune a pat before showing them back up in to the daylight of the main library. "I found two new books that talk about mages using and making jewelry. They are talking about making necklaces to hold power stones like your necklace and cuff. I thought you would like to read them. Also, I found another book on familiars. It's just a book of children's stories, but I thought you might like it." Handing the girl the three books, she grinned. "And let me know if there is anything else you want me to monitor. I know your wards are amazing; maybe you could try anchoring a ward into a necklace. Imagine a protection ward that you get to take everywhere with you. If you manage it, I know I want one." Mage laughed at this.

"Yes, I could have a thriving business making portable wards and have a pleasant house by the sea."

"It could happen, girl. Just remember, I get the first one!" Waving goodbye, Rune and Beryl headed out of the library, laughing at the strange ideas the perky mage came up with.

She had been experimenting with using river stones like Darius used his glass orb and had gotten to where if she concentrated she could feel the lap of the waves and the feel of the breeze on a river or beach, yet it took nearly all her concentration to do so. She would have to keep practicing and see if it got easier. For now, it was not something she could see herself using.

She ducked out of the castle and into town for a few hours hoping to cheer herself up, only to run into a friend of Troche's, Billy, who tugged her into a nearby inn for a game of cards. She settled into the game with a smile, but her mood stayed down, lost in memories of Troche and the games they'd played.

Rune kept his place on her shoulder, watching the other gaming tables. At the nearest table, several guildsmen were having a friendly game full of colorful curses and laughter that the boys nearby were soaking up with wicked grins.

"Liar," Rune murmured in her mind, eyes locked on the table making Beryl glance that way. The men didn't seem to be cheating as they played; why would Rune say "Liar"? Rune so far had only spoken to Beryl a handful of times and seemed to save it for things the cat thought important.

She turned back to her hand of cards and smiled at the young men and woman at their table as she took two cards from the waiting deck, mind still on the other table. "Liar," Rune repeated hunkering down to growl softly against the back of her neck. She needed more information before anyone would believe something her bondmate had told her.

"Billy, who are the men at the next table? Are they Guild members?"

"Yeah, that's Carrow, Jeff's master, and Simmons. The other two are members, but I don't know their names."

"Would someone else?"

"Is it important?"

"Maybe," she said with a huff. "Can you find out?"

"Give me a bit," he said with a sigh, folding his cards and being shouted off the table by the others as he made his way to the jakes. He returned halfway through the next hand with a round of hard cider for the table, causing the others to declare him forgiven.

"The one with the black cloak is Owen; he works at the docks. The other is Luke, a friend of Master Carrow."

"Thanks, Billy."

"You owe me a half silver," he said with a snort. "Help me fleece these idiots, and I'll call it even."

"Deal."

She stayed for two more hands to ensure that Billy was repaid before collecting her pennies and heading out into the night. Rune was a tense weight across her shoulders as she headed for Master James' office. They had to duck the guards once along the way, but they didn't see her in the darkness of a side alley.

"What brings you here so close to curfew, Mage?" James asked showing her into his office.

"It might be nothing, but Rune called a guildsman a 'Liar' while we were playing cards at the Loon."

"Were the players known to you?"

"No, but Billy knew them." She listed out each man describing his looks.

"I've known Master Carrow for years; he's an outstanding man. The others I will have to look into."

"It might be nothing, but Rune was insistent that they're dangerous."

"Many in our Guild can be considered dangerous, my dear, myself included." He held up a hand to stop her protests. "I'm not saying your bondmate was wrong, that he might have misread the situation. What kind of game were they playing?"

"A friendly one with no real cheating that I could see. Master Carrow was quiet, but laughed along with most of the jokes."

"It was a loud group?" he mused, taking a sip at the whiskey in his tumbler.

"Yes, the boys at my table were enamored with some curses the other three used."

"Was it a simple card game or more complex?"

"It looked simple to me."

"Something that could occupy the hands while we talked other things about?"

"Yes, is that important?" she asked as Rune moved into her arms to be held.

"Carrow is a master at the tables, he wouldn't consent to a simple hand without another motive. I will see what I can find out about his guests. For now you had best return to the castle at speed, it's almost curfew," he said with a snort, checking the clock to one side.

"All right, thank you for listening," she said standing and gathering up Rune and her coat.

"Thank you for reporting it to me, Mage. Sometimes minor things can add up in our work. You may have solved a mystery for me," he mused, starting to dig through the folders on his desk.

"Will you let me know how it falls out?"

"Once all the players are in place, you can know. Now, run child, or you'll be dodging the guards the entire way."

"Thank you, Master James," she said with a slight grin as she pulled up her hood and hurried out the door.

She made it to the castle just as the last bells of curfew were ringing out. Trotting though the cold halls, she dodged several servants who sent her disapproving looks. She'd have to tell Darius about her trip into town before the gossip mongers reached him, she thought with a sigh. As she closed her door behind her, Rune jumped down with a meow and padded towards her bedroom at a quick clip.

"Yes, time for bed," she agreed with a yawn, it was Master James' mess to deal with for now.

CHAPTER 14

The trial was quickly turning into a political statement. The crown didn't take kindly to a Mage being injured, and having it happen to someone not yet an adult, seemed to make it ten times worse. The judge was determined to interrogate Jared for every crime he could, but her uncle had never been a stupid man; he wasn't going to admit anything.

It split the crowds outside the court between pitying the poor junior apprentice and vilifying her as a criminal. As the trial dragged on into its fourth day, the public viewing area was full with watchers spilling out around the building waiting on the final verdict. Those against magic protested alongside those hoping for a public hanging.

Charles slid into a bench in the upper rows and scanned the courtroom. The crowd shifted restlessly but seemed willing to wait until they were released to react beyond low mutters and gasps as each piece of evidence was examined. A handful of guards were posted at each level, but the true protections were carved and spelled into the stone and iron that filled the room, keeping the emotions of people to a low boil while they were within the courtrooms.

Jared Voss looked worse for his weeks in the court holding cells, his clothes torn and soiled. Black bruises circled one eye and cheek, showing that his stay had not been without incident. He sat chained to the iron railing that fronted each section.

"You aren't listening. You just want to hear how the poor chits been beaten," Jared spat. "I never touched her. I raised her as best I could when my sister passed, leaving me her kid. What was I to know about raising a mage?"

"Mister Voss, we have healer's reports listing multiple contusions are from a strike or hand hold. Do you deny that you made these injuries?" the prosecutor asked.

"The girl was willful. She was always running off and hiding instead of earning her keep."

"So, you were punishing her for misbehavior?"

"Yes, sir."

"You also forced the girl to work as a mage without Council approval or training. What was done with the money she earned?"

"We lived off of it."

"And how much were you charging for these services?"

"Enough, we got by, but not much beyond that," Jared said, dismissive of the question.

"I have a statement here from the last town you visited, Breyton, which states he charged them five hundred and fifty gold crowns to ward the town. Is this correct?" the magistrate asked, shuffling through a file full of paperwork.

"The cost depended on what they wanted done. Breyton wanted a lot of work," Jared said with a sniff. "Cheap bastards, they were."

"Mind your tongue here, Mister Voss. I will not have cursing in my court."

"Sorry, sir. I didn't mean nothin' by it."

"When you were apprehended you had three gold crowns on your person and had run up a large tab at a local inn which far exceeded your finances. Where did the three hundred go?"

"I don't see how it matters how I spend my money."

"You claim it's being spent on yourself and your charge. However, several of the towns your charge warded have reported thefts or bills left unpaid in the wake of your stay. Do you have anything to say about this?"

"I don't know nothing about any thefts, and we settled our debts when we left a town."

"When you arrived here in Cardu, what were your intentions concerning your niece?"

"I wanted to see her. I'm her uncle; they should allow me to see my niece."

"The guards reported that you accosted her in an unlit corridor and tried to force her into following you."

"I wanted to go somewhere private where we could talk."

"And you decided that dragging a screaming child through the hallways was acceptable?"

"Of course not! I tried to tell her where we were going, but she wouldn't stop fighting me! Then that blasted animal attacked me!"

"That animal is your niece's bondmate; a physical extension of her magic and soul."

"Well, I didn't know that, did I? All I saw was a scrawny stray trying to claw my face off!" he said, gesturing to the still healing cuts littering his head and neck.

"Why would your niece think you were a danger to her safety?"

"I'm not! I never touched the girl!" Jared said, shifting in his bindings, making the chains ring against the stone.

"And yet when she was removed from your care, she had both old and new bruises and hand prints on her throat, wrist, and shoulder."

"She fell. She had a fit and hit her head."

"They documented her injuries from the fall. However, the healer noted many older injuries more consistent with a brawl or beating then a fall."

"We escaped a group of raiders that attacked the village she was warding. It was only days before the fall! She was injured then!" Jared said, standing as much as the chains would allow.

"We shall see. Return to your chair, Mister Voss. The court calls forward the Apprentice known as Mage, apprentice to Master Mage Darius Fremont."

Charles watched as the young woman stood, pushing back her hood to reveal a still bruised face. She moved to the stand, taking a seat and pulling her bondmate into her lap. Several people murmured at the lack of visible injuries, but he frowned, shifting in his seat. Those with magic healed faster than those without, he remembered.

"Apprentice, do you swear by the gods to deliver a truthful testimony?"

"I do, sir," she told them. The only visible nerves were the way she petted her bondmate with a trembling hand.

"How would you describe your uncle, Jared Voss?"

"My uncle is a gambler, sir. As he said, he tried to raise me the best he could, but once he saw how easy it was to sell wards and spells, I became just another way for him to make money."

"Can you point to where your uncle is seated?"

"Yes, sir," she said, raising one arm and gesturing to Jared before returning her hand to the cat.

"Would you say your uncle is abusive in his treatment of you?"

"No, sir. I would say he was neglectful and lost in his own business too often to care for a child." She reached to brush her hair behind one ear, eyes on her lap.

"How old were you when you came into your uncle's care?"

"Eight, sir. My parents died only a week after my birthday."

"And at what age did you start warding villages with your uncle?"

"Nine, sir." Beryl stared straight ahead, ignoring the shocked gasps that echoed in the high vaulted room. Magical exhaustion was often an issue with small children. It was the principal reason they were not trained until their tenth birthday. To craft wards at such a young age could have killed her.

"How many towns did you ward a month?" he asked, once the room had returned to silence.

"It varied but between one and three."

"At three hundred a town?"

"Sometimes less."

"So, on average you would earn what a month?"

"Between two and nine hundred gold." The crowd murmured

again at this; it was enough for a merchant of fine goods or a minor noble to live off of on a small estate.

"And this money was always in the care of your uncle?"

"Yes, sir."

"Were you given any pocket money or expected to deal with any finances?"

"They gave me a few golds a month to buy supplies for our traveling. That started when I was eleven."

"Do you know what happened to the rest of the income you were providing to your guardian?"

"Yes, sir. He gambled it away as we traveled. Sometimes we would stay in a town for a few months while he made investments or tried to start a business, but it never lasted." The crowd rumbled a shocked commentary which earned the room a quick scolding glance from the magistrate.

"Did your uncle ever hurt you in any way?"

"He often gripped my shoulder or wrist too tight, leaving bruises. Sometimes he would push or pull me to hurry me along."

"Do you believe it was his intent to harm you?" the magistrate asked, leaning forward.

"I do not know, sir."

"How often would he leave these bruises?"

"A few times a month, maybe less."

"Did you ever have to defend yourself from your uncle using magic?"

"Only when he was drunk." This earned another rumble of commentary from the audience, causing Mage to glance around the room for a long moment; hands pulling Rune tighter against her.

"And how often was your uncle drunk?"

"If we were in a town with a tavern, he was drinking. The only time he didn't was while we were between towns," she said, hand smoothing the small cat's fur.

"What did you cast to defend yourself when he was drinking?"

"I warded areas so he couldn't enter, or I left if I was able."

"You never used magic or wards to harm your uncle?"

"No, sir."

"What do you believe his intentions were in approaching you at the castle?"

"He wanted me to return to traveling with him," she said, one hand smoothing her dress fitfully.

"Would you have agreed?"

"No, sir," she said, voice hard as she watched her uncle. "I've wanted to receive more training for many years. I want to stay and learn with Master Fremont."

"Is this why you fought your uncle?"

"No, sir. He grabbed me in a poorly lit hall and tried to pull me into a stairway without a word of warning or explanation. I didn't know it was Jared until the guards arrived."

"A likely explanation," Jared snarked loudly. "The bint wanted to leave me destitute."

"Another outburst, Mister Voss, and you will be returned to your cell until the conclusion of this investigation."

"Take her side! She's magic'ed you into believing her, the tramp. She uses her abilities to take what she wants!"

"All members of the courts wear medallions against such spell craft when a mage is involved in an investigation. To suggest that your own niece would stoop so low is an insult to both this court and to your own flesh and blood."

"She's not mine! She's the by-blow of that damn mage my sister married. Look what it got her! Dead in a ditch with his body right beside her! Magic didn't save them, did it?"

"Enough, guards! Remove this man!" the magistrate shouted.

They dragged Jared from the court, spewing curses and ranting about the perversions of his own niece until the door slammed behind him. The magistrate called an end to the proceedings for the day. They would present the final arguments in the morning before the sentencing.

Charles watched Mage making her way out through a side door before he joined the throngs leaving the building. He headed out to an Inn near the barracks for a quick meal before his squads' shift patrolling the town. He doubted he would make it back in the morning for the reading of the verdict with his shift schedule, but he'd at least try.

Beryl didn't bother attending court the next morning. A page found her in the palace gardens and delivered a note from Darius with the verdict. They sentenced Jared to twenty years of hard labor in the mines. Most adolescent men sentenced to the mine didn't live through a ten-year sentence. Twenty for a man of Jared's age was a death sentence.

She would never see the last of her family again, and she couldn't say how she felt about it? Did she want Jared in the mines? No, but he had broken the law, lied, and cheated everyone around him for the entire time that she'd know him.

He'd only ever looked out for himself, even if he had done what little he could to provide for her. She knew he'd seen her as just another way to make a profit, but the time she'd spent at his side hadn't been all bad. He was never fit to care for a child, but she'd survived and learned from it. Was that enough to pardon his sins? She didn't know.

Tucking the note away, she made her way to the stables, Rune a silent presence at her side. She spent the rest of the morning pampering Flox before heading to the kitchens to snatch a quick lunch. Salendra and Robert found her as she headed back to her rooms, stealing her away to play dice with the servant's children for the rest of the afternoon.

* * *

Two rest days passed before Captain Marshal went out horseback riding with Beryl. It was just a quick ride outside of town before they were standing at the door of a small cottage; it sat inside a glen in a wooded area.

Knocking, they were soon ushered in by a small woman who looked to be in her early forties. Seated before the fire was a rugged looking older man, who watched the girl he was supposed to be teaching. Removing the cat from her coat, she took it off. It was a warm day and her sleeves had been rolled back, exposing the scars that ran up her arms.

Charles had explained about the young mage's past. He stated that he was not sure if she could do the training Durn provided. Durn was not so certain. He'd seen all kinds of trauma as he worked his way up through the ranks in the king's army, just as he'd seen soldier written off for the grave rise and fight again.

He'd seen soldiers so scarred from battle that it seemed like they would never walk again, much less be sane. Charles had worked with those same soldiers for months, pushing at them till they were walking and working at some kind of job, even if it was no longer as a soldier. He would try to teach this girl what she needed know to heal, but there were no guarantees with this thing. she may never fight in an actual fight, but he would see if he could at least get her to where she could survive long enough to get away.

Standing, he clapped Charles on the shoulder. "Thank you, Charles, we can get along without you, I think." The captain gave a knowing quirk of his lips and said his goodbyes before leaving.

"When do you want to begin, girl?" he asked, eying the girl's thin build.

"Whenever you can teach me, sir," she said firmly. The cat sat at her feet, nearly at attention.

"Very well, let's start now. Let me see your hands. Do the scars limit your movement at all?" Turning the girl's hand in his, he stretched the muscles, watching for signs of pain.

"I'm stiff in the mornings, but I stretch every morning and night."

He grunted at this. "Good, you will need those. I'll show you a few more to add to your routine. Lissa, get the girl some of your balm for sore muscles. She will need it." He eyed the thin girl's frame. She had some muscle on her, but it was a wiry strength.

"You will never heft a heavy blade, but maybe a thin one like the ones used in Bourdain. You can use daggers, definitely. Before any of that, we will improve your endurance and strength. Here."

He fetched the bars from his desk and handed the girl a flat piece of iron. It was heavy. She looked at him to see what to do. Placing the second one in her other hand, he showed her a series of exercises for her arms.

"Bend your legs, shoulder width apart. Holding the bars up and down, slowly. Yes. You're to do this every morning and every night with your stretches. Ten of each exercise for now, we will add on as you build up some muscle."

Taking the bars, he handed her a leather ball filled with sand and began showing the girl exercises to strengthen her wrist and hand.

"Do these as well in the morning and at night, now for the daggers."

Opening a trunk, he fetched out a wooden box which he handed to her. Opening it, she found wooden daggers carved out of a dark wood, which had been oiled and sanded until they were as smooth as silk. Gripping one by the handle, she removed it from the box. Durn immediately correcting her grip.

"You may use these until you learn to make your own. Handle them like you're holding a real dagger of steel that could cut off your fingers with a missed hold. Carry one around with you everywhere. Get used to the weight and feel of it. Make it an extension of your arm." Showing her to the outside practice yard. He pointed her toward a target in the shape of a tall man.

"Targets for a dagger differ from those for a sword. For a dagger, you want to aim for soft spots, the stomach, the throat, the meat of the back, and backs of the knees or elbows, for cutting tendons." Taking one dagger, he demonstrated the lunge for a strike to the throat.

"See, the foot skims the ground forward, and you just tap the tip to the target. Too hard a hit and you become pinned while your momentum forces you forward. A good dueler with knives is never still, but you do not move just to move. Conserve your strength for the fight. You move to anticipate a blow or to draw the attacker away from what you are doing; however, that is a lesson for another day."

"You need to run on the days you are not coming here. Build up your wind. For now, practice each target twenty times." Handing her the other knife he showed her how to guard with one dagger while striking with the other.

"No, too hard, light taps to the wood; control the motion. Once you get this, we will work on hand to hand and with staffs. My back is too bad for me to do it, but you can spar with my two other students for now. Every middle day I want you to come spar at noon. On the day before rest day, I want you to come once your classes are over to practice the lunges and throwing daggers. That, and your exercises, should keep you busy for a while." The steady tock of the dagger touching the wooden target filled the clearing.

"Good enough for a start. Take the daggers with you and do the exercises I showed you morning and night. Ah and don't forget to balm any sore muscles with this." He handed her a large jar of balm. "My Lissa's own recipe; works like a charm. Now off you go. I will see you again on next middle day." With that, he shooed the girl out the door and onto her horse. Soon, she was heading back to the castle.

Charles had been right, Beryl thought; this would be a lot of work. She plucked at a spot of sweat, making her shirt stick to her skin. She prayed to Ruth it was worth it, and she could protect those around her. Rune poked his head out of her coat pocket and sent her a wave of calm and certainty. He had faith in his mage; she would do what she needed to keep everyone safe, with Rune by her side they had to win.

Beryl's life fell into a pattern of school, working with Durn, sparring with his other students, riding Flox, working with Master James on rest day nights, and collapsing into bed at night. Her sparring sessions with Durn's other students left her black and blue, and she came to love Lissa's muscle balm and the tub in her rooms. Her visions were now more under control, but some unnamed pressure pushed her to learn as much as possible.

Lessons with the other apprentices were going better. They had moved her into all fourth-year classes, except for her one fifth year class. Her work with self-defense was coming along. She'd started sparring with staffs and in hand to hand twice a week. To help with learning daggers, she'd built three small targets in her library for her to practice throwing her wooden daggers.

She was in the middle of learning to make a steel dagger at the forge and would start practicing with real steel instead of wood with her target soon, however she would not be throwing and catching real daggers for a while. The constant practice of using the hand weights and running with Robert had increased her strength and endurance, but she still had to use the bruise and muscle balm after every practice.

She had talked Durn's wife, Lissa, into teaching her how to make the balm, since she was going through so much of it. Between her practice with Durn, and her lessons with Pol learning to track, most of her days were full. When she was not in lessons learning magic, then she was learning how to fight or live off the land. Pol said most of what he was teaching them would not do good for a lengthy stay in the woods, but it would keep them alive till they could find someone to help.

Beryl was sitting in the kitchens with Rune and a cook who was shelling beans on a rare free afternoon. The head cook had grabbed her when she tried to cut through the kitchens to get an apple.

"Why are you so determined to learn such things? Why not be like the other girls, learning to sew lace or to enchant music boxes?"

"Because I want to learn something useful," she retorted, giving Rune a pea shell to chew.

"When are you going to need to know how to shoot an arrow or climb a wall or, Ruth help me, fight!? Don't you dare deny it either. One maid informed me of your 'Lessons' with that horrible man!"

"The former captain of the king's guard is not a horrible man."

"Rolling around on the ground with a girl and boy half his age, and you ride all over the country on that horse of yours, wearing pants, astride like a heathen!"

This made Beryl look at the cook and ask, "So you wish me to wear skirts?"

"Yes, it is not proper for a girl of your station..."

The cook continued to ramble on. The head cook gave her a wink and called her over.

"Ignore the woman; she's a bit stuck in her ways. Help me roll out this dough; we have sixteen pies to make for dinner tonight. If you're an excellent worker, I can teach you how to cook a few simple things."

"Every woman needs to know how to protect themselves, and with you running all over the place on that horse of yours, you need it more than most." She eyed the thin young woman, "There is a healer at Ruth's temple that teaches the adolescent girls how to break hand holds and how to use a knife if you are interested. Her name is Enid. A bit of healing would not be amiss either; what if you are out on the road and you or your animals gets sick? You need to know how to care for them." Rune gave a bleak of agreement from his perch on the Beryl's shoulder.

"Now don't you be getting fur in my pies, Master Cat. I let you in here because you're polite, but I remember when you were just a ball of fluff falling in my pies and getting covered in flour, I do!" Rune ducked behind Beryl's neck, peeking his head out to give the cook a meek look.

"And don't be giving me that look. I know just how much meat goes to your bowl twice a day. I know you're not starving."

At this Beryl burst out laughing, "He's a bottomless pit, I'm afraid."

The cook harrumphed but handed her a roll and a strip of meat for the cat. "Most young things are, child."

Contrary to what the cooks and servants thought, her training with Durn was going well. She was making slow progress in her sparring but had yet to win a bout. What she was showing promise in was throwing daggers and using a sling with stones.

She was deadly accurate in throwing stones, thanks to her affinity with river stones, and Durn was trying to get this ability to carry over to throwing other things. He had her spending half the afternoon throwing wooden daggers or blunt pieces of iron at targets to get her used to the weight that a throwing dagger had.

With her stones, she could hit the center target ten out of ten times; with a dagger she was hitting around five out of ten. Durn wanted her hitting at least eight out of ten before he would graduate her to throwing sharpened daggers. He also had her throwing differing weights of knives, so she never got too accustomed to one balance or type of dagger.

After asking what she could defend herself with now, he'd demanded a demonstration, taking her outside and having her hit different targets until she thought her arm would fall off. The next day he had handed her a sling and told her to do it again. It had taken her a few tries, but soon she was just as accurate without a sling as she was with one.

Later that week he handed her a rough stone and told her to try throwing it. She had missed the target over and over before finally clipping the edge. Stopping, she examined the rock. It was heavy and pitted, looking like no rock that she had ever seen. Weighing it in her palm, she tried to sense it with her magic. Building an image of the stone in her head, she held it while she turned and threw the rock, striking the target dead center.

"Again," he said, waiting until she had struck the target five times before gesturing for her to stop. Durn grunted and gestured for her to hand over the stone.

"Now try this," he said, handing her a strange knife.

The knife had a wooden handle and looked like they made it of some thin black glass that was rippled and chipped. Holding it, she let her magic feel out the blade as she weighed it in her hand. Throwing it, she struck the target to one side. Turning she asked, "What kind of blade was that?" Retrieving the blade, Durn handed it back to her.

"The stone is raw iron ore, and the blade is made from obsidian, a volcanic stone they have in the southern islands. You should be able to use your magic to aid you by throwing a knife and throwing a stone. If not then we may have to get you some stone daggers. The problem with obsidian is that it is very sharp but also very fragile. It chips and shatters easily with a strike and could leave you holding a handle in the middle of a fight. I have a friend of mine looking into other types of dagger for you. If he finds one that works, we can make or buy you a set. However, either way I think you should add magic to the blade to make it less likely to break. there was a reason after all that we went to metal blades."

Over the next few weeks, her aim with metal blades improved, yet her best work was still with the stone blades. They had found a ceremonial dagger that was made of limestone. Still, the blade was fragile, and it was unlikely that she could find a stone blade in the middle of a fight if they took away hers.

She would need to be just as good with metal blades as she was with stone. Now that she was getting proficient with metal, Durn had her throwing knives of every shape and size until she could hit the center of a target at least once in three with any blade put in her hand, and Durn would not be satisfied until she made that one out of two.

* * *

WHILE SHE HAD BEEN TRAINING, the Thieves' Guild had been fighting to defend its territory from attacks that grew steadily worse. The healer's halls were still full of injured and dying from the increasing violence in the streets. Guild members were being attacked during the day now, and a second riot had burned down several homes bordering the waterfront. It was too close to the thieves' guild hall for comfort, yet the Nail refused to give the order to retaliate. She seemed to glory in the chaos, often killing the men who persisted in trying to persuade her to act.

Beryl couched on a rooftop in the thick mist watching the tiny flickers of breaking wards, Rune crouched next to her, his tail flicking as he scented the men they hunted. Most mages were so used to the whisper of magic on skin that they ignored them, even when they were somewhere wards shouldn't be cast. Each flare was another member getting tagged by her spells as they left the "guild house" for Marcus and his thugs.

She'd started it on a whim, marking the known attackers and thugs hoping to find a pattern to the attacks against the thieves' guild. Instead, she had pinned down the location of three hideouts and the key bolt hole for Marcus' men. She slithered back from the edge and hurried to the street, scooping up Rune as she ran.

She arrived back at Master James' office out of breath and flushed from the run. He gestured her to a chair, going back to his papers as he scribbled out a note for the waiting youth to take. When he had finished, he surveyed the young woman and her bondmate, as she draped her coat next to the fire to dry before taking a seat.

"How goes the marking?"

"I marked all four doorways and stayed long enough to watch the marks being added. Are you sure you don't need me to note who's marked?"

"No, we have several adolescent boys and girls who have a bit of magic. They're too young or too weakly gifted for an apprenticeship with the mages, but for now they can be our eyes. No one will think it odd that they're about town delivering messages."

"When will the fight start?"

"Blood thirsty as ever," the man huffed, standing and pouring them each a mug of tea. "We have several marked guild members already. Some are playing both sides, waiting to see who will win. Still, others are in Marcus' camp. There will be no notice about the coming battle, and you will be safe in the castle if I can arrange it."

"I can fight! I've been training."

"I'm aware of your training. While I'm ok with your training now, this will be one fight you will sit out. The guild is falling apart at the seams, and I will not see you caught in the fall out," he snapped, thumping one hand hard against his desk.

"You think the guild will disband?" She asked slowly, shocked into stillness.

"If we fail, then the guild members will have to swear loyalty to Marcus or leave the city."

"And if we win?"

"That depends on how the next few nights play out. You're to stay at the castle until I send for you. We will need you at the Healer's guild once they finish things."

"Are you sure there's nothing else I can do?"

"No, Mage. You have given us our advantage. We're the ones who will have to force it to be enough to route our demons. For now, return to Darius and give him this letter. I've explained the situation and asked that he keep you behind wards until I call for you."

"I still don't like it."

"None of this is something to be liked, Mage. Honorable men and women will die in the next few nights. Forgive me if I want to spare you that."

"Should I leave now?"

"No, warm yourself and finish your tea before you head back out into the mists. It looks to turn to rain soon," he said with a huff. "We all might as well enjoy what comforts we can."

"You think it will be that bad?" she asked, stroking one hand along Rune's back.

"War is never a gentle or pretty thing, Mage. People bleed and die in war, leaving naught but emptiness behind them. It's the ones left after that have to pick up the pieces. We will need your strength then."

Beryl made her slow way back to the castle, ignoring the light rain that soaked her to the skin. Death seemed to be the lot of most of the people she came to love. Her parents had died, Jared was sentenced to the mines, and Troche had died keeping Rune safe from harm. Would she lose Master James as well in the coming fight?

She changed out of her wet clothes before ducking into Darius' office and leaving the note on his desk. According to a page, they closeted him with the King, which meant he'd be busy late into the night. She retired to the rug by her fire and started her exercises. Still, her mind was still with the Guild.

Master James claimed that the Guild would need her strength to help rebuild, but would she be strong enough if he wasn't there to lead her? She wasn't sure she wanted to find out. Beryl needed to be stronger; she was still being pushed and pulled about by the powerful people around her.

Sharp pounding on the door woke her early the next morning. The page darted from her door before she could ask what he needed.

Darius' door was flung open, so she hurried there to see if he knew what was happening.

"Ah, good; go get dressed and head to the Healer Hall, Mage. There has been a fire in the warehouse district, and they need all the help they can get."

"Is it the Guild?"

"That or another riot; hurry, child, they will need every hand they can get."

"Yes."

She hurried to her rooms, pulled on the first thing at hand, and snatched up Rune and headed out at a run for the Healers Hall. They spent the next few days in a blur of activity as she healed those she could and helped bandage those she couldn't. Food and sleep were taken in snatches as more and more injured arrived. The fire spread further into town, and the thick smoke had injured or hurt many as they fought the blaze.

Rune was a constant presence at her side, fetching minor things and lending her strength when she faltered. Many of those she'd helped had been Guild members or people who carried the mark of her magic on their skin, marking them as a member of Marcus' group. Soon the people all blurred together, only noted distantly as she moved from one body to the next.

By the end of the week, she was as exhausted and worn as the injured. The healers sent her back to her rooms at the castle to recover. She made her way back, taking in the smoke-stained sky with a frown. The warehouses were still smoldering. The rebuilding would take months; she staggered to her rooms and collapsed into bed with a groan, only stopping to make sure Rune was settled before letting sleep overtake her.

Darius woke her late that afternoon and called from some dinner to be brought to her rooms. He looked as tired as she did, shedding his robes and dropping into a chair by the fire. Once they were both settled with trays, he sealed the room.

"I have news from Master James if you're up to hearing it," Darius said, once she'd begun eating, making sure Rune was munching at his own plate of fish.

"Please, is he all right?"

"He suffered a slight injury helping others escape the fires but is well enough. He wished me to let you know they have paid your debt to the Guild and you can leave the Guild or become a full member if you wish."

"What of Marcus and his thugs?"

"I'm afraid you must ask him yourself; that was the extent of his message."

"That can't be all?" she asked, looking at him in shock.

"When you've recovered your strength, you can ask yourself." Darius said with a smile, "He's asked for you to visit him in the coming weeks to announce your decision. For now, the city must recover and rebuild, the mages and apprentices will assist with that. They have asked me what tasks would be best for you. Do you have any preferences?"

"What will the other apprentices be doing?"

"Helping their Masters in the rebuilding; those that are skilled in wood and stone will assist with the architects in rebuilding the warehouses and docks. Those with some healing skill will continue to help in the Healer's Hall."

"Where will you be assigned, Darius?"

"I will be here at the castle help procure the needed materials. Dull paperwork that I'm sure you would rather avoid; I would if it were possible."

"I've only crafted minor items in metal and wood, but I could help ward the remaining buildings. I could go back to the Healer's Hall; I was some help there."

"I'd rather you got your strength back before returning to healing, Mage. Frankly, you look worn thin, and I'd rather see you conserve your magic until you're healed from this week yourself. For now, I'd like you to help run messages with the castle runners and to help where you can on the grounds; I don't want you casting magic at all if you can help it for the next three days. After that, you may go back to helping with the healers if it's still needed."

"All right, I'll check with the steward in the morning to see what work they need."

"Thank you, my dear."

The next few days passed slowly as Beryl ran around the castle taking messages here and there or helping move supplies from storage. She was looking forward to going back to the Healer's Hall the next day. She took a shortcut through the kennels on her way to a distant wing of the castle, Rune tucked safely into her hood.

"Hey, girl!" One of the dog handlers called to here, reaching out to stop her as she jogged past.

"I'm running a message, sir," she said with a frown slowing to a stop.

"You asked to see which of the hunting dogs would work with your cat, didn't you?"

"Yes, sir. Master Fremont wanted me to see if any would bond with me," Beryl said, legs itching to be moving.

"The King's hounds are in for dinner. Take your cat down the line and see if any don't try to eat him."

"It'll rile up all the dogs if they realize a cat's in the kennel."

"They'll go back to their meal fast enough. Let the beast out already, girl, I have other things to attend to," he snapped, turning back to filling trays with meat and grain.

Rune took decided her jumping down and starting to wander down the lengthy line of cages. Beryl had to admire the cat's courage as dog after dog charged their wire doors, snarling and barking. They left the smaller terriers and hounds behind, moving towards the nicer parts of the kennel where the King's dogs were kept.

<h1 style="text-align: center;">CHAPTER 15</h1>

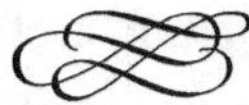

arius swept into the young mage's rooms in a flurry of robes and motion. He had been on duty as an official royal adviser, since he almost never wore his robes of office outside of his days at court. The heavy robes of velvet and brocade may have been beautiful, but they were also heavy and boiling. He was shedding the thick robes even as he entered with a sigh of relief.

"Ah, Mage, I have two more books for you and..." He trailed off, as the massive dog stretched across the floor to one side of the fireplace raised its head, its tail beating the wall like a drum.

With a happy bleek, Rune's grey head popped up from behind the other side of the beast before jumping over its broad back and trotting up to Darius. Twining around his feet, the small cat gave a string of grating cries, ranting on about something. Turning to the girl, Darius looked to his apprentice for an explanation, "Mage?"

Getting up off the floor, Beryl pushed the mass of blankets she was working on to one side and fetched Rune, guiding Master Darius into a chair. Sitting back among the blankets, she hefted one edge and eyed her needle before setting both back down with a sigh. Rune bounced back next to the dog to continue his exploration of their newest member.

"Do you remember how you said I needed to take Rune with me to see the hawks and hunting dogs, and that I should only see the ones most attached to me in case they eat Rune?" she asked, fiddling with a loose thread.

"Yes, I recall that," he said, regarding the gigantic dog with a thoughtful look.

"Well the hound keeper had time, and he let me see which ones would come to each cage door and not react to Rune. None of the hounds did so, so he took me to see the King's dogs. I don't think he thought any would bond with me." The girl's voice had taken on a hysterical edge at this point; her words were tumbling out fast and uncontrolled.

"Now, now, calm down. I take it this... enormous fellow bonded with you?" Darius said shakily.

"Yes, but he is the King's dog. I can't keep him," she said, wadding the blankets in her lap. The dog let out a low whine at this. Quickly, she looked at the dog and scooted so she could rub its head. With a happy wuffle, and a few bangs of its tail, the dog settled back down.

"Don't look so worried child, as a bonded pair not even the King can separate you. I'll arrange to speak with him; perhaps this has happened before. They may require you to buy the animal or work off the debt to the King. However, we will have to see what he will agree to." He sighed, surveying the animal.

"We may need to ask for larger rooms for you," her said with a chuckle. "Now what are you doing with these blankets?"

"I was trying to make Argent a bed since there's no way we can both fit into mine," she said with a stressed smile. Rune walked across the blankets and collapsed into her lap giving a soft meow. "Don't be silly, I love both of you." This last statement left Darius blinking.

"I beg your pardon?"

"That was the other part. Argent keeps sending me images to explain things, and now I can understand what Rune's meows mean."

"You have developed a powerful bond then. Is it just Rune or can you understand all cats?

"I don't know. I guess we will have to test it."

"That can wait until later, child," Darius frowned at the dog, eying his lengthy sprawl. "And what have you named him?"

"Argent." She said with a smile, ruffling the dog's ears.

"Ah, well that is appropriate at least," he said with a smile. The dog's wiry coat was speckled with white, black, and silver, while his lower legs, ears, and tail were a dark grey that faded to black at the tips.

"How was your day running messages before you found your new charge?"

"Fine," she said with a sigh, collapsing against the large dog's side, "I was going to ask if I could be reassigned to the healers again but with Argent I'm going to be grounded again, aren't I?"

"I'm afraid so. You need time to adjust to the new bond. It's just as well, since by this rest day most of the cleanup at the docks will be complete and rebuilding can start in earnest. Only full mages will be allowed to assist with the rebuilding, so your lessons should start back next week. For now, if you feel up to it, continue your help with the castle runners."

The King's final decision was that Beryl would pay for the dog's original cost when he was bought as a puppy. She would work as a messenger for the crown on rest days, and half of her pay would go toward the debt she owed the crown. The rest of her pay was to go to the upkeep of her familiars and to pay for any expenses that were incurred from her being a messenger, such as lost horse shoes and the messenger uniform.

The next day found Beryl running up and down the castle hallways delivering, messages for the house staff, while Rune and Argent trailed along behind her while she waited for the Royal Steward to decide on her rotation of the messenger runs outside of town. Since she owned a horse, she would be using it to deliver messages to the outlying towns and villages that were less than a day's ride in any direction. Once she had proved herself worthy and reliable, she could be given message runs that took her even farther out.

She spent the next day with the dog's handler, learning the commands used with the king's dogs on a hunt. However, with the bond, she doubted she would ever have to use them. The one thing Argent insisted on was a morning and evening walk. He was happy to sit and gnaw on one of the bones she had begged from the kitchens for most of the day, but he was used to being exercised and going out on weekly hunts with other dogs.

For now, they started going on runs in the afternoon with Robert and taking walks every morning before class. This suited Rune as well, as it got him out of the castle more. The only days they didn't go out were those with rain or bad weather. Then they beat a hasty retreat to the barn, so the dog and cat could do their business in a stall without making her room smell like she had a stable of wet animals staying there.

The maids were already complaining; several refused to clean the mage's rooms while the dog was inside them. However, others could not stop talking of how cute it was to see the small cat and enormous dog sleeping or playing together.

Beryl started ducking into the kitchens and grabbing some meat, bread, and cheese for the three to share, while the cat and dog romped around one of the pastures near the castle or inside one of the castle gardens. Robert and Salendra were both taken with the large dog and went out of their way to find time to play with him. She felt a bit bad for abandoning the tentative friendships she'd struck up with Tor and Rose, but her bondmates came before anything else.

The next rest day she was out of bed extra early helping to get horses and dogs ready for the day's hunt. Argent had been allowed to attend as long as Mage kept herself and her horse to the edges. She had no worries about either, but the hunt masters were keeping a stern eye on her as the hunt progressed.

At the hunt, Flox had behaved amazingly. He stepped among the milling dogs without batting an eye. He watched the other horses stream away from him with some concern but had been willing to stay with the dog handlers who were walking or riding with the hounds, waiting for the lead hounds crying howls to signal that it had found a scent.

The horn was sounded and the rest of the dogs were released. This was a small game hunt, so the large hounds like Argent were not being used. A handful of larger dogs were allowed to run alongside the horses as the hunt moved farther afield, but they were not the ones doing the hunting.

The larger hounds were only used if they flushed a deer or a boar during the hunt, or to hunt water fowl or to retrieve downed birds. Otherwise the smaller, faster hunting hounds ran along through the brush, tracking their prey. Argent was happy simply to be out amongst the other hounds.

Beryl grinned, happy to bask in the warmth of her bonded's happiness. Rune purred from his spot draped across her shoulders. It was a good day, she mused, relaxing as she watched her new bondmate, stepping carefully among the smaller dogs waiting for them to find the scent.

* * *

BERYL WALKED down the street happy to be allowed back into town finally. The bond with Argent was settling quickly and with how well-mannered the dog was proving to be Darius had agreed to allow her to head into town to see Master James. Rune dashed along ahead of them as they wove their way along back alleys and side streets.

She nodded to several guild members she knew as she made her through the inn and up the stairs to James' office. The inn was bustling with business, Guild members sat eating or gaming at nearly every table, while young runners dashed from the back rooms on their way about town with messages. She knocked and grinned when Rune darted through the door when she opened it at James' rough permission.

"Mage, come in," James said, rising with a grin. He rounded his desk giving Beryl a quick hug, even if he hesitated for an instant as Argent entered the office, "Darius said you'd gained another bondmate but not that he was so intimidating."

"Master James, I'd like to introduce you to my new bondmate,

Argent," Beryl said with a smile, while Rune purred from his spot on the hearth.

"Please to meet you, lad," James said, ruffling the large dog's ears before he returned to his seat behind the desk to straighten some papers.

"Are you alright? Darius said you'd been injured in the fire?"

"A few burns that have already been healed, nothing to fret over," he said, waving away her concern as he rang for a pot of tea.

He waved away her questions until they were both seated by the fire with cups and the serving boy sent away. One of the reasons that Beryl was growing to love the older man was his care and attention to her bondmates. Most people just saw them as dumb animals and treated them as such. Each animal was currently enjoying its own cup of tea, while a bone and some ham had been brought up for them both to share.

"Will you tell me how things fell out with Marcus and the Nail?" she asked, setting her cup to the side.

"Before I can, I must know your answer; do you wish to become a full member of the Guild or to leave our halls?"

"I would like to be a full member, but you know I won't be able to stay in town once I finish my apprenticeship with Master Fremont."

"Not all of our members stay in the capital. Some travel the nation helping by sending us rumors and news. While you're in Cardu, you would be expected to check in and help as you are able, but you would still be a member even if you leave; The guild is for life."

"I still want to join."

"Good, I'll arrange for our wizard to be available to give you the Guild mark later this week. For now, I'll take your word at its worth and tell you what transpired in the fires."

"Is everyone alright? I saw a lot of members in the Healer's Hall."

"As well as can be expected. We lost about twenty members and nearly everyone had at least some small injury. Most of the names you wouldn't know except for Vadna."

"The Nail is dead?" Beryl said blinking in shock.

"And most of her major supporters," James said with a nod.

"Then Marcus won?"

"No, Marcus died in the fighting as well."

"So, who won?" she asked, hugging Argent when he shuffled over to lean his head against her shoulder.

"No one," he said with a bitter smile. "The two Guilds have agreed to combine. The Day and Night watchers will continue to deal with day to day issues among the Guild, and the members will meet once a month to decide on important issues or problems."

"Who will make the final vote?"

"A council of peers voted in by the members. For now, it consists of the Day and Night watchman from our Guild and two members from Marcus' Guild."

"Has a new Hall been chosen, or will we meet somewhere different?"

"For now, we are meeting here at the Inn. It will be closed to non-Guild members once a month while we meet."

"So, what will we be doing now?"

"For now, we rebuild and continue your training," James said, tugging out a stack of paperwork. "I've heard that you will be working as a King's Messenger?"

"Yes, I have to pay back the cost of Argent since he was the King's dog."

"While you are running messages, we may add some notes or packages to your rounds. Otherwise, on the days you're not busy, you will be training with me."

"Will I be learning anything different?"

"You could say that. You've learned the basic skills of a street thief. Now it's time for you to learn the other half of our work."

"The respectable side, you mean?" she asked with a grin, rubbing Argent's head.

"Exactly. We work as a merchant house mostly, and you will be learning the skills a daughter of such a house would be expected to know."

"So, bookkeeping?"

"And managing small accounts, learning the ins and outs of shipping, and how other black-market traders get around the rules the King and international ports put in place."

"Sounds like I'll be busy."

"Once we know exactly how the Guilds are going to combine, you could be called in for more warding; but I'd like to keep your presence to a minimum. If Marcus' old supporters realized that you helped craft the plan that brought him down, it could put more enemies on your tail."

"I seem to collect them these days," she said with a sigh.

"Then let me do what I can to keep them at a distance," James said with a huff. "Here, your study material for the week. I'll send you a note when your lessons have been arranged and when to come receive your Guild mark."

"Where will it be placed?"

"I was thinking on the back of your shoulder. It's more discrete, and you won't have to constantly flash your mark like some of our members."

* * *

BERYL STARTED ADDING cleaning and preserving runes to the leather of her saddle and bridle since she was going to have to start using them nearly every rest day riding around town and to the neighboring towns. She added protection runes as well, which she hoped would help lessen any injuries that her mounts might get. She'd been studying with the priests of Ruth for the last few months and was doing well in healing small injuries with magic, an ability that had been sorely tested after the warehouse fire.

After the healers had praised her work during those long weeks, she'd begun to work with one of the mages who worked in the Healing Ward in order to learn healing runes. It took energy and magic from both the patient and the mage casting the spell for a healing to work, and many mages spent years learning how to do it. It was easy for a new healer to burn themselves out by using up too much of their own energies as they fought to force a healing.

Because of this, she was restricted to using magic directly on the patient only once per week. For now, she was working on two small runes that acted as a cleansing spell to clean out any dirt or infection from the wounded area so that it could be bandaged. This kind of rune could be stitched into bandages to keep infections from setting in, and it would be handy to know when she had a month off in the coming new year.

She wasn't sure what she wanted to do, but she was thinking of traveling with Argent and Rune to another city to see what she could learn there. The constant traveling with Jared had created in her a desire to travel; one that got worse the longer she stayed in one place. She wanted to travel and see what she could learn in other far off places. Maybe she could visit a few other mages and see how they enjoyed their jobs and where they lived.

One thing she'd really come to enjoy was her tracking lessons with Argent and Rune. With Rune cuddled inside her hood, his sharp gold eyes would notice details she missed, and Argent's nose could track down the trail of what they were hunting with a speed that none of the others could match.

Salendra and Robert said that using her familiars was cheating, but she could no more cut off the flow of information and images that Argent sent her then she could cut off her own hand. The others realized this but could not help but rib the mage about it whenever possible. Robert's training had finally started showing some improvement, and his body was filling out with a bit of muscle.

Salendra had started joining them on their morning runs, and soon both girls were looking fit. To the scandal of the servants and her mother, Salendra had cut her hair short to her head. But, she was stubborn, and once she got the idea in her head, next to nothing would have stopped her. She said she enjoyed it, and offered to cut Mage's long hair. But Beryl refused, saying she liked her braid. Plus, with the coming winter, it would be rather cold; a notion Sal shrugged off, declaring that if she could wear a hat if she got cold!

One nice thing about bonding with Argent that she hadn't anticipated was that the small pushes and shoves from the other apprentices in the halls stopped completely. No apprentice dared to touch her while Argent walked beside her, his massive feet sounding like boots hitting the ground. She moved her work to the back table in every lesson, so that Argent would not be blocking the way and no one would be near enough to step on a his tail or paws.

She still was shunned by most of the older students, but she had too much to do to really worry about it. The small slights and barbs hurt, but she'd had worse at Jared's hands. She'd keep going and do the best she could; the rest could fall as it may.

She got into the habit of waiting for everyone else to leave so that she would not have people crowding her bondmates or glancing out of the corner of their eyes and seeing a massive dog right behind them. Argent had caused no small amount of panic the first few times she had taken him somewhere. The one place he was welcomed without reservation was the stables, since they were used to dealing with the hunting dogs of the various riders.

Her first few messenger duties had sent her scurrying all over the castle. Thanks to Rune's eternal curiosity, they'd found several hidden servants corridors and unused rooms, that the three of them could use on occasions when the weather was too nasty to play outside. With all the work in the castle, she was learning the ins and outs of the castle better than the back of her hand.

They had also discovered that both animals could travel alone throughout the castle, because everyone now knew of the mage's animals. The bond would only become strained if they traveled beyond the castle, so there was a limit to how far away they could be from one another; the limits were still growing and settling, however. As time passed, they were able to go farther and farther away, until Beryl could be in the castle while the dog went out hunting and running with the other hunting hounds. The bondmates still preferred to be near each other, but it was good to know they didn't have to spend every waking moment with each other.

Winter set in with frost every morning as Beryl began her message runs outside of the capital. Her first run was to a forge outside of town that needed to be notified of a new order of weapons for the latest batch of recruits for the King's army. In the spring, the tournaments would begin to see who would be judged worthy to join the king's guard, and most of the new recruits were planning to compete. Her lessons for tracking and hunting in the woods had tapered off until the first big snow; Pol had promised to teach them how to deal with tracking in snow.

As the month progressed,, she was sent farther and farther out away from the town. She took Flox to get him used to having a massive dog running next to him, but the horse was nonplused as he generally was with everything else. The people she met on message runs were a different story. They were always shocked to see Argent loping alongside her horse as she trotted into town.

She'd gotten laughed out of many a tavern when she stopped to get a mug of barley water for her dry throat. The sight of Argent padding beside her tended to silence a room, but as soon as Rune popped up out of her coat and sat on the bar or lay down on Argent's broad back, the occupants would crack up.

Everywhere she went she was asked about the dog and cat and why she was running messages with a menagerie in tow. She would explain as best she could without outing herself as a mage, and then get back on the road, but the next time she was out that way, those that had met her before would introduce her to their friends.

Rune was a great conversation starter and would fearlessly approach just about anyone, always looking for a bite to eat or a pat on the head. Few could deny the tiny cat's desires. He had finally grown out of his kitten looks and was a sleek grey tabby, with charcoal colored stripes and bright gold eyes. However, he had not grown much in size. He still was small enough to ride comfortably in the pockets of the great coats or on his bondmate's shoulder.

Argent was known to snatch up the small cat in his great maw and tote him to there destination if the cat was being obstinate. This terrified people, as they were always convinced that the monstrous dog was eating the tiny cat. Beryl was constantly getting him to drop Rune to show that while the cat was now covered in dog spit, he wasn't harmed. Before Beryl caught on and made them stop, Argent and

Rune had even made a game out of it for a while, seeing how many women they could get to scream.

She held her hands out closer to the fire. Weather like this always made her hands and back ache. It had been raining all day, and a harsh biting wind numbed her face and cut through her wet coat.

They'd been sent on message runs throughout the town and outlying areas. They were finally able to stop and dry out at an inn near their last delivery for the day. If the rain didn't stop soon, they would have a wet ride back to the castle grounds. Rune and Argent lay before the fire, steam rising from them as their coats dried. Rune groomed himself, while Argent laid mud splattered and filthy, his body taking up the entire front of the fireplace. There was no point in him cleaning up when he would get just as dirty on the trip home.

The other customers of the Inn spoke in low, tense tones, eying each new arrival with suspicion. Everyone was unhappy with the rumors of war approaching. More and more soldiers were being moved to the North as news arrived daily about attacks happening up and down the coast.

Picking up her cup of hot cider, she finished it off and went to the bar to hand back the mug. Soldiers filled most of the bar, chatting or huddled at the tables in quiet misery. They were all wet and mud splattered from the road. At the table closest to the bar, a group of soldiers were eating bowls of stew and talking loudly about the possibilities of war as she passed.

"It'll be all out war come spring. The King will have no choice but to call out the garrisons if the trade caravans keep getting attacked going over the mountains," one of the soldiers said loudly, while waving to the barmaid for a refill.

"I say leave them to the mountains, it's not our country. Let them kill themselves," another said with a huff, hunched over his mug.

"That hasn't stopped them from attacking every farmer and fort for miles around the boarder. They're not attacking their own people."

"Their people are starving, and the refugees are dying in the passes. They say the forts and towns are sending them farther south, too harried themselves to deal with the extra mouths to feed."

"Half the supplies the army sends get stolen on the road. The refugees they want us to help are stealing everything they can find," he said with disgust, only to snap out of his slouch as his commanding officer stepped up.

"We're pushing through for Cardu. Finish up and start getting the horses ready," she said with a cough, tossing back the last of her mug.

"Yes, Ma'am," one said with a nod, tossing several coins on the table to cover their meals. "What do you think of the coming war?"

"That no matter the outcome, we'll be marching to cover the border before long. Get moving, I want to be in a real bed tonight."

"Yes, Captain," they murmured snatching up the last few bites and thunking down their empty mugs before trooping out of the inn and into the rain.

Beryl cast a discrete warming charm on her clothes when she settled back next to Argent, hoping the faint glow went unnoticed so close to the fire. One of the things her traveling had taught her was never to flaunt her abilities; people feared what they saw as different. She and Jared had been run out of a few towns that didn't trust the services of a mage.

Rubbing her hands together, she thought about getting out some healing balm for her hands but dismissed the idea quickly. It was in her saddlebags, which she had left in the stables along with a small charm so that no one would bother them. It probably wouldn't help anyway. The cream was for cuts, not old scars inflamed by the cold.

Giving the barmaid a small smile, she collected her damp cloak from the fire, tucking a disgruntled Rune into the hood before leading Argent back into the misting rain. They were in for a miserable ride back to town. The stable yard was a churned pit of mud from the passing troops, and it took some urging to get Flox to leave the dry stable.

They made slow time, slogging their way back to the stables in town. She rubbed down both Flox and Argent to clean them off of most of the mud and water, giving Flox a warm mash once he was settled in the stalls. Once in her rooms, she hung her cloak and clothes by the fire to dry while she took a hot bath. Argent and Rune curled together in his bed near the fire, watching as she stretched and did her exercises.

They spent the next two days quiet since they'd been given an extra rest day after the horrible weather continued to ruin the roads. Since being outside was out of the question, they continued their explorations of the castle and its many rooms. To the delight of the castle errand boys and stable hands, the moat was frozen solid enough to skate on the next morning. Games were held out on the ice every rest day and most afternoons. Beryl happily pulled out the thick green winter coat for her messenger runs and for walking the drafty halls of the castle.

* * *

BERYL RETURNED from a study session with several of her lower-class friends later that week in a pensive mood. Tor was looking more and more run down, constantly having to work late on projects for her Master or doing punishment assignments for various slights. Watching the young woman become more and more stressed left Beryl hunting for small things she could do to help.

Tor's master pushed the child to progress constantly; nothing ever seemed to be enough for the man. Tor would say nothing against her master. He had found her in an orphanage after her parents had died of spring wasting sickness. She wouldn't do anything to lose his care, no matter how meager it was.

"I'm afraid there isn't much that I can do," Darius said with a sigh when she approached him with her concerns. "We would need examples of the witnessed incidents with at least two witnesses to even bring up the matter with the Mage's Council. They would have to be the ones to remove Tor from her current Master and assign her to a new one. Tor's Master, Claude, is a harsh man, but unless he physically abuses her there is little I can do. I will make sure to keep an eye on her and see if I can find a way to give her a safe place away from him should she need it. I will speak with Mage Altria. She may be a better choice to be a shoulder to lean on then an old man she hardly knows, and she could use her as an assistant."

"Thank you, Darius, maybe it will help."

"My dear, I know we haven't spoken of your time with Jared but if you need a shoulder as well…"

"Thank you, Darius, but it's behind me now, and I would like to leave it there."

"Be careful, child. Nothing buried stays there forever." She gave him a sad nod and a smile before pulling the next book towards her and starting to take notes.

Her dreams of the rest of the month were full of danger and old hurts. She ran from unknown pursuers, or old memories of Jared cornering her while he was drunk and angry. She would wake shivering, curled against her bondmates, blinking at the stone walls around her until reality returned. She barely could keep herself and her bondmates safe; how was she supposed to protect the others around her when even her dreams sent her running?

She went on with her duties and tried to do what she could to cheer up both herself and her friends, but lately she so was so busy she barely saw them. She was either in lessons, working on projects for Darius or the Guild, or running messages. She just didn't have the time or energy to devote to anything else, no matter how much she wanted to. She'd have to trust that Darius would keep an eye on the situation and step in if he could.

Beryl's sense of foreboding didn't fade as time passed; it grew, as tensions increased in town with the threat of war overshadowing every part of the day. Beryl's dreams and visions were full of war and desolation: scenery blasted and destroyed, bodies ripped and broken. She tried to do as Darius suggested and direct her visions, but she would still get pulled back at the end of her visions sometimes to find herself standing in a wasteland devoid of life as biting cold cut at her face and hands.

Mages drew their magic both from themselves and from the natural magic inhabiting their surroundings. An area that had been drained of magic was a desolate and forbidding place. The Black

Sands Desert was one such place, the site of a massive duel of mages. The area had been stripped of its magic in the final blow used to fell the rogue mage Larkin.

What was once a pleasant plain was now a desert of black sand, where plants refused to grow. Water and previsions brought in to the area would rot and foul within a day, as the void sucked all magic out of any object brought into it. Mages would sometimes bring unstable or dangerous magical objects into the desert to be destroyed. It was speculated that if enough neutral magic could be funneled into the area it would eventually revert back into a normal plain. For now, however, it was an area to be avoided.

Did her visions mean that she was headed for a magically destroyed area or was she seeing destruction that she would eventually cause? She didn't know, and it left her stomach in knots. She tried to research similar areas and how to prevent their creation. Her visions had become nothing but portents of death and destruction. Only the fact that she didn't recognize anyone in them gave her a bit of comfort. Maybe they were for a distant future she wouldn't have to see.

CHAPTER 16

The current rumors percolating around the capital were all about the Queen. She and the King had been trying to have a child since their marriage began, but the few times she had become pregnant, she'd lost the child early in her pregnancy. Now, the royal physicians had asked that she stay confined to bed until it was certain or not if this pregnancy would last. Beryl was helping in the kitchens, while Rune watched from one shoulder.

"Mage, you've been working with the healers. Have you heard anything about the Queen's condition?" a sculler maid named Mary asked, the others pausing in their work to catch her response.

"Mary, you know even if I heard anything, I couldn't say. We do not allow healers to talk about the people they treat."

"But with it being the Queen, no one would think anything of it."

"She may be the Queen, but she is also a woman trying to have a baby. Would you want your healer to go spreading tales about you around the city? Anyway, the last thing the Queen needs now it to have to worry about what everyone else is thinking about her pregnancy. She needs rest, not people gossiping in the halls." Rune shifted on her shoulder, and for a moment she saw a brightly lit hallway filled with tapestries. Then the bond was silent again.

"Rune…" she whispered, rubbing his ears. "What was that? Do I need to go there?"

Rune gave an unhappy grumble, rubbing his head along her jaw. She had not understood him. Beryl sighed. The bond continued to deepen as the weeks went by, but she and the cat rarely seemed to understand each other. Some days she would know what her bondmates wanted or were trying to say, but other days it was just a blurred set of images, scents, and emotions that was little more than noise coming across the bond.

Over the next few days, Rune took to disappearing for a few hours at a time while Beryl was in lessons with Darius. When she asked him about it, she would again see the hallway. Her rest day saw her searching the castle for the hallway with Rune in tow.

He was no help. He enjoyed finding old dusty corners to investigate or unfamiliar smells to track down, while Argent followed along, content to explore and smell the unknown places. She found out where he had been going from Darius several days later. They were in his workroom inscribing runes into a silver plate that prevented the user from being poisoned; the runes would glow if the contents would harm the eater. They were often given to minor nobles as gifts, and several members of the court had requested one for them.

"My dear, I've had an unusual request for your services," Darius said, while he inspected her latest attempt.

"What kind of request? Does another Master need something made?"

"No, the Queen would like to speak to you. It seems that your bondmate has been keeping her company at times during the day, and she wished to speak with you about it."

"Has he been disturbing her? I can try to talk to him about it, but we don't understand each other much right now," Beryl said with a sigh, glancing to where Argent and Rune lay to one side napping.

"Actually, it's more of the opposite. She has enjoyed spending time with him and would like to continue to do so. Since your second bond is still new, I didn't want to allow him too much time away from you, so I suggested that you both spend some time in her presence. She agreed, and you're to meet with her each morning after breakfast for what time you have before classes. If this is acceptable with you of course?"

"Yes...but Darius, what will I be doing?"

"She is the Queen. However, she is also a woman confined to her bed; talk to her, my apprentice."

"Yes, Master Darius," she said with a frown. She went back to her work. What could a Queen have to say to an orphaned mage and apprentice?

The next day, Beryl smiled nervously at the Queen from a chair next to the bed. Rune had already jumped up onto the bed with his normal grating cry, before making himself comfortable against her side. Argent lumbered to the fireplace before stretching his grey and white body across the large hearth. Beryl fought the urge to try and straighten the skirts she was wearing. Apparently, one did not see the Queen while wearing a tunic and men's pants, no matter how nice the material and cut.

Propped up by pillows, Queen Marie sipped her tea on the bed. Her night shirt may as well have been a dress with the embroidery and ribbons sewn to it, her stomach rounding the covers in front of her. To Beryl's surprise, while the room was large and well-appointed, there were no displays of overt wealth; no gold or jeweled decorations, only pleasant embroidery and tapestries, thick carpets on the floor, and goose down pillows and blankets on the bed. The Queen had a large embroidery hoop to one side, so there was a fair chance that much of the work in the room was from her own hand.

"Tell me about yourself, Mage. What have you been doing out and about the castle this week?"

"Nothing of great import, my Queen," Beryl said with a blush. "Nothing that would interest you—simply study and message runs."

"Humor me, Mage," the Queen said with a sad smile. "There is only so much embroidery one can do when ones trapped in bed and the hours pass slowly. Tell me of your day, I can assure you it was much more exciting than mine," she said with a small laugh.

Beryl remembered what Darius had said; she was simply another woman about to have a baby. She smiled back hesitantly and began telling the Queen about her week. She told her about the men in the inn eating lunch after working in the fields, skin dyed red from the clay they were digging.

She told about the boys she saw playing among the massive stacks of hay bales, waiting to be put up before the rainy season hit, leaping and dodging as they leapt from bale to bale, hair covered in chaff. She spoke of the kindness or arrogance of the nobles who accepted her messages and packages, the tradesmen she encountered, and the common folk who greeted her by name whenever they saw her riding into town.

The village children loved roughhousing with Argent while she delivered her messages, and Rune charmed the maids and servants with his calm presence. The Queen laughed as Beryl told of Rune falling into a pie as a kitten and how the children always were scared of Argent before they learned that the most he would do was lick them on every part he could reach until they collapsed in giggles.

* * *

"THANK you for coming this afternoon, Mage, you've certainly cheered me this day. I'm afraid that I have kept you too late; please ask your Master to pardon me. Next time I will make sure to keep better track of the time. When are you next free?"

"Not for another two days in the afternoon, but Rune can still come to visit you while I'm in lessons if you like, ma'am?"

"That would be most appreciated, thank you Mage," she said with a smile.

"Thank you for tea and listening to my stories Queen Marie. I hope you have a good night," she said, giving a quick curtsy before opening her arms to catch her bondmate as he made a flying leap from the bed. He rode her shoulders as she left the room, tail jauntily ticking back and forth as he rumbled a purr in her ears. His bonded had done well.

* * *

HER VISIONS WERE BECOMING MORE and more prevalent as news of the brewing war on the Northern border reached the capital. It seemed like every time she closed her eyes she was pulled in to watch another battlefield coated with snow, ash, and blood. Captain Marshal and his squad had left to man the boarder several weeks ago, and he'd started sending her letters as the weeks passed. He recounted Healers Wards full of injured and sick soldiers. They were wounded in skirmishes with enemy fighters who swarmed in and attacked, only to melt back into the snow and woods like shadows.

They were fighting a two-fronted war. Farmers and trappers in the North were desperate after constant attacks, becoming little more than outlaws themselves as they stole what they needed to survive. The soldiers fought to maintain order and distribute the much-needed supplies to the people, only to have the supplies stolen or destroyed by enemy and outlaw alike. He told of the weather mage, Merrick, who was traveling with them, and how even he struggled with the massive winter storms pounding their lines.

Beryl watched as in vision after vision, the forests burned, and a snow of ash fell on the bodies frozen into the mud. She watched as mage worked against mage trying to give their troops the most ideal fighting conditions. It was all for naught, as the brutal Northern winter sent the snow banks higher and higher. Soon the passes would be closed for the season, and the war would have to wait until spring thaw. Snow could not stop the ships that were attacking the Northern coast, however.

She spent her days trying to prepare for the coming violence as she could. She trained and worked her body to exhaustion each afternoon when she wasn't riding on messenger runs. She could tell she was worrying Darius and James as she pushed herself to do better, to be stronger. But she couldn't stop. Dangerous times were coming, and she needed to be ready.

The only real reprieve she had was the quiet evenings talking to the Queen, or late at night when she curled with her bondmates by the fire, unable to sleep. No one else seemed to see the pressure she felt building around her. She'd tried to explain it to Darius, but he'd advised her to not worry about things she couldn't control.

She might not be able to control anything, but she could control herself, and she was determined to be ready for the coming storm. It would be up to the gods if they survived, but she would do everything she could to protect those around her. She would heal and fight as long as there was breathe within her chest. With her bondmates at her side, how could she lose?

CHAPTER 17

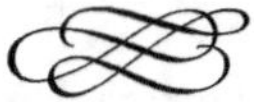

The hawk master arranged for her to meet with his friend who sold exotic birds. Everyone doubted she would bond again, but Darius was insistent that she at least try. The day before she and Rune were to go to Master Ion's friend's store, she sat down with Rune to discuss his behavior in the store.

The three bondmates had decided that Rune should be the one to accompany her into the store while Argent waited outside. Rune could hide in her coat if the birds got spooked by a cat, while Argent might simply be too large to get through the shop without knocking anything over and scaring the birds. Beryl had given Rune a stern lecture on his behavior while in the store. The last thing they needed to do was to antagonize the shopkeeper, who was also a friend of Master Ion.

The store was on the east side of town in a wide, white-washed stone building with green shutters. An enormous sign in red letters over the door proclaimed the place to be Augustus' Exotic Birds. Gesturing to the window, the mage opened the door, while Argent settled himself where he could see inside.

Beryl stopped just inside the door. Cages lined every wall as far as she could see, filling the shop with half-seen movement and sounds.

Cages sat on stands or hung from the ceiling. She was just stepping up to a cage to examine the large red and green bird inside when the shop owner emerged from a back room carrying a large crested white bird.

"Oh, hello," he called. "Feel free to look around. I just have to return Hans here to his cage." Coming back a moment later, he stopped in front of her, wiping his large hands on a towel. "Now, how can I help you?"

"I'm Master Fremont's apprentice, I was working with Master Ion, the hawk master for the King, and he recommended that I come and see your birds."

"Ah, yes. He told me you might be coming. Come, come, please have a look around. You are the young mage correct?"

"Yes, I am"

"I have the birds of prey in here, and the others in the next room."

"Sir, I was told I might not bond with a bird of prey; none of the hawks would take to me."

"Bah, there are more birds than Hawks. Once the bonding starts, the animals get smarter and act less and less like regular birds. Had a chap I know bond to a falcon. Never thought I would see a falcon begging to be petted and fawning over a boy like it was its chick."

The man was broad chested and muscular. With a deep booming laugh, his blond hair and beard marked him as a northerner. Following him through the shop, she was hard pressed not to gape. Birds of every size and color lined the walls or sat on stands fanning their wings. There was a constant cacophony of tweets and calls echoing off the walls.

Beryl sent a steadying wave of calm at Rune as he watched the birds, murmuring deep in his throat. With Rune riding her shoulder, they began to examine the various birds. After examining both drab and bright birds, she worked her way to the back of the shop.

She found the water birds just past a row of small birds that were hopping and bouncing around their cage, flashing turquoise wings, like sparrows who had fallen into a painter's pallet, Ducks and other birds swam and dived in a shallow pond, which was blocked from the rest of the store with fine netting. Her magic fluttered in her chest, pulling her toward the small pool.

* * *

"I SEE you have found my pool. What do you think? Nothing like it anywhere else in the country," he said with clear pride. "The water birds do better when they can get wet and bathe. Keeps them and their feathers happy."

"Why is that one-off by itself?" she asked, pointing to a grey bird that almost seemed to be trying to blend in with the wall.

"Can you see the chain attached to its foot? That is a Shiro. They are like the eagles of the sea. They hunt fish and small birds or animals. This one was injured and has healed up nicely, but isn't taking to the indoors well. Savage things they are-- I've the scars to prove it." The man frowned, seeing the young woman eying the fierce bird. Taking her elbow, he drew her away from the enclosure.

"Perhaps you would like to take a look at the parrots over here." Beryl glanced back at the regal looking bird, yet obediently let the store owner guide her away.

Rune had no such problem. Jumping from her shoulder he raced to the netting, ducking under a loose edge. The water birds immediately burst into the air trying to escape the cat in their midst. Rune ignored the chaos he was causing and went straight to the Shiro, sitting before it. The two engaged in a staring contest, while Beryl and the owner were trying to get to him before he was injured or the birds died of fright.

Seeming satisfied with whatever had been exchanged between the bird and cat, Rune turned and jumped the pond into Beryl's waiting arms. Cuddling him close she scolded him for scaring her. The owner quickly put the netting back. However, the Shiro hopped to the end of its chain and shrieked, rustling its wings. She looked up to watch the bird, feeling her magic flickering in her chest like a flame.

"Sir, I need to see the Shiro."

"Miss, that thing is wild, she will tear you apart. I can't let you!" he snapped, refastening the netting. Turning to him, Beryl glared.

"Yes, you can and you will. That is a bondmate of mine, and I intend to buy her." She felt the Shiro's approval; the bird's mind was like standing in a forest fire of rage and power. There was no middle ground with this creature; you were either friend or enemy, and enemies were meant to be destroyed.

It took some more arguing, but eventually the owner allowed her to go to the back entrance of the tank and collect the Shiro. Rune gave up his perch so that she could carry the bird on a falconer glove which the store owner had given her. The bird was the size of a small hawk or owl, yet had a wicked looking black beak and claws. Turning its head, it watched her every move with unblinking blue eyes. Beryl left after paying the store owner, who angrily shooed them out, while Rune and Argent marched beside her. She balanced her new bondmate on one shoulder when her arm began to ache.

She went straight to Master Ion to see what she would need to take care of this new member of her family. He apologized for his friend when she told him what happened, but said he was very sensitive about his birds. He would have to spend the next few days getting them calmed down and tending them extra because of the stress Rune put them through. Master Ion assigned Salendra to assist her in learning how to care for the bird and how to train it. For now, they would try to teach it like it was a hawk and see how it went.

Master Darius excused her from class for the rest of the week, so that she could learn what she needed and to bond with the volatile bird. She couldn't have it attacking people.

Beryl sat watching her new bondmate inspect the perch she'd been given. She set it up on her desk, which she moved in front of the window so that the bird could come and go as needed. She left the window open for now, but she would need to figure out something different soon. Perhaps she could craft a spell that would open and close the window when the bird touched a rune. She would have to see. The grey bird finished its inspection of the perch and desk, turning its eyes back to its new bondmate.

Beryl watched the bird, feeling its mind ruffling through hers like a swirling breeze. The bird's coloration was perfect for hiding; it blended into the stone wall of the castle, making it hard to see in the shadows. When it flew it was hard to spot from the ground, blending into the pale blue of the sky or hovering on a thermal till you thought it was a cloud. The Shiro was fiercely protective of anything it considered its own, from its territory to its chicks. Shiro were known to attack mountain lions or bears that came too close to their nests.

The bird gave a soft creeing cry as she watched it. The mage leaned forward and rested her chin on her hands as she watched the bird. Reaching out along the bond she tried to send the bird a thought, asking if it needed anything.

A kaleidoscope of images swirled and broke into shards before the girl's grey green eyes; she was struggling to make sense of the barrage when it suddenly ended. Looking back up at the bird she picked a single image, that of the sea in a storm, lashing against the black rocks of the northern coast. Concentrating on that scene she sent it back to the bird.

Rune jumped up on to the desk and settled down, watching the two of them. The mage felt Rune send all of the bond members an image of the bird and girl sitting there. The Shiro hissed at the cat, causing Argent to give a low whine. Beryl got up and sat on the floor next to him for a moment stroking his head.

Once he gave her a long-suffering look and a few bangs of his tail, she went back to her chair at the desk, Argent followed her and settled down where he could rest his massive muzzle on the edge of the desk. The Shiro shifted on its perch eying the large dog. The dog sent images and feelings of hunting and being outside with the mage, of going on messenger runs with Sparrow or Flox, and of them taking walks out in the woods. The Shiro responded with images of the sea.

Beryl frowned, thinking. She could feel the others following her mind, trailing along as she thought this out. Her cousins lived in a fishing village on the coast to the north. She had never been there herself, but she had heard stories of the pounding waves, tides, boats, and fishing whenever they had come to visit when she was a child.

She felt the yearning for the sea coming from the bird. Frowning, she looked at the others.

There was only one place for mages to apprentice--here at the capital. She couldn't leave the capital except for short trips once or twice a year, until she finished her fifth year, passed her test, and was deemed to be a full mage. That would be in another year or two.

Once that happened, she had to decide what she wanted to do as a mage. She would probably apprentice herself to another mage to learn her career craft. She didn't know where she would end up until then. She could be sent anywhere in the country and as a King's mage, and she would have to obey. Even if she bought a home on the coast, there was no guarantee that she would be able to live and work there. The Shiro gave a mournful cry at this.

Beryl reached out a hand and ran her fingertips along the back of the bird's neck with a feather light caress. She sent a picture of the Shiro flying above the water while Rune, Argent, and she walked the cliffs. She would find a way for the Shiro to be near the sea, even if she had to become a weather mage to do so.

The Shiro leaned into the light caress as they shared the vision of the cliffs and sea. This seemed to decide for the Shiro, and it hopped off the perch and approached the dog, inspecting him as she had Rune while in the shop. Once satisfied she ran her beak through the hair along the top of the dog's head before turning to the mage that had brought these three animals together.

"How am I to carry you? You can't fly through the castle, and I don't know if I can keep letting you ride on my shoulder if I'm to have any clothes left." She eyed the shredded cloth of her cloak and the scratches the bird had inflicted on her shoulder as they had walked from the store back to the castle.

"I need a glove like a falconry glove, but one that covers my shoulder. That might work."

She sent an image of what she was thinking to the others. The Shiro wasn't happy with being carried everywhere; it wanted to fly. The mage responded with images of the bird trying to fly through tight hallways and twists and turns of the stairs. The bird ruffled its feathers in indignation. It could fly through that.

Beryl sent images of the Shiro flying through the halls with people cowering out-of-the-way. The bird gave a shake of its head, snapping its beak. That was where people should be when dealing with it.

The mage sent her images of Darius reprimanding her and threatening to cage the bird. The Shiro shrieked at this. Sending out waves of calm, she assured the bird and her other bondmates that she would never let anyone cage them. She might not be able to stop them from trying or casting her out of the castle if the animals did not behave, however.

"You can still fly and go where you wish. I only ask that you return to me. That's all I ask of any of you," she said fondly while looking at her three bondmates.

"We do need to decide on a name for you. What do you call yourself?"

The bird sent images of a massive storm that covered the skies with clouds so dark it seemed night, winds that howled and shrieked swirling the clouds and sea in a deadly dance. The girl frowned, thinking back to the stories her cousins had told about the many dangers of the sea and the killer storms that would hurl ships to their deaths.

"I think that is the Kuro, the stalking storm that will sweep in on a clear day and break ships in half or pick the small boats up and fling them on to shore. Can we call you Kuro?"

The bird considered this before sending out agreement along the bond.

"Very well Kuro, do you think if I padded my arm and shoulder with leather you could ride there to travel in the castle? I would like to take you to the library so that Brennan can meet you, and so we can look up your kind so I know how to take care of you." The bird sent a shaft of rage at this. No one cared for it; it cared for its self.

"I mean that if you get injured we will know how to treat you. What food we can offer you that will not make you sick, and how to care for you if you do get sick?" The bird puzzled over this but agreed warily. Going to her work tables, the mage pulled out some scraps of leather and a needle and thread. Concentrating on what she wished the product to look like and how she wanted it to work, she drew her magic up and into her hands.

Sometime later she came to herself as she was making the final stitches. She smiled, looking at what she had made. The falconer glove was attached to a series of strips of leather that were reinforced with runes and cotton padding, protecting her shoulder and giving the bird something to hold on to.

Simple buckled straps held the leather to her arm in three places, and a belt-like strap went across her back and under her other arm before attaching back to the other side of the padding at her shoulder. She frowned at the glove for a moment, before she realized that the fingertips of the glove had been removed to allow her to handle things. Grinning, she tried it on. She could fix it so that she could use this as an arm guard for her archery as well. It felt uncomfortable and strange, but she would get used to it.

Digging through her pack she found the travel jerky that she had carried on her way to the castle. Placing some in a pouch, she tucked it into her belt and offered her hand to the bird. Kuro sprang from her perch and gracefully glided to the girl's fist. Settling the bird on her shoulder, Beryl smiled. She offered the bird a small strip of meat to nibble while the four of them made their way to the library.

* * *

IN THE WEEK since she had bonded with the Shiro, Beryl was learning how the bond worked. She'd been afraid that the bird would not be able to fly very far before the bond forced it to return, but they'd discovered that while the bond would only work to a certain distance, Kuro could fly farther than that, reconnecting with the mind of her bondmates once she was in range.

They also discovered that they could see through each other's eyes for a time, feeling like they were in the body of their bondmate as they flew or ran along a field. Kuro was ecstatic that she could fly to the sea if she wished. However, Darius reminded her that if they were apart for too long a time, they would start feeling the pain of the separated bond and be forced to find each other.

The bondmates decided to try and wait till the end of the year after the fifth year's testing for that year. All apprentices were allowed to take a month off before lessons began in the spring, and the mage was determined to make her way to the coast for a few weeks. She could try to track down her cousins in Arbor while she was traveling, but primarily she needed to go for the sake of the bird.

There were many areas in which a mage could specialize. Warding and protections were just small components that most mages could do to some degree. Mages tended to lean toward one element or another.

Darius, who was good at working with glass, was also skilled with fire spells. He had learned how to craft glass sculptures, goblets, and bowls before he had become involved in the Mage's Council and advising the king. Other mages who were skilled in fire often worked in areas prone to forest fires or learned to work with molten metals. Others had an affinity to earth and worked at farms or growing rare herbs in areas they would not normally grow. Earth oriented mages were often called by the crown to go to areas of famine or drought to help get the area's crops revived and growing.

Mages that were skilled at manipulating air or wind became weather mages. They lived on the coast and worked to tame and control the severe storms that hit the coast. Mages who were skilled in working with stone often apprenticed to stone masons or builders and learned to ward homes or to sculpt in stone. The one thing that every mage must do regardless of their skill was answer the call to war if the King commanded it. All mages were taught the basic shielding and warding spells that were used to protect areas under attack.

In ancient times, there were mages who only learned spells of attack and defense against attack, but those spells had been outlawed along with most of the other spells that came from the dark period of history when mages attacked other mages and wars raged for tens of years at a time, decimating the country side.

Mages cast spells to warp themselves into monsters so that they could attack the enemy, only to turn and attack their own people once the enemy was exhausted. These War Mages had all but destroyed the known world before it was decided that they must be destroyed, and the spells and books that taught war magic locked away, never to be used again. In current times, the main purpose of a mage was to serve his or her country in a way that protected or increased the production of that country.

There was no magic used on the battle field, except for shields around the areas that were close to villages or towns to prevent stray shots or arrows from hurting innocents. Most fights were now decided on the tournament field with leaders having their soldiers fighting one another in combat or by jousting for their leaders.

Those that won the yearly tournaments that were held in every major town came to the capital at the end of the year to compete against the best of the king's army. Those that won or showed themselves worthy were often offered positions in the king's army or even his personal guard.

SALENDRA AND BERYL had begun trying to train Kuro as a regular hawk, but so far the only thing that the bird would tolerate was lure training, and that was only because the mage had told her that it would make her an even better hunter. Right now, the bird spent its days hunting or flying around outside while the mage was in lessons or inside.

Kuro only came in to roost for the night or to accept a ride with Beryl to the library, so that Brennan could coo over it and feed it strips of dried meat. The librarian mage was completely smitten with the bird and was talking of trying to bond with a bird herself, perhaps an owl.

In lure training, the bird flew above the trainer, who twirled a ball of fur or piece of meat on the end of a thin rope or string. The bird had to dive on command and try to catch the lure that was twirling around the trainer. If they caught it they got a reward of meat.

They had also begun hunting rabbits, while Beryl and Rune watching from a distance, while Argent flushed a rabbit or grouse and Kuro tried to swoop down and catch it. If the bird missed, Argent sometimes would catch the animal and kill it, allowing the mage to divvy out the meat between the three animals.

The strangest thing about adding Kuro to the bond was the sudden addition of the four bondmates sharing each other's dreams. It didn't happen every night, but when one of the bondmates was having a strong dream, the others would be sucked into it and dream it alongside the others. Most of the dreams were harmless: flying with Kuro, running through the woods chasing rabbits with Argent, stalking the castle hallways with Rune. They could watch and even change things to a small extent, but normally they just let the dream run its course; unless it was a nightmare.

The night that the three animals were pulled into a dream of the attack that Beryl had suffered when she was a child was different. She'd been lost in the dream, until she heard barking. Looking to one side she could see her bondmates waiting. Standing over her, the man laughed pulled out his knife and taunted her to scream.

As the knife cut into her she screamed. Somehow, this released her bondmates, and they had attacked the man who was harming their bondmate, tearing into him until he disappeared into mist and smoke. When she woke, sweat cooling on her skin and chest heaving for breath, the others were pressed tight against her. The heavy weight of Argent covered her legs. Rune draped across one shoulder while Kuro nested on the pillow next to her head.

CHAPTER 18

*H*er metal-working was slowly progressing. Beryl could craft basic jewelry, and as promised, her first nice piece made with a ward stone was given to Brennan. She was slowly learning to craft things other than necklaces and was always keeping an eye out for something to try. She was surprised when Durn asked if she had thought of learning to craft weapons beyond the training daggers she had made. He thought with her skill in runes she could spell a dagger to be ever sharp or help to improve its balance. He would work on getting her a teacher.

Her weapons' training was really progressing. She could only spend one or two days a week training, so she added the basic forms and stances to her morning stretches. She couldn't shake the sense that she was preparing for battle and pushed herself all the harder, so she would be ready when the danger showed itself.

Beryl sat on the stone wall surrounding one pasture, rubbing Flox's long nose and scratching along the bottom of his jaw. Argent and Rune were playing a game of hunt and pounce, the large dog delicately bounding around the cat making happy wuffles as he pranced back-and-forth chasing after the cat before letting the cat pounce on him and streak away to be hunted by the dog, only to pounce at him again once he got close enough. Kuro soared high above, sending glimpses of things she thought interesting down the bond.

Kuro was slowly learning how to identify things on the ground from a bird's-eye view. The perspective was so strange that it was hard to say what was being seen. By focusing on something, and sending those images, they were slowly learning how to spot roads, men, animals, and other objects from high in the sky.

Flox wandered to a nearby tree in the pasture to doze, allowing Mage to get back to her work. Turning the band in her hand, she continued incising runes into the leather. Every night this week images of her bondmates had haunted her, both hurt or injured in an attack.

She would bolt out of sleep each night just as she was pushing her body in between that of her bondmates as the final blow fell. She started crafting the collars after the second nightmare. Each would be powered by the magic stored in one of the three stones they had given her. They would heal minor injuries, shield the animal from arrows or thrown objects, and act to locate them should they get lost or separated. All her visions said pain and terror were coming. Idyllic days like these gave her the determination to prepare. She would make sure they survived the coming firestorm.

Classes were still awkward with her three bondmates attending. Kuro rarely came, preferring to fly or roost outside the castle. As the year had progressed, more of the other apprentices had gained familiars, much to the chagrin of Marietta, who still had not bonded to anything. She had gotten particularly nasty to the group of mages that she ate dinner with.

Tor had bonded to a small terrier, and Rose had bonded to a robin, which she called Sol. The bird stayed in constant motion, chirping at Rose or hopping around the table. Tor's dog was called Bastian. The small, white and black dog was a glutton and would sit under the table waiting for the smallest crumb to fall. He could be found at any other time in Tor's lap, his black beady eyes surveying the room.

Dogs that went to war with their masters often wore a leather harness, sometimes made with metal or bone spiked collars. Other times they were made with shark skin to prevent people from grabbing them. She decided she needed one for Argent for when they were out traveling. He already had a leather breast-plate and harness for when he went hunting.

She had taken the collar to a local leather worker in town and explained what she wanted. It would mean spending the last of her gems and coins she saved from when she lived with Jared and all the coin she saved from her allowance with Darius but lately she hadn't been able to get the crushing feeling of something about to go wrong to go away. The tightness hadn't eased at all until she went to the leather worker. So, she had ordered the harness and ignored the cost. If it kept her bondmate safe then it was worth it.

"Durn, do you know where I can get a set of daggers?" she asked hesitantly. If he refused to help, she would go to Master James.

"Aren't you soon to make your own? I thought your Master was arranging lessons?" he asked, eying the target she had been using.

"He is, but it will be months before I have a set worth using," she said, beginning to practice under his watchful eye.

"And you can't wait, I take it?"

"Something's coming, Durn. I need to be ready."

"And you need a set of daggers to do so?"

"I think so." He watched her for a long moment before turning back to examine her target.

"Are you certain that you cannot wait?" he asked finally, gesturing for her to stop.

"Yes."

"Then I have a set you may borrow until yours are ready. Clean up and come inside."

He went into a back room and returned with a set of daggers, arm guards, and a pair or fingerless gloves. He refused her money, saying to consider it a loan until she could afford to buy another set. They went to the back and practiced throwing the daggers till it was too dark to see the targets clearly, no other words needing to be spoken.

Kuro was fond of the old man merely saying that he was steady, however she enjoyed watching the sparring matches between her bondmate and Durn's other students. After one such match, Durn had helped her up, while clapping her on the back. "I see you finally learned to channel some of that rage. Good, now do it again."

Later she realized what he meant. She was throwing herself into these fights, pouring her frustrations and angers of the week into them. In the process, she was finally learning how to fight hard enough to win a bout, which made the other boys fight all the harder against her. They didn't like being shown up by a girl.

A small part of her had always held back, knowing that this was just a practice fight. However, since her bonding with Shiro, she was able to start fighting like it was to save her and her bondmate's lives. She did not hold back for fear of hurting her sparring partners, only holding back the moves and blows that she knew could seriously injure a person or break bones.

The stable boys stared at Argent's new harness when Beryl went to collect Flox for her message run. The happy bouncing monster that they normally saw had been transformed into a true monster; one that could take off a hand without moving his head. The harness ran thick leather straps along his chest and belly holding the flexible leather and shark skin that covered the dog's back.

She was wearing her leather great-coat with Rune riding in one pocket, along with the leather arm brace that she used with Kuro. Kuro was flying high above the stable watching the road ahead for dangers. All of the bondmates were worried, the tightness that Beryl had been feeling in her chest had gotten worse when she was handed this package. She was delivering it to a remote estate that sat in an isolated part of the region. The nearest home to the estate was several miles down the road, and the estate itself was several miles off of the main road through a forest.

The ride was normal, except for the stares they received. Beryl had her bow and quiver hooked to the saddle but doubted she would be able to do much with it if anything happened. She was counting on the short sword and throwing daggers she had strapped to her waist and wrists if she needed a distance weapon.

They made it to the manor without any problems and delivered the message packet, receiving a small packet of meat for her bondmates from the cook. They set out on the road to return to the castle, eyes wary. They were nearing the main road when it happened. Kuro screamed from above, Beryl threw herself forward into a crouch on Flox slamming her heels in to his sides with a shout.

An arrow hummed through the space she had just been in. She hung on as best she could as the horse bolted down the path. Argent lunged off the road, dodging between the trees. Rune dug his claws into Beryl's shoulder and tried to stay on as the horse galloped down the rain soaked road, most of his body still hidden in her hood.

Kuro sent the images of two men on horseback pushing their horses to catch up to them, while another man rose from the bushes holding a crossbow. Flox was pounding down the path, but he was no match for the lighter horses behind him. They needed to go faster if they were going to get away!

Argent sprang from the bushes, slamming into the first horse. The horse reared and staggered as its rider was dragged to the ground with a scream. The horse slid and slipped in the mud, the rider abandoning his mount to stagger to his feet, drawing his sword. The rider behind them was unable to stop in time and slammed into the ground when his horse tripped.

Beryl wheeled Flox and brought him back to the downed men. The one Argent had downed lay moaning, holding his leg, while the other was getting up, sword sliding from its sheath. Dismounting, leaving Rune on the saddle, Beryl pulled her long knife and a dagger. Argent had faded back into the brush, waiting on an opening where he could assist his bondmates.

The sudden shriek of Kuro had Beryl spinning to throw her dagger before her mind had registered the action. The man with a crossbow took the blade to the throat, collapsing with a horrible gurgle, choking and gasping as he died. She had no time to react to his death. Turning, she barely blocked a blow from the sword wielder with her short sword. The man was strong; her arm ached from the blow. Half falling, she feinted with her sword, pulling another throwing dagger with her free hand.

Beryl fought to breathe through the fear and burn of the fight that was surging through her veins. She couldn't stop the thought that this was a fight she could not win, but she couldn't leave her bondmates to carry on alone. Her breath came in gasps as she forced her body to move. She threw everything she had into each strike, each parry, she would not leave them alone!

The gems in her belt and arm cuffs flared to life. The man, fight, and dagger in her hand became distant and strange. Her attacker fell back, crawling away from her in the leaf litter and mud. Time seemed to slow as the link between the bondmates widened into a sudden river of information flowing between them, until they were no longer separate. They were four bodies controlled by one mind and heart.

The man recovered and lashed out with a bellow. She sent the incoming blow skittering away with a flick of the wrist and Argent loomed at the man, crowding his left side. She watched the fight from four sets of eyes; Kuro from above, Rune from behind, Argent from the side, and facing her attacker with her own. Four sets of lungs breathed as one. The man raced away through the woods shouting about demons.

Just as suddenly as it happened the joining shattered. With a cry Beryl collapsed, dropping her blade. Her body felt ravaged and broken, her mind a mass of broken glass shifting and splintering with every heartbeat, every breath. The bondmates lay huddled together in the middle of the path, Kuro gliding to a stop a few feet away and awkwardly hopping to her bondmates.

Sometime later, Beryl moaned and tried to stand, only to collapse back to the ground, her head pounding in time with her racing heart. Argent whimpered and leaned against her, propping up her back. Reaching out she pulled Kuro and Rune toward her, letting the Shiro cling to her shoulder while Rune went in the pocket of her coat. Her hands shook as she took up her blade. It took her three tries to sheath it.

One of her attackers gave a moan a few feet away. Staggering, she managed to get to Flox and slowly turn the horse toward the main road. She walked with Argent the next few miles back into the edge of town. Beryl begged a stall from the first Inn they found, and once Flox was seen, collapsed into the hay alongside her bondmates.

They did not wake till noon the next day, and then it was because a concerned innkeeper was worried that a King's messenger was going to die in his stable. She waved away his concern and paid for the use of the stall. She saddled her horse and headed for the castle. She needed to tell Darius and Sir Derrick, who oversaw the messengers, what had happened.

Argent was still in his mud-stained harness, and she needed to clean all the tack. She was exhausted, but the horrible headache was gone. Moving like a broken marionette, she made it to the castle stable and got Flox settled. Dodging the stable boys' questions, she headed to the interrogation she was sure would happen.

* * *

SHE FOUND Darius in his rooms. He took one look at her before bundling her and Rune into a chair near the fire with a cup of sweet tea and a blanket across her lap. Kuro sat atop the high back of a chair, head tucked under a wing, while Argent was sprawled next to the hearth, his head resting atop one of Beryl's feet.

"It is troubling that you were attacked at all. Messengers are held outside of most conflicts. This appears to be simply men attacking a lone traveler, hoping for some quick wealth."

She watched Darius pace, idly stroking Rune's back. She was not sure of Darius' conclusions. She was attacked while on the estates' main road, not the road to town. The attackers would have had to see her head down the side road and follow her to set an ambush. Or, perhaps they had been alerted by someone at the estate while she was held up in the kitchens.

"Now, tell me again about the bond and how the gems glowed."

Beryl tried to respond with as much detail as she could, but the ride in had sapped the small amount of energy she had gained since the attack. Darius paced back and forth across his study. He whirled back to ask another question only to find the girl and her bondmates asleep. With a small snort, he stopped. With a wave of one hand he banked the fire and dimmed the lights before heading to speak to the King. As soon as they thought they understood what was going on with this young Mage, she would shatter their plans all over again.

Beryl woke to a dark study and no sign of Darius. Waking her grumpy bondmates, she picked up Kuro and Rune, hobbling down the hall to her own room and a hot soak. Coming out of the bathroom in a cloud of steam, she was surprised to see her coat and weapons harness hanging alongside Argent's harness, all oiled and cleaned. With a shrug, she sent a mental thank you to whatever stable hand had done the deed, as she wheedled Argent into the bath for a scrub.

An hour later they were as dry as they would get. After leading her menagerie out for a quick bathroom run, they trooped to the kitchens for a late lunch. The staff was as full of gossip and scandal as always, but strangely there was nothing about the attack. They just thought she had been on a rough message run.

Day to day life continued at the castle as if nothing had happened, but Beryl was not willing to leave it alone. Someone had tried to harm her bondmates. Having a bondmate was the best thing to ever happen to her. They were a constant source of comfort and support; she couldn't lose that.

The constant mental presence of her bondmates had taken some getting used to. As time passed and they grew closer, so did the bond shared between them. Each issue was analyzed by four minds, each voicing possible solutions. The fact that the animals were still coming to slowly understand human motivations led to some truly hilarious suggestions at times.

After the night she overhearing Darius and the King talking, she kept an eye out for similar meetings. She could not follow Darius in the castle, but Kuro could when he left. One afternoon a week he went to different pubs throughout the city. He met and spoke with different people at each pub in no visible pattern.

On market day, he wandered the vendors buying items at random. Why would a male Master Mage need lace? Or a pound of salt? It was maddening. She had given up on figuring out Darius and his work for the King for now and was trying to just find out what she could.

The message she had delivered was from a minor noble who lived in the city to the Baron de Marco, a man with his wealth mainly in land and estates, with very little hard coin. He was the son of a soldier who had won several land grants and eventually been given the title of Baron as a reward for service to the crown. She hadn't been able to find out why the title was given as it did not appear to be common knowledge. Even the gossips did not know, but the rumor was that he had saved the previous King or Queen's life.

She didn't know what the content of the letter had even been. There were no rumors at all about the noble who had sent the note. He was the bastard son of a Duke, who had been given a small estate to manage, presumably to ensure he kept out of the Duke's affairs. He lived a quiet life and did not hold the constant parties and dinners that most nobility deemed necessary. In truth, he was rarely seen off of his lands.

* * *

SEVERAL DAYS AFTER THE ATTACK, Beryl was summoned to see the Queen. She had been visiting the Queen once or twice a week since their initial introduction. Rune went at least once a day to check on the pregnant woman himself. They received the summons as soon as she dismounted from another short message run.

"The Queen has asked for your presence in her chambers as soon as you arrived."

"Do I have time to change or get cleaned up?" she asked, handing Flox off to one of the waiting stable hands.

"I was told immediately," the boy said, before turning and leaving.

Beryl examined her muddied cloak and pants in despair. Argent was covered in water and mud from the road. With a sigh, she grabbed a stiff brush and worked on getting most of the mud off her cloak and boots before brushing Argent and toweling him down as best she could. She would just have to hope the Queen was forgiving.

As she worked, she conversed with her bondmates, seeing who wanted to attend. Argent and Rune were content to go; neither was willing to leave their bondmate so soon after an attack. Kuro agreed, even though she disliked being walled in within the castle. She took her place on her bondmate's shoulder, where her sharp eyes would see any danger long before it happened. Beryl sighed. It seemed they would be smothering her with their dedication for a while longer.

Deciding they were as clean as they were going to get, she let Rune climb into her hood where it hung against her shoulders. Giving Argent and Kuro a stroke, she made her way to the Queen's chambers. The royal physician waited with her next to the bed, where the Queen sat against a mound of pillows on the headboard. The physician's eyes widened as she was announced and entered. Rune immediately jumped down and then up onto the bed next to the Queen.

"My Queen, I must protest! Such filth should not be near you in your condition."

"Physician Davies," the Queen drawled in a voice that radiated command, her eyes hard. "You are here to make sure that this conversation does not tax my condition and nothing else. I may be pregnant, but that does not change my intelligence or station. Please keep your comments to yourself," the Queen snapped stroking Rune. "A Mage's bondmate is not filth."

"I apologize, my Queen," he said with a stiff bow. "I meant no insult, Mistress...Mage."

"If I may my Queen, we'd just returned from a message run when I received your request. I was told to come immediately, or I would have cleaned up more. I can assure you, Rune is quite clean. Argent and I, however, took the brunt of most of the rain and mud on the ride, I'm afraid. If you wish, we can return after we have cleaned up."

"Nonsense, Mage, you're here already," the Queen said with a smile and a much warmer tone. "I am sorry if the message was not delivered correctly. I simply wanted to make sure you were alright. I heard of your ambush two days ago and wanted to make sure for myself that you were not injured." Beryl blushed slightly and advanced to stand beside the bed at the Queen's gesture.

"We're fine, my Queen. Argent was scratched up a bit, and we were all a bit bruised, but it caused no lasting harm." The Queen took her hand, turning it so she could see the yellow bruise that adorned her forearm; a small cut marred one cheek as did another darker bruise.

"Are you sure you would like to remain a messenger? I have spoken with the King, and we would be willing to forgive the remainder of your debt if you are no longer comfortable riding the messenger circuit."

"Oh, no my lady, I couldn't let you do that. I intend to pay back the price of Argent to the King and yourself, my Queen. I enjoy taking messages to people. It lets me get out of the castle and see the area. I'm not used to staying in one place for so long after traveling with my Uncle for so many years."

"If you are sure, Mage, I will inform the King of your decision."

"Thank you, my Queen."

She spoke with the Queen for a few more moments before the physician reminded the Queen stiffly that she was supposed to be resting. Gathering her bondmates, Beryl restrained a chuckle as she heard the Queen begin what was surely a harsh dressing down of the Royal Physician.

SHE STOOD by a window breathing in the breeze that was whipping her hair back from her face. Argent rested his massive head against the window sill, sending her the scent of rain on the breeze. A dark band of black clouds was marching its way closer to the castle.

The tangy scent of lightning was shared among the bondmates, causing Kuro to scream her joy at the coming storm. The sea-bird loved the raging winds and sheets of rain that came with a fierce storm. Riding a thermal, she soared high above the castle. As the rain began to fall, she shared her exaltation with her bondmates; they flew above the ground, dodging walls of rain and wind as one.

The storm heralded the official start of spring. At the end of the month of Bear, on the last week of Rabbit, the fifth-years and those being considered and trained for the King's personal guard would go through the testing. On the first day of the new year, the tested warriors and mages would stand before the King and proclaim their loyalty to him and their country.

The month was moving quickly; the testing for the fifth-years was only a week away. They would start their practical tests before the Council of Mages tomorrow. Once a Mage passed his or her fifth-year exams they were declared a Kings Mage.

Everything the Mage's did was at the whim of the monarchy. They could be ordered to move, change professions, even change names and identities with a word from their ruler. Mages were largely outside of the law. They could not be held to judgments or accusations that were not from the Mages Council or decreed by the King.

While the Mages Council dealt with the day to day issues that arose, the King had final say in any and all judgments they made. He did not often use this power, and in the last two generations of peace many Mages had come to forget how all-encompassing their vows were. A Mage's duty was to the crown. They were magically bound to this as their final step before being officially declared a full Mage. They were bound by their own magic to answer a King's command to service.

"Darius, how can apprentices die of the fifth-year testing? I thought it was just a test of your skills?" Beryl asked, pushing away the books Darius had given her to study.

"I see the fifth-years are already spreading rumors about the testing this winter," Darius said with a chuckle. "It is part of the tradition of the testing to withhold information about it from those who have not yet undergone it. I will say, however, the final test is not a test of skill. The apprentice is asked to step into a rune circle and activate it. It can only be deactivated by the apprentice. Those that are unable to deactivate the circle are those that die."

"You said it was not a test of skill. Isn't knowing how to deactivate the circle a show of skill?"

"It is not; it is a test of character and strength. If the mage is weak, then they will fail. That is all I or anyone here would be able to tell you."

Several of the students that Beryl knew were taking the test this winter. Mariette and Lucas were the two she was worried about. Lucas, a fifth-year who often ate lunch with Mage, was due to take his testing in a few weeks. He was skilled in memory and had perfect recall. He wanted to become one of the Mage Council's researchers or to work in the Magician's library here in the capital.

If the final test was one of character would the quiet, bookish boy pass? Would Mariette pass when she was such a mean-spirited girl? There was no way to truly know. Those taking the test would be isolated from the other apprentices while they were being tested. The testing would last a week, with the final day on the first of the new year being a ceremony where they would be bound into service for the King and Country. Those that passed would receive their placements after the start of the new year.

Many of the younger apprentices had left to return home for the week of the testing. Beryl watched from her perch in the stable loft as another carriage left. The memories of her parents had faded with the years, and at times it panicked her to think she might forget them entirely one day.

Kuro sent a wave of protectiveness along the bond which Argent and Rune echoed, lacing theirs with affection. She gave them a small smile and returned the emotions. She may have lost one family, but she gained another with bonds that went even deeper than blood.

The end of the year testing began tonight for the fifth-year mages. Beryl would not be allowed to even ask to take them until next year. She watched as many of her fellow classmates picked at their dinner before being escorted out of the room by their masters.

They would spend the night in mediation or prayer with their master. At dawn, the testing would begin, and it would last for three days. The rest of the castle would not find out who had achieved their mastery until the fourth day, when the successful Mages would be presented before the King and Mages Council in a grand ceremony.

In the end, all the mages tested that year passed; there would not be a day of mourning for those young mages that died this year. Mage was leaving at the end of the week for the month of holiday the apprentices were given.

CHAPTER 19

Spring was coming to Arden, and with it the month sabbatical that all apprentices were given to return home each year. As she had promised Kuro, I headed us to the Northern coast to stay with a friend of Darius', Valerian and her apprentice Ren, weather mages for that section of coastline.

Beryl rode Flox at a steady pace, while Argent trotted beside her. They made excellent time. Darius and Sir Derrick, who oversaw the king's messengers, had given her several letters and packages to drop off on her journey. As a result, she could use the relay stations and inns along the way to rest her horse and catch some sleep in a proper bed. Both she and her bondmates were ready for a bit of a rest from the day-to-day life in the castle.

The trip down was wonderful. They took their time. Everyone was fit and moving at a good pace after all the message runs they been making. Kuro strained to get there faster; each day closer to the coast made her jittery. All bondmates found her energy infectious and were soon hurrying just as much, waking earlier each day and staying on the road longer.

Kuro screamed her joy at the first sight of the ocean and sped her way to the sea, leaving her land bound bondmates to catch up as they could. They shared her joy as she dove to kiss the waves with her talons before spiraling back up to massive heights, using the wind coming off the cliffs.

The Shiro continued to wheel and dive as they made their way down the coastal road. By midday they had reached Blake's point, the compact harbor town where Valerian lived. They stopped for lunch at a small Inn by the waterside; the locals making hearty jokes over the mage and her companions.

"What need have she for a man with a beast like that?" one laughed, gesturing to Argent.

Beryl ignored them. The bondmates had heard it often enough during their message runs. They were used to the taunts and jabs from locals. King's messengers were adolescent men, not a young woman old enough to be married. And most weren't accompanied with a trio of animals.

It was assumed that she was a fallen woman, or they treated her as a bit touched in the head. At least Argent kept the taunts to harsh words by his presence. It took a lot of drink for even the most foolish to ignore the exposed teeth and deep threatening growls coming from his barrel chest. This inn was proving to be the exception; three drunken sailors had approached her already.

They packed the inn. Several merchant ships had docked, and their crews were competing to see who could consume the most ale. The barmaids were hard pressed to fill their mugs fast enough. They had already broken up two brawls had already, the inn's owner was a massive ex-sailor himself.

Beryl had snagged an out of the way table for Argent, Rune, and herself. The barmaid, Helen, had been nice enough to bring bowls of water and stew for the animals to share. They would have left quickly enough if a storm had not rolled in. Kuro was reveling in the erratic wind and sheets of rain, but even she was forced to land as the storm got worse, riding it out on the mast of a ship. For now, Beryl and her bondmates were stuck in the inn, along with everyone else as the wind and sea roared outside.

The door banged open, letting in a blast of rain and a water-drenched traveler. He fought the door closed before facing the room and pushing his hood back. He had a fine boned face and long, blond hair pulled back in a low tail. Working his way to the inn-keeper at the bar, he removed his cloak exposing a lute case. Clearly, he was a musician.

Once he was toweled off and seated by the fire with a hot mug of spiced tea, he opened his case. To a rousing cry of approval from the sailors he began his first song, a bawdy one about the ways a man tried to tempt a mermaid to come aboard with him.

Rune was fascinated by the music, watching intently as the minstrel's fingers flew across the strings of his instrument.

"Can you do that?" Rune asked his human bondmate. Mage laughed softly stroking the small cat's back.

"No, but I could learn, perhaps," she replied, watching as several men began staggering about, dancing she supposed. Rune continued to watch the musician.

"Can we talk to him?" he asked softly along the bond.

"Once he finishes, perhaps," Mage agreed. Argent banged his tail in agreement. Kuro was listening to the music as well, but preferred the howl of the storm to the man's voice.

As the evening wound down, the sailors slowly staggered to their beds. The minstrel began to play slow ballads and older songs, songs of the gods when they were alive and among men. When he finished his current song, he sent the mage a smile before beginning the ballad of Togin, who struck a deciding victory in the last mage war, sacrificing his life to destroy the enemy who had killed his fox bondmate, Kellrin.

As the last few sailors were shooed into the steady falling rain or up the stairs to the packed rooms of snoring boarders, the minstrel set his instrument back into its case. He happily accepted a wide bowl of stew and a mug of ale from the barmaid. Beryl brought her own mug of spiced tea with her to stand next to his table.

"Can we join you? I'm Beryl, and this is Rune and Argent."

"Please, have a seat. My name is Jacob," he said with a smile. "I was surprised to see a mage so far from the capital, especially one with bondmates. What are you doing sleeping amongst the commoners, fair Mage? With a word, you could have the finest room in this Inn." Beryl blushed softly and concentrated on stroking Argent's ears for a moment.

"I may be a mage, but I am also a King's Messenger. I don't spend my message runs dining in manor houses and sleeping on silk sheets. I was born a mage, but I see no point in lording that fact over anyone."

"You would be the first mage I have met that thought so," Jacob said wryly, as he took quick bites of his stew.

"I'm the daughter of a mage who married a poor merchant's daughter. We lived a simple life without the pomp and pressures of society. When my bondmates and I settle down, we want but a small home by the sea. Nothing more, Jacob." He watched her with a sudden, serious demeanor, as if this earlier jovial countenance had been nothing more than a mask used to settle the locals.

"Well said, friend mage. What did you wish to speak to me about, or did you merely come over to share ale with me?" he asked with a grin, signaling the barmaid for a refill.

"No," she said blushing. "Rune would like to know more about your instrument and what you do as a traveling minstrel." She wasn't used to dealing with men that flirted so openly. This minstrel changed masks and faces in the blink of an eye.

Jacob grinned wider at her blush. "Ah, Master Rune, do you wish your mage to become a minstrel? It is a hard life, sir cat, not one suited for many. It means traveling from town to town, never having a true home. For you must travel to hear the newest tales and songs, no matter the weather or if there's no one to sing for. You sing what your audience wants, sea chanteys for sailors, and ballads for the rest. It is rare that you truly get to sing what you want. I write my own music, but few ever hear it. On a good night, you might get free food and a seat by the fire, but on a bad one you get tossed into the rain bruised and broken. I've had my instruments and money stolen while I slept, and I've been forced to play at sword point. It's a rough life, but it does have its rewards."

"As for my instrument, I learned to play at my Grandfather's knee and broke my parents' hearts the day I started wandering. It's a life I love, and I wouldn't trade it for a calm life in a town for all the riches in the kingdom."

The talk drifted from his life and travels to the rumors about the war. More and more soldiers were being called to the Northern coast and borders. They had finished several mugs of ale, and the minstrel had pulled his lute back out, fingering slow patterns and songs that Beryl did not recognize.

"I've heard rumors that the northern coastal towns have been attacked. Bainbridge was set on fire last month. The Northern waters are not safe to travel. The ships are being boarded, and the crew members killed or put to ransom. The King of Orlean continues to deny that these are his ships. He says they are pirates or mercenaries. The coastal islands are being hit the hardest."

"What about the northern border? I have a friend, a soldier, who's stationed there, and he says the attacks are random."

"The problem is the land in the North has been ravaged in the last few mage wars. Nothing really grows there. It's a land of ice and rock. Those who live there hunt for their livelihood. They live a hard life with little hope of it ever getting better. A new war lord, called Roth of the red hand, has rallied the clans. He sends out raiding parties to harass the hunters and trappers who live on either side of the border. The men and able women are given the choice to work for his army or die where they stand. They have the chance of work and food if they agree; few turn him down."

"Now enough of this grim talk, what will it be? The ballad of Marvis the Great, Garrick the bold, Roger the cunning, or Anya, the Voluptuous?" he asked with a roguish grin.

"None of the above," she said with a mock groan. "What do you know about mages with multiple bondmates?" she asked curiously. Surely a minstrel would know a few stories at least.

"You're the first I have seen in my lifetime with more than one bondmate. Bondmates themselves are rather rare anyway. The stories about mages with two or more bondmates tend to be the larger than life kind. Rescuing entire kingdoms, making the deciding blow in a war, destroying entire kingdoms for that matter, take your pick. It's never something small. They seem to be destined for greatness in one way or another."

"Take the Mage Luthor for example. He bonded to a pair of twin fox cubs. He traveled disguised as an old peddler to spy on a warring nation. By chance, he was discovered in the same manor that a kidnapped princess was being held when he healed a maid who had been beaten almost to death. He healed the maid, freed the princess, and ended the war in one day. She then went on to marry our Prince Leon III, who had almost thirty years of peace. Luthor became the Royal Mage and dressed in silks for the rest of his life, or so the story goes."

"There are a few tales of bad mages with bondmates, but there are quite a few stories of those who failed and failed massively in their quests. Mage Roderick was one such fellow. His bondmates, a sparrow and a dog, were captured and tortured--the pain drove the Mage mad. The skies rained fire, and the earth swallowed the entire castle where he was being held, killing himself and everyone else in the area. Bad things tend to happen to those who mess with mages or their bondmates."

"Take your cat, Master Rune, for example. He doesn't act like a true cat. He is smarter than normal, smart as a human I would guess. Problem is that it shows. One glance at him, and people know that he's not a regular cat. Now the dog still acts like a dog; he could blend in if not for his size."

"What does he mean I'm not a normal cat? Am I strange" Rune asked plaintively, slipping across the table to sit at Mage's elbow.

"He's trying to keep us safe. If people can glance at you and know you for a mage's bondmate, then they know they can hurt you to hurt me. If you were able to play at being a non-bonded cat, then no one would think to use you. Don't worry, we can think on it later." She tried to reassure the small cat.

"But I am a mage's cat," Rune complained softly, jumping to his mage's shoulder and draping himself along the back of her neck.

"Yes, you are mine, as I am yours."

The mental conversation had taken only a moment, since sending across the bond was much faster than speaking. But it still was enough of a pause for the observant minstrel to notice.

"Were you two talking just then?" he asked softly, eyes sliding from her face to the cat on her shoulder.

"Yes, I'm sorry. He thought you were insulting him since he is a mage's cat," she offered with a small smile.

"Now, Master Rune, I mean no harm. It's just a bit of advice from one traveler to another. Sometimes you need to wear a mask to keep those you travel with safe, to keep yourself safe," he assured them with a grin.

It was late that night when they bid the minstrel goodnight and headed to their bed in the stables, the storm having finally spent itself. The next morning, after a quick bowl of porridge and some leftover stew for Rune and Argent, they were on their way. It was mid-morning when they approached the cliff side home of Valerian and her apprentice.

The home was stone, built into the side of a hill. A steady wind swept the garden that sat to one side; only the hardy herbs were able to stand the harsh nonstop wind coming off the cliffs. A pale blue windsock fluttered atop a high pole--wind mage colors.

* * *

BERYL LAY in bed watching the mist roll through the open window. Valerian had given them the loft bedroom while they were staying. Argent was managing the narrow stairs, but sounded like he was falling down them more than climbing. Kuro roosted on the foot board, cleaning her feathers.

The windows were always open at the cottage. She'd asked Valerian about it and was given a wry smile in response. "You can't stop the wind around a Weather Mage. It'll break windows and move boards to get in. It's not intentional, I can assure you. Elements that are strong in a Mage react around them. An Earth Mage will be surrounded by plants even in the most arid desert. A Water Mage will have springs bubble up near them, and a Weather Mage will always be in the path of breezes. But notice, have you been uncomfortable, too hot, too cold? No, and you won't be here."

Both Valerian and her apprentice sang and played several instruments. They introduced Beryl to a few; however, she seemed to only have ability for the wind instruments and pipes. She was given a small set of wooden hand pipes to practice with and told that later she could learn to use a mouth blown flute if she liked.

Controlling the wind was strange. You couldn't stop it or reverse the flow. You had to work with the wind. By pushing your magic into the air by voice or instrument, you could speed or slow the air currents. Weather mages that were fully trained could send messages or send their awareness out along the currents of air and view areas far inland or out to sea.

The nice thing about using windblown instruments was that they could be spelled with runes to enhance the spells cast with them. She was using a wooden hand pipe right now: two rows of hollow pipes that were blown from above; each tube produced one pitch. She wanted to try and make one out of metal so that she could add runes. She was still learning to spell and add runes to wood, but hers were still too weak or unstable when she placed them into piece of wood.

She tried to help out around the cottage by placing runes for strength and cleanliness on metal utensils and tools. Valerian's strengths were in air and earth, so most of the things she owned were made from wood. Darius used mainly metal and glass since he was proficient in fire and earth.

Beryl had yet to find a specialty. She was training in earth, air, and fire. She would start working in earth more when she returned from the coast. Being linked to Kuro gave her a small advantage in learning Weather Magic, since she was used to seeing through Kuro's eyes as she flew. Kuro was also able to follow her view of the winds and make suggestions on where they could be moved or sped up.

Storms couldn't be moved or directed. If rain was removed from one area to another, then the plants in the first would wither without the water they needed. She was learning how to slow the winds and to spread storms out so that they couldn't maintain the pounding rains and screaming winds. With so few wind mages of any real strength, not every storm could be changed.

Beryl was given the morning off to observe the ocean and the winds that came off of it. Rune, Argent, and Beryl were exploring the tidal pools, while Kuro soared farther out to sea. The booming of the surf on the cliffs farther up the beach kept a steady measure that vibrated Mage's bones as they drew closer. The wind was a constant presence, buffeting her face and teasing strands of hair out of her braid.

She watched Valerian and her apprentice weave their weather magic with ease. They sat on one of several stone benches that had been lined up along the bluff facing the sea in front of Valerian's home. The weather mages sat in a deep trance, while their minds and magic roamed the coast near them.

Beryl sighed before beginning the breathing exercises to enter her own trance. She could feel the magic being worked near her but could not see or manipulate the strands of wind as Valerian described them. She gave another sigh and stood up; she was too worked up to even get into a light trance. Argent wagged his tail at her, but continued his search along the cliffs hunting mice with Rune.

With another small sigh, she moved to a flat patch of ground and began going through her weapons exercises and stretches. She forced herself to go slow, making her breath match her movements, focusing on feeling the full extension or contraction of each muscle before moving on to the next move.

She lost track of time and her surroundings as she moved; she let her mind see only the current movement. It took a sudden blast of wind, which nearly knocked her over, before she realized that it was almost dark, and Valerian and Ren had already gone back to the house.

Argent gave a happy bark and bounced to his feet from where he and the other bondmates had been waiting for her. Beryl spoke her apologies for making them wait so long before collecting Rune and Kuro and heading toward the house.

"Ah, good. I was wondering if you were going to stay out there all night," Valerian said with a wry smile. Beryl murmured a soft apology while setting Kuro on his perch next to the fire, bowls of chopped meat and water already waiting for him and the other bondmates at their spots on the hearth.

"What exactly were the movements you were practicing, Mage?"

"Weapons exercises that I am learning from Durn, the previous Captain of the King's Guard."

"You were quite absorbed. Do you normally focus so entirely when practicing?"

"Not always, but I like to go through the exercises slowly like that at the end of the day. It's relaxing," she confessed with a small blush. "I do similar stretches each morning, but those are for the injuries I received as a child."

Valerian made a soft humming sound as she dished everyone a bowl of stew. After they had been eating in silence for a while, Valerian set her bowl aside, turning to Beryl.

"I have a rather unorthodox idea that I would like to try tomorrow if you are willing. I know your training in weather magic isn't progressing as you would like. Considering you have a bird bond-mate, I assumed it would come fairly naturally to you, So, I have been training you in the manner I was trained. "

Ren's gull bondmate, Twist, gave a raucous cry in the background, which brought a smile to her lips, "Yes, Twist, the same way I trained Ren and you. However, I think having your other land-bound bond-mates has complicated your training. If you are willing, in the morning we will begin again and try to include all your bondmates in the lesson."

"I'm willing to try," Beryl said, her bondmates echoing her accent with small sounds of their own.

"Good, then I suggest you go and get some rest, for tomorrow we start from scratch," she said with a laugh.

The next morning they were awakened early by Valerian and shown out to the benches yet again.

"I have two methods I want you to try today," she said gesturing for

Beryl to take a seat. "The way Ren and most mages who have bird bondmates cast is by following the bird into the air and learning to feel the currents of air and magic that move and flow around the bird." She held up a hand to stop the girl from responding. "I know this is what we have been trying for the last week; however, I want to try this with a small difference. This time I want you to pull your other bond-mates into the bond as well. Try this for a time, and then we will try the second method after we break for lunch. I will be here if you need me but will not interrupt you until it is time to stop. Agreed?"

Beryl gave a small sigh, but nodded, settling herself into a comfort-able position on the cold stone. Kuro had launched herself out over the ocean as soon as they opened the door that morning. Rune made himself comfortable in the hood lying against her back, as Argent plopped down with a sigh to lean against her legs; no mouse hunting this morning, it seemed.

Closing her eyes, she gathered her two four-footed bondmates and reached out to Kuro, pulling them all into her mind. They had spent a fare bit of time learning to see from the sea hawk's eyes and not let vertigo seize them, but Beryl had never tried to work magic as she did so.

She drove Kuro crazy for the rest of the morning, as she fell in and out of the bond while trying to shape a rune for air. She dropped out of the bond again, cursing under her breath. She stood and stretched for a moment before plopping back down to try again.

This time she simply tried to draw magic to her eyes while looking through Kuro's vision to see if she could see the currents of magic layering the sky and earth--nothing. She tried over and over, only stopping when Valerian called a halt for lunch.

Beryl stumbled to the cottage, head pounding, trying to limit the bond so that her bondmates wouldn't have to suffer as well, but she doubted that she was very successful from how subdued they were. Valerian interrupted the rubbing of her temples, hunched at the table with a touch on the shoulder. While she had been turned inward, they had set the table and served lunch; a cup of willow tea sat steaming at her elbow. Beryl drank the bitter brew down quickly and began picking at her meal. By the time they headed back outside her headache had faded, and she hoped Valerian's next trick would produce some results.

"Since the other technique didn't work, I want you to try something different. I want you to go through your weapons stances slowly like you did yesterday. While you are moving, try and sense the currents of magic under your feet and through the air that you are moving your arms through." She paused, tugging at a strand of hair that had worked its way out of her braid.

"I met a fellow weather mage during my earlier years while I was an apprentice, who used his entire body to assist in his spell crafting. He had been trained from birth as a dancer and tumbler. His magic was discovered in his late teens, and he struggled for many years before discovering that he could work magic while he danced. I have lost track of him in the years since, or I would send you to him for training." She shook her head, frowning for a moment. "Well, we must continue as we are able for now, maybe in a few years you can try and track him down yourself. His name was Abram of the Zune Clan. He lived in Orlean when I knew him, but he was always on the move studying different kinds of magic. Begin your practice when you are ready. Ren and I are going down to the village for supplies, and we will return before dinner. Have faith," she said with a smile. "Some magic simply takes time."

* * *

LATER THAT NIGHT, Ren came bounding into the cottage after his screaming gull. "Some thing's wrong; the town is on fire!"

"What?" Valerian gasped. "Outside, now!" she snapped, running toward the cliffs. From there they could see the flames and smoke rising from the town, some two miles down the road. The flames lit the dark sky.

"Goddess," she breathed. "Ren, help me. We need to call up some rain."

"I'm going to town to see if I can help," Beryl said.

She dashed inside for her weapons and coat, some instinct making her grab Argent's armor and buckle his bristling form in before bolting down the path. When she got closer, she could see several of the fishing boats in the harbor were also in flames. This was not an accidental fire, then. Kuro soared above the flames and smoke, showing them the fighting in the streets, men in dark clothes with swords tearing through the houses, stealing and killing those who tried to stop them.

Unknown to the bondmates, the stones in their collars began to glow softly. The bond stretched tight between the four as they ran toward the town. Mage passed people running to and fro with buckets of water before she found her first body--its face and chest coated with blood.

The screams and clash of swords directed her to the next. Rune jumped down and ran into an alley, curling around the legs of a boy too terrified to move. "Kitty," he said softly, watching as the cat turned and went farther into the alley, away from the fighting. Stumbling, the small boy followed Rune toward safety.

Argent stayed at her side as she pulled out her sling. Quickly loading a sleep spelled stone, she took aim and loosed it. The small stone struck a dark clad man just as he raised his sword for the final killing blow. He crumbled to the ground, sword falling from his suddenly slack hand. His opponent turned to help the next fighter as she loaded another stone.

Rune continued to lead the children away from the fighting, while Kuro showed him where they were hiding. Argent rushed those who dared to turn and attack his bondmate, giving her time to sleep spell them in turn. Suddenly, lightening split the air, and it began a steady downpour. Kuro was forced to land on a ship's mast that had avoided destruction, but she still was high enough to give them some idea of where the fighting was occurring. She directed them to the next group of fighters and warned them about possible ambushes.

The fighting had been pushed back to the harbor as the rest of the town fought the flames and smoke. The worst was the local Inn, which roared with flames as the tar used to seal the walls and floors burned.

Suddenly, Rune darted through a gaping doorway, "Rune!" Beryl cried, dashing around the people trying to quench the flames or hugging burned limbs to dash through the doorway into the blistering air within, ignoring the cries of those outside trying to stop her. Her drenched coat and clothes began to steam as she scooped Rune up and tucked him into the inner pocket of her coat.

Argent paced behind her as they slowly crept up the stairs. Rune swore there was a child there. Lines of flame licked up the walls and table tops, broken beams and bits of burning pitch from the roof covered the floor and dropped from the ceiling as she checked each room. Most were in flames, the beds a funeral pyre for any left within them. Rune steered them toward a door near the end of the hall that was open a crack.

Mage could feel the heat stretching the skin on her cheeks and hands. She sent Argent back down the stairs to wait for them as she entered the room, his paws raw already from the heated boards. Smoke was filling the hallway and swirling around the room. Two small bodies lay curled together in the space under the bed. Pulling them out, she doubled over coughing. They all needed to get out now.

She pulled the two limp forms to her chest and shoulder before staggering out the door and down the hallway, trying to protect the children's heads from the falling flames. The railing of the stairs was on fire, and a fallen beam canted over the steps forcing her to duck and crab walk her way down. The heat and smoke was overwhelming. Argent bounded up barking and grabbed her coat, pulling her down the stairs and guiding her through the smoke to the door.

She fell out the door into the rain, as hands reached for the children. Rising, she staggered to the other side of the street, coughing up the smoke from her lungs. With trembling, black-stained hands, she pulled Rune from his pocket and checked the cat over.

He protested the rain with a weak meow, but let his bondmate fuss over him. His paws and face were singed but he wasn't truly hurt. Argent also suffered from a few small burns and cuts on his feet. Beryl wrapped the worst injury in a strip cut from her shirt so that it would not get more dirt in it before it could be treated. Scrubbing her hands and face in the falling rain, she leaned against the next building, getting her breathe back.

"Goddess bless this rain," a man said from one side of her, watching the embers slowly smoldering.

"Goddess bless Mage Valerian and Ren," Mage said, standing. "The weather mage outside of town sent the rain. It wasn't due to rain for several more days."

"You were the one spelling the attackers to sleep," another said, eyes wide with awe.

"I don't know enough weather magic to help, so I helped how I could, nothing else," Mage said tiredly. Gathering Rune up, she called for Kuro.

"Who are you?" one of the others asked.

"I am called Mage," she said, raising an arm to let Kuro drop in and land to the startled cries of those nearby.

She set the sea hawk on her shoulder. Cradling Rune in her other arm, she turned and headed back up the road toward the cottage. Argent trudged beside her. She would need to make sure that Valerian sent word of the attack and asked for more healers to come; the town would need them.

The next few days were a blur. She stayed in the village working in the temple to help with bandages and healing where she could. The temple chambers were full of the injured and dying. The temple hall itself had been converted to temporary beds for those who had lost their homes.

"Mage, can you craft a sending stone to Darius? I want to let him know about the attack."

"You mean my messenger stones? Yes, Darius has a receiving circle, so I can send him one. How large of a package are you sending?" she asked, patting her pockets to see if she had a pebble handy. She came up empty-handed.

"Just a letter," Valerian said.

"Let me go find a stone, and I will do it now. Once it's done you just place a drop of blood on the stone to activate it."

"Wonderful, bring it to the healer's office once it's ready."

Beryl gave a nod and finished rolling the bandage she had spelled before gathering Rune and Argent to head outside. It only took a moment to find a smooth stone. It sat in her palm like a small heart as she poured the spell into it, sealing it with a quick rune.

She ignored the children that watched in awe. They'd taken to following her whenever she was outside of the healing rooms hoping to see some small bits of magic. She had obliged them a few times with small spells that floated and pulsed with magic like soap bubbles before imploding in a soft, glowing shower of golden sparks. She gave them a smile and scooped up Rune to take with her back inside, while Argent happily romped with the children. None of them would come to harm while he was their watcher.

Making her way to the healer's office, she raised her hand to knock on the door. Voices within made her pause. Rune's sensitive ears relayed the conversation to the other bonded. Valerian was talking with a man, his voice rough and deep, booming loud in the small room.

"When do you think she'll be brought into the web?" he asked.

"Perhaps once she graduates. She's a powerful mage who would make a good addition. She cares for those around her, not like most mage-gifted, I hate to say," Valerian said ruefully.

They continued talking of the attack and what supplies were needed as Mage gathered herself, smoothing her face into a mask. Then, she knocked lightly on the door. The conversation stopped immediately. Valerian opening the door a moment later.

"Ah, Mage, come meet Merchant Richard Brooks. He'll be traveling to the capital tomorrow and is willing to offer you a billet on his ship if you would like to head back a few days early. It would cut a fair amount of time off your journey. He can take your horse as well. Once you are farther south, you can either set off on your own for the final few days, or you can join his wagons when they head in. It is up to you."

"Surely you need my help with the injured, Valerian," Beryl said uncertainly. Rune gave a soft bleek from his spot inside her hood where it rested against her back. The man gave a start at the sound, before breaking into chortling laughter as he spotted the small cat.

"While I would never turn down a helping hand, the healers from the south are due in tomorrow. I'll have no time to train you farther until things settle down, which could take weeks. If you wish to ride to the capital you can, but it will take you almost two weeks and the spring storms are soon to hit; by boat it takes but a handful of days."

"It's a generous offer," Beryl said softly. "I could hardly refuse. I just don't want to leave you or the injured suffering because I accepted."

"Good, then that is settled. Did you bring the stone?"

"Oh, yes. I'm sorry, here it is," Mage said, handing over the small stone.

"How simple…and you simply tie the letter to it?"

"Yes," Mage murmured, watching as Valerian tied a thick letter to the stone before setting both on the table. Taking a straight pin, she pricked her finger and let one drop of blood fall onto the stone. With a flash, stone and note were gone on their way to Darius' receiving table.

"How soon will it arrive?" she asked.

"As far as Darius and I can tell it is nearly instantaneous," she murmured, watching Valerian and Merchant Brooks from under her lashes.

* * *

THE TRIP back to the capital had been easy, and the four bonded slipped back into lessons and message runs like they had never stopped. Beryl had hoped to learn more about the web while traveling with Merchant Brooks, but nothing else had been said in her hearing. She was sure it was the same web she'd overheard Darius speaking about long months ago.

Mage dismounted at the edge of the wood, trying the steady Flox to a branch. She didn't worry about him trying to graze, there was no grass or greenery to speak of, and the forest was dead. Dead pine needles and leaves crunched beneath her feet. Bare branches arched above her head.

No sounds disturbed the forest except the soft patter that Argent and she made as they walked. Rune crouched inside her hood, his whiskers tickling her neck and ear where he peered out. This wasn't a good place he rumbled softly in her ear. Mage agreed. Everything about this place felt wrong, broken. Kuro watched in a tree by the road, refusing to go closer.

Argent waited just beyond the carcass of a deer. No insects marked its hide; it lay undisturbed, unmarked by predators of any kind. The scent of the decaying flesh alone should have brought scavengers, yet nothing had touched this meat. Turning, she continued toward the center of the wood. Here the tree trunks were black and weak, crumbling at a touch. Pulling out a small pouch she gathered samples of wood and dirt to bring back to Darius for study.

A few steps later she found the epicenter of whatever had caused this ring of death and decay. A dark ring of ash almost five feet across sat in the middle of the wood, undisturbed in any way. She couldn't bring herself step into this ring; it took all her nerve to take a small sample of its fine grey ash.

The center of the ring was shiny and black, like the rock had been fused by great heat, but this was not caused by lightning or fire. What fire would strike the center of the wood and kill everything around for almost a mile? As best she could tell, it looked like a rough, circular bite had been taken out of the forest. Shuddering, she forced herself to walk the parameter of the circle before heading to the other edge of the blighted area. Along the way, she passed bodies of squirrels and birds lying as untouched as the deer had been.

It took all her willpower to stay in the circle of death and examine it fully before making her way back to the horse at a fast walk. All her instincts screamed that she should be running away, not walking. Even Flox was antsy and snorting by the time she returned, and he broke into an extended trot the moment her weight was in the saddle, snorting and blowing his displeasure as they put more distance between them and the forbidding place, Argent galloped alongside as best he could until Beryl managed to convince the horse to continue at a slower pace so that he could catch up. None of them wanted to delay their return to the castle.

Once at the stables, she gave Flox to the stable hands. For once, she did not take care of him herself. Urgently, she rushed on to Darius' lab. Opening the door, she barged in without knocking. She was ready to tell him everything, but she realized he was not within. The energy that had sustained her flight left her in a rush making her dizzy for a moment. With a sigh, she sat the bag of samples in the center of his desk and left to take a bath.

Much to their disgust, she bathed both Argent and Rune as well; she didn't want the slightest taint from that forest left on her bond-mates. They suffered through her scrubbing before being toweled dry and curling with her in front of the fire she stoked as hot as she could make it. She felt chilled to the bone. To a mage's sight all life held a faint glow of energy or magic, even in death, the trace of energy lingered.

The forest Darius had sent her to investigate was dark to mage sight, worse it almost seemed to be trying to leach the energy and magic from anything that entered the area. The grass and trees on the edge of the circle had been grey and dying, as the magic in them was pulled toward the empty soil. It was like magic was trying to correct the balance of what was missing.

All large works of magic pulled energy and life force from the air and earth around the mage. That use had to be balanced, however. Too large a pull of life from an area, and the ground itself would begin to leach magic and energy from the mage and anyone else near in an effort to restore balance. The small magic most mages used day to day pulled from their own heat and energy.

Large castings such as warding a town or village pulled from both the land itself and from the townspeople to power the wards. Once such wards were set they took very little energy to maintain, the average energy given off by a person just in breathing could power a small personal ward indefinitely if it was not challenged.

The larger the town, the more people a ward had to pull energy from, and the stronger it would be against attacks. If a mage lived in a town, it was enough to power most simple spells in every home, since a mage gave off more energy than the average person. This is what allowed them to cast spells, since they could pull from this well of energy for power.

Once a spell was completed, the energy that made it dissipated back into the environment, replacing what the mage removed. The forest had been a negative place for energy, sucking at every bit it could, trying to regain its balance. It would take years, but eventually the balance of the area would be restored as new energy filled the gaps left by whatever had happened.

No mage would ever dare to try and funnel that much energy into a spell. If there was nothing to ground the energy, then it would burn the mage from the inside out. Energy gathered like that must immediately be sent back out as a spell or the heat would build in the mage until they burned alive.

To kill a mile's worth of forest, someone must have cast a massive spell. There had been no reports of anything unusual, however, beyond the dead zones of forest that had appeared in different parts of the world. Darius said they had encountered several farther north, but this was the first to be found within riding distance of the capital.

CHAPTER 20

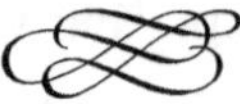

The entire castle was subdued. The Queen had been in labor for two days. She had carried the child eight months after spending most of the pregnancy in forced bed-rest. This was the longest any of the Queen's pregnancies had lasted. To lose the child now would be devastating. The political pressures were not helping. Many of the King's councilors were pressing for the king to divorce and remarry in hopes of a more fertile match.

Beryl fretted more than most. During the months of the Queen's pregnancy, they knew each other, speaking of their pasts and the idle gossip of day-to-day life. Beryl became the Queens lifeline for news beyond her confinement. She wasn't sure if they could be called friends, but the Queen had earned her respect and trust.

She sat in the kitchens, helping to make apple pies from the hard apples that had been stored through the winter. The head cook was determined to use up the last of them, expecting to get a supply of berries in the next few weeks as spring arrived.

"Mage, have you heard anything of the Queen?" one of the scullery maids asked quietly. The room fell silent as everyone looked at the girl with hope rising in their eyes.

"Sorry, I haven't heard any more than you have," Mage said with a slight grimace. A slight commotion arose as Darius strode into the kitchens.

"Pardon the intrusion, ladies. Mage, you're needed. Bring your bondmates, please," He said, gesturing her out the door and urging her to keep up with his quick stride as he rushed down the hallways.

"Darius, I thought you were staying with the King."

"The Queen is asking for you, as is the Head Healer of Ruth. She heard of how calm the Queen has been while Rune was visiting and thought it might help now. You will assist the healers as you can. I must go back to the King—Ruth, be with you." All the royal counselors were closeting with the King until the birth.

Beryl glanced down at herself, activating the runes stitched into her clothes to remove stains and keep the material smelling fresh; she was covered in spots of flour and dog slobber. She was wearing one of her older shirts with ragged sleeves, since she had been working in the kitchens. She paused outside the Queen's chambers to roll up her sleeves and re-braid her hair; it would have to be enough.

She pulled on one glove so she could let Kuro perch on the leather shoulder guard she wore over her shirts and jackets. She scooped up Rune and tried to brush him and Argent down before nodding to the amused guard at the door. She was sure he'd seen worse. Argent gave a slight whine and sent her the scents of exhaustion and blood coming from the Queen's rooms.

They stepped into the room just as Queen Marie and two healers were moving slowly across the room, the healers supporting the Queen as she walked. She was pale with stress and pain, dark circles framing her eyes as her hair clung in sweaty clumps to her neck and shoulders. She wore nothing but a thin shift that was drenched with sweat.

Candles and a roaring fire illuminated the room. Very little magic was being used beyond the basics to keep the Queen warm. Herbal drinks were dulling her pain. It was thought that too much magic used on a woman in labor would affect the child and its magical potential.

Argent slunk to the far wall, whining softly as the Queen paused, gasping as she rode out a contraction. She grasped the healers hand with a white knuckled grip until it had finally passed. Rune gave his grating cry once the Queen began to move, drawing her attention.

"Mage, thank you for coming," she said, extending one arm for the young mage to take.

Beryl quickly settled Kuro on a chair back, depositing Rune on the floor before taking her arm, ignoring the healers gasp at the scars exposed on her forearms. Beryl let the Queen lean against her as they circuited the room before returning to the bed. The Head Healer of Ruth, Radha, quickly helped situate the Queen in bed, accessing the position of the child. The royal physician wouldn't be allowed to attend the birth since he was male.

"Thank you for coming to help so quickly, Mage. The Queen and the healers you have worked with at the temple have spoken highly of you. Let me introduce my assistants, Althaia & Amaltheia."

"It's an honor to be asked to assist. How can my bondmates and I help?"

"I hoped that your cat bondmate would help the Queen relax for a time before we continue turning the child. The child is laying wrong, and we must help move it to where it should be. Once the Queen has her breathe back, we will try again."

Rune hopped up into bed by the Queen, quickly settling and starting to purr. The sound seemed much too loud to have been coming from such a small animal. Kuro's sharp eyes watched as the healers wiped the Queen's sweating face and neck, while Radha pressed at the Queen's swollen stomach to see how the child was positioned.

"Just a bit more. You must relax, my Queen, the more relaxed you are the more relaxed the baby will be."

"Yes," the Queen agreed, her voice rough with exhaustion, stroking one hand along Rune's back.

Over the next few hours it seemed they walked miles of laps around the bedroom. Argent followed for some of the laps, leaning against Beryl when they stopped for the next contraction. He would whine each time the healer pressed and pushed on the Queen's abdomen; she groaned in pain with each attempt.

Beryl talked as they walked, telling the Queen stories of her travels with Jared or of the antics of Rune and Argent on messenger runs. She had talked herself hoarse when the child was finally deemed ready, and the Queen placed back in bed.

Amazingly, after the days of wait and worry, the birth went quickly now that the child was in position. With a flush of fluid, the baby's head slid out, the healers supporting the small body as it left the Queen's body. The room quickly filled with the child's cries—it was a boy! He was quickly cleaned, while the afterbirth was managed.

The bed was cleaned, and the queen clutched her new baby. Beryl helped carry the soiled linens down to be burned. Blood magic was no longer a common threat, since it had been outlawed over one hundred years ago. Still, certain precautions were carried out. Some would be willing to risk calling up the old magic if it meant that they had control over a royal family member.

CHAPTER 21

It shocked Captain Marshal to see Mage standing on the edge of the street, staring brokenly at something down the road. He often forgot when dealing with her how she had been hurt and abused. She was so happy and confident as an apprentice that he couldn't see the broken child within. Now it stared back at him. He'd returned two days before for a quick leave to see his family.

She stood there staring, struggling with herself. She must be wrong, that could not be him. After her attack, she had nightmares for years of him coming back and realizing she had survived. She had tried to picture herself screaming out what he did once she broke the spell. Now, he was walking down the street from her, and she couldn't move, couldn't say a thing. It was like having a wound you thought was healed and reaching down to discover that you were covered in blood.

She stood, one hand clinging to Argent, while Rune followed the one who had hurt his bondmate. Kuro raged and shrieked from the sky, fighting to gain height for her attack; only then did Beryl come around. Crouching down, she called her bondmates to her, asking them to leave the man alone. He did not know that she was alive. Attacking him when she could not accuse him would accomplish nothing. Turning, she bolted for the castle, not hearing the Captain's cries behind her over the roaring of the bond.

She tried to warn Darius and several others, but no one would listen. The man she was worried about was a minor nobleman who had arrived for the celebration of the birth and presentation of the King and Queen's child. He wasn't a mage, and no one in his family had magic. Deloran was no one's suspect.

* * *

"WE WATCH," Kuro murmured along the bond. The others sent a wave of agreement.

"From a distance only," Beryl said firmly. "He has heard of a young mage who was en-spelled as a child. It wouldn't take much to realize that one of his victims survived."

She did not remember much from the attack, but she remembered his anger. He hadn't hurt her until his spell failed. He'd slashed and stabbed until she lost consciousness. She'd been an accident; somehow his plan had gone awry.

She slowly approached the library, unsure of how Brennan would react.

"Mage! I wasn't expecting you today… is something wrong? You're pale, are you ill?"

"No, I need a favor, Brennan," Beryl intoned. Rune jumped down to bump Brennan with his head, while Argent leaned against his bonded, his large brown eyes sad. "Do you keep records of mages and their families? I want to find a few children I remember." Brennan eyed the younger girl.

"Are you looking for attacks like what happened to you?" she asked gently, pulling the young mage into a nearby chair. "I've already checked. There are no records of children of Mage Families being attacked."

"No, what I'm looking for is families with a history of magic, who suddenly have children who test without magic; the ones who were thought to have magic as a child." Brennan looked at her with wide eyes, blinking as she processed that.

Hours later, they sat surrounded by dusty books and records. Argent gave a whuffling sigh from his spot stretched out in an aisle.

"Mage, how does this all fit together?" Brennan asked, rubbing her eyes.

"I don't think the attack that happened to me was random. I think he wanted something from me, but his spell didn't work. He spelled me to silence, even though I was laying there dying. It was almost like it was habit."

"Yes, but what about the other children? How can there be so many?" she asked softly, looking at the long list of names they had found.

"What if I wasn't the first he attacked? What if I was just the one that didn't work?" Beryl whispered, stroking Rune as she forced her eyes away from the list of names. "Over thirty children suddenly stop exhibiting magic, and years later test as magic-less. I think he's stealing magic, Brennan. He's stealing the magic from all those children. I just don't know how to prove it." Rune rubbed his head along her chin before jumping out of her arms and to the floor; it was time for his shift to watch the Man, so that Kuro could hunt.

* * *

A FEW HOURS before the ball, the King and Queen would present their child to society, Mage followed at a distance as Delorean walked the gardens that bordered the inner castle wall. Losing him for a moment, she wandered the garden until a blaze of magic burned her mage sight.

The wall of the castle was burning with magic as some mage forced raw magic into the spell weave. She could see the spells on the stones trying to absorb the magic, but they were failing. As the magic pooled in the stones themselves, it overcharged them, causing the stone to fracture and chip, as the magic sought to ground itself.

Running to the wall, she sent Argent and Rune to keep people from the other side. She sent Kuro flying to find Darius. If she could slow the spell long enough, he might know how to stop the wall from giving way. Not bothering to slow she slammed into stone, breathe bursting from her lungs.

Focusing, she began directing the excess magic into the ground, plants, and anything else nearby. It wasn't enough. She focused inward, pouring more and more of her strength into stabilizing the wall. As she did, she fell into herself and into the magic. She was the light pulsing through the wall, she was the spells holding the stones together unraveling, slowly stretching and fraying like twine, she was her bondmates driving those in the Ball farther away from the wall, and still the pressure built.

Her hands burned and the smell of burning cloth and flesh filled her nose. The gems on her belt and collar blazed as she pulled every bit of magic she had into grounding the magic running riot around her. She made her own body the conduit for the excess magic, forcing it through her and into the ground. Cracks riddled the wall and the ground around her as the very air burned and glowed with the wild magic pouring off of her.

With a snap, the balance tipped and the first strands of spells parted with whip cracks of energy, flaring into light that even non-mages could see. Magic roared through her body as she felt each spell strand part like they were bones in her body, drawing a scream from her throat. Her vision slid to black as the weave of spells crumpled and back-lashed causing the stones in the wall to explode.

She woke up lying farther in the garden where someone had dragged her after the explosion, curled with her bondmates. Once she was sure they were all right she struggled to sit up. Every part of her body felt like debris had pummeled it.

She was covered in grey dust and minor cuts. She also was under guard. As soon as a healer had a look at her and pronounced her fit for questioning, they dragged her to an inner room deep in the castle and questioned for hours. She couldn't explain why she was following Deloran or why she was in the garden that day. She couldn't voice her suspicions, he caused both her attack and the attack on the castle. Her curse struck her mute at the slightest reference to him.

She sat, arms curled around her knees, on a thin straw mat that reeked of mold. Argent lay curled around her hips and back, ready to take her weight if she wanted to lean on him. Rune sat at her feet using as much of his small body as he could to warm her them. Kuro raged outside that they had sent away her. The young mage had ordered the bird away when she was captured by the guards. She had promised that she would never let her bondmates be caged and a cold, dark prison cell was no place for a bird.

It had all gone wrong since she saw him that day in the market. She had tried to warn Darius about him, but she had only given vague answers when questioned about her dislike of him because of the curse. She had done her best to watch him.

The upcoming ball for the presentation of the young Prince had the castle in a state of uproar, letting her or one of her bondmates trail the man constantly. For weeks, he'd done nothing. He was a nobleman who held a small holding in a backwater area of the kingdom. He had enough standing to be invited to important events such as the ball but had no genuine power or duties outside of those for his land. They sent her to a cell in the dungeon till they could prove she was trying to stabilize the wall like she claimed. She was there for three days. None of the guards spoke to her, and no one visited.

On the third day, the door clanked and opened, allowing a cloaked person to enter. It was late, and the small beam of light from the high window had long ago gone out. The bright glow of a torch in the entryway blinded her for a moment so she did not see the person enter and instead sat blinking black spots from her eyes.

He knelt down next to her, setting a bundle down as he did so. There was the sound of ruffling cloth punctuated with the bang of Argent's tail. She may not see who it was, but Argent knew him. A light globe flared bathing the cell in a soft golden light, illuminating Darius' face as he crouched next to her.

"My dear child, I am not sure what to make of this."

"Darius, you know I would not hurt the castle."

"The Mage's Council has decided that I am too involved in the situation to give a testimony that would not be clouded by sentiment. They have decided that you are a danger to the castle and are to be removed from your Apprenticeship. You have been remanded to the custody of the crown. The King is to decide your fate."

"Darius, you know who did it!"

"There is no proof, child! As far as everyone knows, he is not a Mage! They tested him as a child like everyone else and found to lack magic in a high enough level to be a mage. Even with training he wouldn't be able to cast a spell of that magnitude. He just wouldn't have the magic to do it," Darius said, gesturing her into silence, "Now, I've spoken with the King, and he will allow you to continue working on your education but there is a price."

"Darius, I didn't cause the explosion. All I've ever wanted to do was learn magic. Why would I attack the place that was teaching me? I'll do whatever the King wishes of me if it means I can still be an apprentice."

"The price of your education will be high I'm afraid," Darius said, rummaging through his bag as he handed her some bread and a wedge of cheese. He also pulled out some meat and cheese for Argent and Rune. "I do many things for the King, but ..."

"You're his spy-master, aren't you?" she said with a slight grin. Darius gaped at her for a second before shaking his head with a huff of laughter.

"I told him you would be an excellent one to recruit. You could call me that. I have placed Mages and non-mages in almost every court there is around the world. They are at every border we control, and some we don't. It has taken a lifetime of work, but we have a net of people in place to pass messages and information around the globe. What I wouldn't have given to have you message stones ten years ago," he said with a rueful smile.

"If you agree to this, then you will be placed with another member and trained for a time before heading to Orlean court. There you will pass on information as you come by it, while training under the court's mages. I cannot say how long you will be gone or how long you will be in that court. If you are revealed as a spy, or in danger, you will be moved to another court and start again there. You'll receive a visit from me or another royal Mage once a year to assess your progress. When it appears you're ready you will undergo the fifth-year testing and be bound in loyalty oaths to the King, so that even if you leave his service you won't be able to betray him." Darius sighed and handed her a flask of water.

"I'm hoping that in a year or two the situation may be calmer, and we will bring you back to the capital. Until then, this is the best I can offer you. The other option is that your magic is bound, and you live out your life as you wish--as a non-magical."

"So, my options are to live and work as a spy for the King, or to live without magic for the rest of my life? You know I can't do that. If they bound my magic it could kill my bondmates. I can't allow that to happen and you know it!" She gave a low bitter laugh. "I guess I'm becoming a spy. What happens now?"

"Now, my dear, you're to rest. Later tonight a guard will come and collect you. You'll be taken to another member of the web. They will take you to your last destination and explain more. There's no time now, they can't know I visited you. I wish there was another way my dear, but I think you'll grow to enjoy the work. Now, there are clothes and a few things I thought you would need in the bag.

"Now I must leave you. I hope to meet you again under better circumstances, my apprentice. May Ruth guide you."

Darius quickly ducked out the door taking the light with him. Glancing at the door, Mage drew a weak rune for light on one of the floor's wide stones. She explored the bag's contents by its flickering light. She changed into the warmer clothes and laid her cloak on the ground for Rune and Argent to lie upon.

Next in the pack were her green and leather great coats that was folded and tied into a bundle. They had taken her blue coat when she was arrested. They also packed the bag she normally carried on message runs with traveling food, flint and tinder, herbs and bandages for injuries, and an assortment of other minor things such as bow strings and candles.

At the bottom of the pack was a wrapped bundle. She felt tears coming to her eyes as she unrolled Argent's armor, her arm guard for Kuro, and her daggers and spell stones. Darius had outfitted them for a journey. They get just had to get Flox without drawing attention and see where they were headed...

* * *

CONTINUED in Shattered Stone (The Stone Mage Series Book Two)

ABOUT THE AUTHOR

Amelia G. Sides lives a double life in Columbia, SC. Quiet clinical information system programmer by day and daring fantasy writer by night. Amelia and her four legged companion, Reuben, can be found on most evenings sitting in front of her computer screen plotting out her next book.

The first in a new series, **"I don't want to fight!"**: A GameLit Novel, will become available the summer of 2024.

https://linktr.ee/asides3

www.ingramcontent.com/pod-product-compliance
Lightning Source LLC
Chambersburg PA
CBHW061154210726
48294CB00006B/1670